MR WHITE T-SHIRT MAN

GARY BARRACLOUGH

Gary Barraclough
gary.barraclough1960@gmail.com
Dubbo, New South Wales, Australia

First published in Australia, 2025.

Cover design by Ashley Chau
Cover photograph by Jordan Leist
Typeset by Nikki M Group

ISBN 9781764067607 (print)
ISBN 9781764067614 (ebook)

A catalogue record for this book is available from the National Library of Australia

Contents

Still life

December 2023

Lucy Barnes had her chair pulled in close to the bed.

She was dressed in tight black slacks with a white silky top that hung loosely. She had on a short-waisted woollen coat and brown suede boots. Her long hair was pulled back in a ponytail. She wore very little make up but looked pretty and was dressed in clothes that her daughter Susie would say looked 'mad'. Ever since she met Harry, he encouraged her to dress nicely and look good. He didn't mind when she spent money on clothes and often used to help her shop.

Her initial introduction to Harry was difficult for her to explain, so she just told anyone who asked that they met late in 1981. The truth was she had been infatuated with him since 1978, and they married in April 1983. But as she sat alone, she thought about their astonishing, incredible initial meeting years earlier in September 1978. She had often spoken to Harry about this meeting, but he had absolutely no recollection whatsoever of the event, and this caused her angst. She desperately wanted Harry to remember it, but he remembered nothing, he said.

Years ago, without Harry's knowledge, Lucy had spoken to his mates Max and Steve from Harry's hometown of Rasp. They saw a lot of Harry in 1978 and they told her what she already knew – that Harry was oblivious to anything that happened from around September 1978 until around the end of January 1979, and that during this time in their lives, Harry's behaviour was inexplicable.

It was about 9:30 am and Lucy was waiting for the neurosurgeon to check in on Harry and provide her with an update when she was surprised by their daughter Susie. Harry was in a Sydney hospital and Lucy was staying in a nearby bed-and-breakfast. She wasn't expecting anyone else to visit as the hospital was about five hours' drive from home. She also thought that friends were now used to her 'no change' feedback, interpreting that there was little point visiting unless they were in Sydney for another reason. Lucy was vigilant about visits and did not encourage people to drop in. She was concerned about Harry getting a bug or virus, which would be difficult for him to fight in his present state.

But seeing Susie after a few weeks by herself was heartbreaking for Lucy. They hugged and tears welled, but Lucy was becoming more stoic as the days turned into weeks, and now the weeks into months.

'How's Dad?' Susie asked. Lucy was still holding Susie close and said softly, 'Well he still hasn't woken up. You know how stubborn your father can be when he wants.'

Susie pulled up a chair next to her mother's, close to Harry's bed, and they watched him. He looked like he was sleeping peacefully, but he had been like this for three months now and every day Lucy became more worried. She tried, however, to hide this worry from her children. They had work and things to do and were making their way in life. 'I'll worry about Harry' was Lucy's approach.

Harry was still the same ambitious, determined guy he had always been, and that's what she loved about him. When he was younger, some thought of Harry as arrogant or aloof, but Lucy put that down to his naturally shy nature that he used to try to hide. He had always been kind to those in need, and he had not lost this special trait – but Lucy knew that Harry never forgot if someone crossed him.

Physically, he was still tall and slim. He had lost most of his hair, but he was a young 63, Lucy thought. They were both active; they liked to walk and go camping together. Harry used to say, 'Let's do stuff while we can, because tomorrow, we might not be able to.' She thought they made an attractive couple, and Harry liked it when Lucy dressed nicely for him.

They had three grown children – Ben, Susie and Albert. Ben was a builder, married to Evelyn, Susie worked in child social services and Bert was a pilot. They all lived close to one another in Donvale in central-west New South Wales.

Ben, the eldest, was like his mum. Careful of other people's emotions and ready to help anyone in any way he could. He was tall and took after his father, with thinning blonde hair and a wiry physique.

Susie's personality was more like Harry's than Lucy's. She didn't inherit her father's intellect, but she was a streetwise girl, didn't suffer fools, and was liked by everyone. She was tall and very pretty like her mum, with long hair and casual good looks. Susie only lived about 500 metres from her parents', with her boyfriend Dusty.

Bert was the youngest child and a surprise for his mother and father. Lucy had reason to do a pregnancy test one day and left the result on the kitchen bench where Harry would find it. She didn't relish telling Harry that another baby was on the way, but Albert was warmly welcomed. Lucy reckoned that he was a dreamer with big ideas, and Harry's mother said that Harry was like that when he was younger as well. Bert was similar in statue to his older brother and father – tall and slim with thinning hair.

The three children had good relationships with each other and a close relationship with their mother and father. Every Sunday evening, Lucy cooked a roast dinner and everyone was invited, together with any friends they were hanging with at the time.

Susie was frightened that she would lose the dad she knew and loved. A fear that Lucy also thought about. The doctors continued to tell her that other than his broken tibia, which had now mended, he was physically well – apart from problems caused by his inactivity. Harry was losing muscle tone, and Lucy continually worried about a complication such as pneumonia. But all the doctors commented on his resilience, which was pleasing. Harry was an adventurer and used to say to Lucy, 'Don't worry about me if am lost somewhere or go missing – I'll survive and make my way back to you.' She now clung to Harry's comment. Harry was in there somewhere and struggling to find his way back, she knew it. Susie's fear was more basic: 'What if Dad wakes up but his memory is gone, and he doesn't know us and he has no basic cognitive functions?'

The treating neurosurgeon had told Lucy several times that tests indicated Harry's brain was functioning well. Thankfully, his brain-stem sustained no damage – the medulla oblongata was fully intact and functioning. The doctor also determined that the hippocampus and amygdala were not damaged and said there was no reason to believe that he would not make a full recovery. He added, however, that as time went on, Harry's chances of recovery would diminish because of other medical issues that could arise as a result of the coma he was in.

Harry's doctor, Peter Lynch, was due to see Harry at about 10.30 am. Lucy liked him because he was always positive and gave her simple, candid feedback. Lucy had also Googled his resume and decided he was up to the task, and that it would be difficult to find a better-qualified doctor to treat her husband.

Lucy and Harry had built up considerable assets over the years and Lucy was in a position to be able to afford whatever Harry needed. Harry called their financial position 'comfortable', but Lucy never gave much thought to it. Harry always said to her, 'I'll let you know when to worry', but such a time never occurred. When they first started 'going together', Harry had nothing in the bank: instead, he had a car loan, a motorbike, a crockpot, a doona and a pillow. Lucy, on the other hand, had some savings, and this is what got them started. They worked together for many years in their restaurants after Harry left the bank, and did quite well.

Harry worked for the Australian Rural Bank from late 1977, when he left school, until 2010, when he resigned to open three restaurants.

At the time, Harry determined that there was more to life than making money, so he challenged himself by starting his own businesses. Harry packed up the family and they moved from Sydney to Donvale in the central-west of New South Wales to open their restaurants. Lucy figured that Harry had always been a country boy at heart and it was good for him to leave the cut-and-thrust of the financial world.

Then his mate Bill's inheritance in 2016 provided them with a significant sum. Lucy often wondered why Bill left Harry so much money. The executor of Bill's estate had contacted Harry shortly after Bill's death to inform him that he was to be a beneficiary. Harry had said to Lucy, 'It's probably his golf sticks or something like that,' and didn't think about it again. When the estate was wound up, Harry received around $8.7 million dollars, along with a personal note from Bill that said, 'Thanks for the tip, Buddy.' Bill used to call Harry 'Buddy'. They often played golf together, from around 2000 until Bill's death. They were also on the golf club board for many years – Harry as honorary patron and Bill as treasurer.

Harry wasn't aware that he was to be a beneficiary of the will and protested to Bill's family when he received his share: he didn't want to take from Bill's family. He met with Bill's eldest daughter about the bequeath and told her he was uncomfortable with such a legacy. 'Don't worry about that Harry,' the daughter had told him, 'there is more than enough to go around.' She added that her father had told the family many times that he was indebted to Harry for his success.

Lucy and Harry had discussed this over and over again. Harry did not have a clue why Bill left him money and had no idea what the message included in the will meant. Lucy had her suspicions, though. Harry couldn't remember their meeting in 1978 – in fact, he couldn't remember anything about the last three months of 1978, which his best friends had confirmed to her.

Harry maintained he only met Bill when he was around 40 – around the year 2000. Lucy wondered perpetually, what tip did Harry give Bill that was worth $8.7 million? Harry and Bill always talked about business and share prices, which is why they got along so well. Harry was about 25 years younger than Bill and he looked up to him as a mentor.

Lucy remembers when they went to Bill's 85th birthday – all Bill's old friends were there but Bill had said to Harry, 'Your chair is up here next to mine, Buddy.'

Lucy always thought that Harry may have visited Bill in 1978 and talked to him about his visions. If this was correct, could Harry have mentioned companies whose share price increased many times over during the years between 1978 and 2016? And what else did Harry get up to that he doesn't remember? Lucy did speak to Bill's daughter, June, who also worked with Harry when he first joined the bank.

'June, when did Harry first meet your father?' she had asked. June said: 'They became close friends around 2000, but I know that Harry and Dad did meet before Harry left Rasp, so maybe that was around late '78 or early '79, because I remember Dad saying he had played golf with Harry, and had asked me about him.' So, Harry could have met Bill when he was seeing the future mused Lucy. I bet he said something to Bill about investing – I've always had my suspicions, she thought.

Lucy's thoughts were interrupted when Dr Lynch came into Harry's room, saying 'Hi' to both her and Susie, whom he had met shortly after her father's accident. He was accompanied by a senior nurse and a resident doctor, and together they looked briefly at Harry's chart. Dr Lynch had previously told Lucy that Harry's condition was difficult for him to understand. He couldn't be sure why Harry was comatose. His brain appeared to be free from physical injury, and that augured well for a full recovery.

Today, he told her what she already knew from her own observations: that there was no change to Harry. Again, he said he would be concerned if Harry remained in this seemingly vegetive state for much longer. He reiterated that Harry was in a state of post-coma unresponsiveness or PCU.

Lucy considered Dr Lynch's words carefully, understanding that time was both their enemy and their friend. Time was needed so Harry's brain would fully recover, but that time was against his physical condition. It was like walking a tightrope. Dr Lynch said he would talk with Lucy again in two days' time, unless summoned by the resident doctor. He and his team then made their goodbyes and left.

It was December 6, 2023. Lucy remembered Harry saying to her at about 11 am on Saturday 9 September 2023 that the day was so nice he was going for a ride on his Indian motorcycle. Harry had bought himself a candy-apple-red Indian Challenger motorbike after he retired. He thought the red was a 'bit out there', but he told Lucy that at least he would be seen by other traffic and therefore he would be safer. 'Will you?' Lucy had replied sarcastically.

Harry always had bikes. When they were younger, Lucy used to get on the back and they would ride in the bush. She wasn't a big fan, but did it to be close to Harry and share in what he liked. She remembered when they were young, he never used to have passenger foot-pegs, so she would have to curl her feet around his legs to hang on. It was most uncomfortable, but she thought of it as a leg-and-thigh exercise.

This new bike was the complete opposite of those early dirt bikes. The passenger seat was very soft, there were passenger foot-pegs, and it even had a stereo. Harry bought the Indian because he liked the old-school look, but thought that an old bloke on a Harley looked a bit like someone having a midlife crisis, and that they were common. His boys also thought it was cool because it had a very large 1768cc engine. In his youth, Harry had a 125cc bike, so this was a behemoth compared to it. Harry had had lots of experience on bikes and usually didn't ride fast, so Lucy had no issue with him riding. Even though it had passenger foot-pegs, Lucy didn't ride with him very often. She was okay with riding in the bush, but didn't like traffic much.

He sometimes liked to be by himself and would often ride, but only on days that were nice and sunny. Lucy wasn't worried until she received a call from a police officer around noon, saying that she needed to come to the hospital as Harry had been in an accident.

Lucy and Harry had a particular dislike for hospitals. After they were married, but before they had children, Harry was diagnosed with carcinoma of the sigmoid colon. Harry was progressing well in his career with the bank – but with one single sentence a doctor had brought their world crashing down. The doctor had summoned Harry and Lucy to a meeting after a regular visit and told them Harry had cancer. Harry had a left hemicolectomy days after that, and then had to have chemotherapy.

The couple were warned that the treatment could affect Harry's ability to reproduce and recommended they bank sperm, which they did. It was an awful period in their young lives. Lucy was worried Harry would die and that she wouldn't have any of his children to love when he was gone. Harry thought about Lucy being lonely: he determined that once he was well again, they would have children.

Harry's body didn't cope very well with chemotherapy. He was constantly nauseated, yet was allergic to the drugs that treated the nausea. The doctor had recommended 12 months of chemotherapy, but Harry discontinued it after about six months. He was exhausted from feeling unwell, telling Lucy, 'I just can't do it anymore.' Lucy accepted his decision: she had seen him vomit just at the sight of the hospital. He also vomited when he received the injections and would be bedridden for two days after the weekly routine.

Like a miracle, about 12 months after Harry ceased chemotherapy, Lucy fell pregnant without medical intervention. Harry often thought that maybe the big fella upstairs was repaying him for all his trouble over the past 18 months. After that, Harry didn't go near a hospital for many years.

Harry was unconscious when Lucy rushed to the hospital after the police called. They were concerned about the possibility of a bleed on the brain and wanted her to agree to transport him to Sydney immediately. The police said that he was found on the side of the road. It appeared that as he had come around a bend, his bike had slipped on a trail of water leaching from one side of the road. It didn't seem as though he had been riding fast – he was just unlucky. He had his leathers and helmet on and was protected from more serious injury, but when a passerby found him, he was already unconscious.

When he arrived in Sydney via air ambulance there was swelling of the brain but no bleed. It was then that Lucy met Dr Lynch. At that time, he was confident that Harry would make a full recovery. He had said the brain needed to rest and recover and that they had put him in an induced coma to allow this rest and prevent secondary damage.

Lucy and Susie continued to watch Harry breathing rhythmically and talked to him about everyday things – Dr Lynch said that any stimulus was good stimulus. Lucy uncovered Harry's feet and gently massaged a foot and his calf, not only to provide some stimulus to Harry but to feel better by touching him. Both women felt they were crying on the inside.

After her short discussion with Dr Lynch, Lucy reinterpreted his message. Time was their enemy now, not their friend.

(02)

Harry

August 1978

It was a sunny and warm August afternoon, a Sunday, and Harry was waiting out the front of his mother and father's house for John Webb to pick him up. Harry lived on the last street on the western side of the town of Rasp, and all there was in front of his house was bush. This was really convenient for Harry and his brother Ryan, because before they had their licences, they would hop on their dirt bikes and charge out of town. Ryan was now an apprentice mechanic in Darling, and they would see each other about every two weeks.

Harry's father Geoff was also a mechanic, in Rasp, and his mother worked in a preschool. His parents weren't rich, but they provided a good home to Harry, Ryan and their sister Melinda. Harry respected his father, for his work ethic and the way he helped so many people with his mechanical skills. Harry's mother Tania seemed to be always going crook at his father, but they had been married for many years and enjoyed travelling in their camper now that their children were making their way in life.

Harry had lost his licence for three months about two months ago. He was on his 'P' plates and had left his blinker on, and the police highway patrol had given him a ticket. (On your Ps as a new driver, it only takes one indiscretion to lose your licence.) Harry was dirty about the copper booking him. 'It was only a minor infringement,' he told the policeman, 'and the blinkers in my car don't automatically cancel.' The highway patrol copper didn't give a shit, thought Harry. Now it was difficult to get to work and difficult on the weekends to get around when all his mates were busy.

Harry started work on 12 December 1977 at the Australian Rural Bank in Rasp, and now most mornings he would walk to work, unless his mum had time to drive him. The loss of licence irritated him because he loved his car. It was his first car and he kept it spotlessly clean. It was a bright metallic blue, two-door, 1968 HK Monaro GTS with a 186s engine. It had black racing stripes up over the bonnet and was a bit lairy – which probably caught the eye of the cops, Harry had reflected. He had bought the car in early 1978 and replaced the engine shortly after with a modified 186s motor that had triple carburettors, which made a lot more horsepower. He had put wide aftermarket wheels on it and covered the black vinyl seats with white woollen seat covers. The dash had faux wood trim and a tachometer on the centre console. Someone offered him an eight-track cassette player and he mounted that under the dash. Harry loved his car because it looked good, it was fast and he reckoned that girls were attracted to it.

Before buying the Monaro, Harry had occasionally borrowed his mum and dad's car to take girls on dates, but it was so much better in his Monaro. He had had a number of girlfriends since leaving school and all of them had liked the Monaro. No licence now made it difficult to date, because he couldn't go and pick up girls or even take them home. He had had casual sex in the Monaro a couple of times – but without a licence his freedom and love life were curtailed. He still met girls at the disco or pubs, but was disadvantaged without the Monaro. However, he didn't have a girlfriend at the moment.

His last girlfriend worked in the main street, as did Harry, and one day she walked into the bank and asked Harry if he had been using contraception when they last went out together. Harry recalled the night particularly well, and although there was groping and touching, he hadn't actually had penetrative sex with her. She told Harry that her period was late and that she was worried. Harry spoke with his best mate Ben about it, who said 'Don't worry too much yet. Wait a week and see if she is okay.' She had her period a few days later and Harry was relieved, but he broke off their relationship, then soon after lost his licence. He had been without a girlfriend since.

Ben worked in the bank with Harry but was transferred to the north coast of New South Wales shortly after the girlfriend incident. They were very good mates at school and both successfully applied for a job at the bank when they finished. Harry really missed Ben – probably more than he missed his girlfriend. Now, he hung out mostly with Webby.

Webby was a good mate. He had a different personality to Harry, apart from sharing the same sense of humour and doing what they called 'stupid things' together. Webby was loud and seemingly more outgoing than Harry, but with girls he was more reserved. At about 178 centimetres, he was shorter than Harry and carried a little more weight. He wore wire-rimmed glasses and had collar-length straw-blonde hair.

Webby liked playing cricket, not golf like Harry, and would often mix with his cricket team at the weekend while Harry hung out with his two other mates, Max and Steve. Sometimes, Webby seemed like a bit of a loner and unsure of his future. He worked at an office supply business and seemed happy in his job, repairing and selling photocopiers. There were two high schools in town: Webby went to one and Harry the other, due to where they lived. Max and Steve both went to the same school as Harry.

The previous weekend, Harry had bet Webby he couldn't drive all the way to his home from one of the local clubs in top gear. Challenge accepted, Webby roared his car and tried to set off by slipping the clutch. They both laughed when the car jerked and stuttered away from the kerb. Webby leaned forward over the steering wheel, acting like an old man who had forgotten how to drive, slipped the clutch, and revved his Torana again, until finally it had enough speed to accommodate top gear. Harry roared with laughter again when he saw they were approaching a red light, because he knew they would have to start the process all over again.

There were only three sets of traffic lights in Rasp. Located in far-west New South Wales, Rasp had a rich mining heritage and had been declared a 'city' in 1907. Mining sustained the city for about one hundred years, and there was evidence of this everywhere. Running through the centre of town was an old slag heap, piled 50 or 60 metres high, right beside the rail line that had been used to transport minerals from the city to ports in South Australia. The main street was on the north side of the slag heap and 'South Rasp' on the other. The slag heap was probably a kilometre long and half a kilometre wide.

The mining industry provided most of the jobs in Rasp, and Harry thought that in some ways the general population took the mine for granted. Most blokes who worked in the mine followed in their father's footsteps. It was a dangerous business, but they were very well paid and the community benefited from the sporting ovals and club facilities that were subsidised by the mine.

Harry had joined the bank because he didn't want to spend the rest of his life in Rasp – or ever work in the mine. Harry often thought there was a big world out there, and he was keen to explore it. He knew that after a year or so the bank would offer him a transfer, which he would keenly accept. While he was in Rasp, he would continue to live with his parents, but he looked forward to one day having his own house. Max and Steve were doing very well at the mines, but Harry figured that one day he would 'climb the ladder' in the bank and earn very good money. His time would come, he thought.

Rasp was a very dry city, with less than 250 millimetres of rain each year. It was dry, hard, rocky country, and in summer temperatures often exceeded 40 degrees Celsius. The city was located where they originally found minerals – without any thought given to practicalities such as water, or to niceties such as greenery, trees and any sort of vegetation. Rasp pumped water for daily use from a river about 100 kilometres away.

Rasp was also isolated. It was about 1100 kilometres west of Sydney; the nearest city was about 300 kilometres south. This isolation suited Harry and his mates, because they all liked to ride dirt bikes, and there were thousands of square kilometres on which to do it. Most weekends they would go camping, riding bikes and shooting.

Harry and his mates all left school at the end of 1977, about eight months ago, apart from Steve, who had been out of school for over two years. Steve didn't like school and wasn't good at it, so he first got a job as a roustabout, then one on the mine in Rasp.

The boys all had cars now and all were involved with girls – or *a* girl – and this new activity ate into their time a little. They would all meet up on Saturday afternoon and talk about their plans for that night or for the following weekend, which now somehow had to be configured around girls.

Webby arrived in his six-cylinder Torana. He had altered the exhaust system and the car was loud and sounded much better than it actually went. Harry and Webby were going to see Max and Steve, thinking they might just cruise and see what was happening around town.

Steve Taylor was a little taller than Webby, but shorter than Harry. Slim, he had short dark hair that seemed to be receding even though he was only 19. He had a steady girlfriend, Debbie, but it seemed he was 'in lust' rather than 'in love'. Not that he would tell Harry, Max or Webby about his feelings. He just wasn't a talkative, emotional sort of guy. He would talk about everything and anything but emotions.

Despite not liking school, Steve was very intelligent about some things, such as war history. If Steve was interested in a subject, he was knowledgeable about it. He 'went bush' for some two years, working in woolsheds with a shearing team on sheep stations around Rasp, but didn't much like the isolation so came back to Rasp when he landed a job with the mine. He was now a diamond driller and was on a salary about five times that of Harry. Steve worked on a mine roster that rotated between day and night shifts over a seven-day period.

It seemed that when Steve wasn't working, he was with Debbie. She didn't have a job and was always available to be with Steve. Steve lived at home with his parents, but when they were at work, he'd bring his girlfriend over and they'd have sex. When his parents were home, they'd have sex in Steve's car. Harry used to say, 'Steve's always on the nest.' All the boys were a bit jealous that Steve had a girlfriend that allowed him regular sex.

Max Bruce, the shortest of the four, with short legs, had what Harry reckoned was like 'a white man's afro'. It was kind of stupid, but one day they were going into an underground carpark with a sign that said 'Max. headroom 2.5 metres' – from which point 'Heady' became Max's nickname.

Max was a bit more studious and conservative in his outlook, and when he left school he got a job on the mine as an apprentice underground surveyor, which suited him perfectly. At school, he was always good at maths – an analytical guy who usually thought before he did, so he was a good foil for his mates at times. Max didn't have a girlfriend but was always keen to go out to a party looking for a girl. He liked tinkering with motorbikes and doing modifications to his car, a baby-poo-brown Toyota Corolla that had two huge spotlights on the front. Max lived at home with his parents, about a block from Steve.

Max and Steve didn't play team sports such as football, which was popular in Rasp. Steve was too busy with Debbie, but Max and Harry played golf, and the remainder of their time was spent riding their motorbikes or 'out bush' camping and shooting.

Harry and Webby pulled up at Steve's place just as his mother was going crook at him. Steve was always getting in trouble from his mother about something. He had a much better relationship with his father, but Steve knew how to 'press his mother's buttons'. Webby yelled to Steve that they would meet him at Max's instead.

When they arrived, Max was under his car doing something. Max liked cars just as much as Harry and he would often be found working on his car.

'Hey boys,' he yelled.

'Steve will be here in a minute,' Harry said. 'We were just at his place, but he was having a blue with his mum.' None of the boys were big drinkers. They would sometimes really get on the grog, but on 'nothing weekends' they usually just had Coke. (Steve liked Pepsi because it was cheaper, despite being the richest of them all – go figure, thought Harry.)

Harry's mates all called him 'Flash'. He had a red Golden Breed windcheater with 'Flash' emblazoned across the back in white. But that's not how he got his nickname. In Year 11, during a game of football, a classmate pulled Harry's shorts down while he was waiting to catch a ball. Everyone thought it was a great joke and 'Flash' was born.

Harry enjoyed his nickname. It was something different and stood out. Even teachers knew him as Flash, and in Year 12 the art teacher drew a picture of Harry running in an overcoat with nothing on underneath.

When Steve arrived, they all sat on the edge of the back veranda and talked about the trip they were planning to a small town called Darling, about 200 kilometres east. Harry was born in Darling and knew someone who owned a large sheep station just north of it. They were leaving on Friday 8 September and at this stage, Harry, Webby, Max, Steve and Harry's brother Ryan, and a mate of his, were going.

They had borrowed a large tent that would sleep everyone. Steve and Harry would take their cars and tow bike trailers with the bikes. There was beer and meat to organise, and someone needed to bring a flat barbecue plate they could use over the fire. Steve and Harry each had rifles they would bring, and Steve would also bring his spotlight. Harry loved the country around Darling, knew the way to the property and would ring the owners in advance to let them know they were coming. It was about three weeks away and the boys were excited.

Eventually, Steve got up and said, 'All good then, I've got to go and see Debbie.' Webby, Max and Harry then said boyish things like 'Give her one for me' as Steve left grinning like a Cheshire cat.

Max was still working on his car as they talked, and as it seemed he wanted to get his project finished before work the next day, Webby and Harry left to cruise the main street and see who was about.

03

Harry infatuated

August 1978

Rasp was usually 'pretty dead' on Sunday afternoons. Webby did a few laps of the main street and they said 'Hi' to some acquaintances. The main street was only two kilometres long with two sets of traffic lights. They would travel all the way to one end, do a U-turn and go back again. The traffic lights were usually the place to hang around on Friday nights, as blokes would bring their cars out and challenge each other at the lights for a main-street grand prix, and girls would be hanging out with their friends. But today there was nothing happening, so they pulled over near a café and Harry went in and bought hot potato chips smothered with gravy.

They laid the chips out between them on the front seat so they could share and soon had gravy everywhere as they enjoyed the snack.

From where they were parked, they could see the bus station, on the same side of the street about 200 metres away. People were getting on the one bus at the station – the weekend bus to Adelaide, the capital of South Australia, about 550 kilometres away. Generally, people caught the bus for a weekend trip, to visit family or perhaps go and see a medical specialist. Lots of students from Rasp also used the bus to travel to university and home again.

Webby had a high-quality car stereo his father had given him. He enjoyed music and was playing Pink Floyd's *Dark Side of the Moon* album. It was a few years old, but both he and Harry thought it was a great album.

Harry watched, still snacking, as the bus pulled out and people waved their goodbyes. As the small crowd started dispersing, Harry saw a shapely young woman walking their way. He watched her intently; he didn't know her and hadn't seen her before. Rasp had a population of around 27,000: most people you'd seen somewhere around town before.

Why haven't I seen this girl before? Harry thought. She was short, with shoulder-length brown hair, parted in the middle and left loose. She wore tight, dark-blue jeans with open-toed clog sandals and a long-sleeved dark brown T-shirt – clearly without a bra. She walked confidently, seemingly without a care. Her nipples were showing, but it seemed to Harry she wasn't doing it to show off, but because she was comfortable.

Webby was mumbling about something but Harry wasn't listening. He was engrossed in this girl. As she got closer, Harry could see she was at least his age, or maybe a little older, which deflated him a little. If she was older, she wouldn't be interested in me, he thought – she would have a boyfriend about three or four years older.

'Hey, Flash are you listening to me?' Webby jolted Harry back to reality, but he continued to look at the girl. He had already assessed that it would be great to meet and talk with her, but thought, I can't just get out of the car and talk to her. Maybe I could just say 'Hi' then try and find out who she is, who her boyfriend is, where she works – all those things.

'Yeh,' said Harry finally in response to Webby, without paying the slightest bit of attention to his mate. 'Yeh, I'm listening.'

'I'll show you something really cool,' said Webby, then called out to the girl, 'Hey Bridge!'

Fuck me, thought Harry, confused. 'You know this girl?' he asked. Harry thought, How long has this been going on – Webby knows a really hot girl!

'You know her?' Harry repeated.

'You bet I do,' replied Webby, and turned his attention to the girl again – to 'Bridget'. The girl looked at the car, recognised Webby and started to walk more purposefully towards them. Harry had all of about 10 seconds to get any gravy off his face and look cool as she approached the kerbside passenger window where he was sitting. She took one side of her hair in one hand, bent over, looked past Harry, smiled and said 'Hi' to Webby.

This is a dream, Harry thought. Such a fantastic-looking girl with a beautiful smile – and she seems so nice. As he feared, she did appear a little older than him and Webby – maybe 19? She smelled so nice. Webby said something and she giggled a little. Then he introduced them: 'Bridget this is Flash.'

Harry felt privileged to put out his hand and touch hers. Harry realised he was already in over his head, managing only to say 'Hi, my name is Harry.'

'Would you like some chips and gravy?' Webby asked, grinning. They both knew that she wouldn't stick her fingers into that mess. She declined and as they started talking, Harry wrapped up the chips, excused himself, got out of the car and put them in a nearby bin, hurrying so he wouldn't miss anything.

'Bridge and I work at the same place,' said Webby. Harry thought that she would be out of Webby's league and was pleased with the explanation. Great, he thought, now I can go and visit Webby at work and talk to her.

Bridget accepted the offer of a ride home, giving Harry an opportunity to talk to her about what she was doing at the bus depot, and about her work. She had been saying goodbye to a friend who was enrolled in university in Adelaide. Harry knew he was right about her age then, if her friend was already at university. He told her he worked at the bank. She was chatty and seemed to enjoy his conversation.

She is so mature and smart, Harry thought, as he absorbed as much of her as he could.

The ride was way shorter than Harry would have liked, but he learned that Bridget had her own flat and had left school two years before he and Webby. She seemed comfortable with Webby's company, but he sensed no spark between them. Bridget lived in a small flat on the first floor, above where she and Webby worked, and he wondered why Webby hadn't mentioned this girl to him before. Maybe he was keeping her for himself, he thought. Maybe he is keen on her?

They arrived at the flat and Bridget invited them up. The building was on the main street, with a door opening onto the street footpath and leading into a foyer. Next came a very steep, straight stairway to a landing outside her flat's entrance. It was a one-bedder with a kitchen and living room. Sparsely furnished, it had a lounge and coffee table on a large rug. The lounge faced three tall windows, with a stereo underneath, that looked out onto the main street.

Bridget liked music and put on a Santana album, which they listened to while talking. They had a Coke and then she made them each a Kahlua and milk cocktail.

Bridget had gone to the 'other high school' that Webby had attended, but left school after Year 10. The two only met when Webby started at her work. She said she didn't have a boyfriend, but Webby raised his eyebrows when she said this. Harry caught the signal, but didn't understand what Webby was alluding to. He would ask him later. She wasn't keen on 'going out bush', didn't really watch sport but loved reading and eating, she said. Bridget put Chicago on the stereo and coaxed Webby to dance with her – as they did, he laughed and she giggled.

Such a great afternoon, Harry thought. He wasn't worried that it was now getting dark and that he would be late for Sunday dinner at home. Harry and Bridget had some more Kahlua, but Webby declined because he had to drive home. Harry danced with Bridget and got close to her by putting his arms around her lower back. She looked up at Harry and put her arms around his neck. Harry was smitten: This could be a great relationship, he thought. She wasn't some young girl; she was mature and witty and they connected on so many levels. She looked Harry right in the eye and moved her head up to kiss him, and he responded as the dance became more of an embrace. They kissed passionately.

Harry heard the front door close and knew that Webby had left. He didn't feel bad about what was happening. He would talk to Webby later. Surely Webby knew Bridget wasn't interested in him.

The music continued as they swayed in time and kissed. Bridget looked at Harry again, reached around and took one of his hands from her back and led him to her bedroom. It was dark outside now, but he could see from the light in the lounge room that she had a dresser and wardrobe on one wall, and that there was a window on the other wall and a bed in a corner. Bridget pulled her jeans off, leaving just her panties and T-shirt on. Harry took off his jeans, T-shirt and underpants. She then pulled her T-shirt over her head and took her panties off. Harry could see she had a beautiful body with full breasts, small brown nipples, and dark trimmed pubic hair. The sight of her took Harry's breath away. He already had an erection as they laid down on the bed on their side facing each other. Bridget had a single bed with a timber bed head, and green-and-white sheets with zodiac signs on them.

Harry touched and stroked her gently around her thighs and vagina as they kissed, and found she was ready to make love. He moved so he was on top of her. She took his cock and bought it to her vagina. It seemed all the foreplay had been done in the lounge room. Harry wanted to be gentle and to make her feel good, because he didn't just want sex, he wanted her as well.

He raised himself on his hands and knees so he wasn't putting any weight on her, brushed his chin against her breasts and suckled on her neck and nipples. He kissed her again and she moved her tongue inside his mouth. Harry reciprocated and their tongues touched. She was making soft, comforting, murmuring noises, as he lowered his head and gently kissed his way across her breasts. She was moving under him, inviting him to fill her up. He raised himself on his toes and moved his cock inside her. It was all too much for him. She was so giving and so beautiful that he couldn't hold back the ejaculation coursing through his body. He thrusted as he was coming so that the pleasure would not all be his and she responded, moving back and forward in time with him and trying to hold him inside.

They were both breathless as they finished. Harry rolled to her side, but he was embarrassed that he had come so quickly, and apologised. 'I'm sorry I didn't last,' he said. 'You are so beautiful and I couldn't control myself.' Bridget told Harry that she had felt wonderful as well and within minutes Harry had recovered and was intent on being better. She was on her back and he reached around under her and grabbed each cheek of her bottom with his hands, rested his head on the pillow beside her head and fucked her as fast as he could for as long as he could. Bridget's head rolled to one side and her cheeks filled with colour as quiet sounds again emanated from her throat as she moved against his cock. Harry was very happy afterwards when she told him how good she had felt.

They laid together for some time, touching each other and talking about the day. Bridget told Harry she wanted to be with him as soon as she saw him, and Harry told her how beautiful she was. Harry asked if he could see her again.

'Yes of course,' she enthused. 'I would have been disappointed if you didn't ask.' Given the look he received from Webby, he asked if she had a boyfriend. She told Harry that she had lived with a guy for a short time but that was now over, hence living in the flat by herself. Harry was happy with that answer: he could pursue Bridget and build a relationship with her.

Then they talked about Webby ('John', as Bridget called him) and how he had left. Bridget explained that while she liked John, her feelings for him were really only that of a friend. She hoped John would understand that they would never be a couple, even if Harry hadn't come along. Harry was pleased that they would approach their friendships with Webby together. He didn't want to think that he had intervened with Webby's hopes.

Harry had to go: it was by now early in the morning and he had to get home and catch some sleep before work. Earlier, they had talked about him not having a licence. Bridget had a licence – but didn't have a car. Harry ran home that cool night, and many nights after that.

He felt so good he thought he could run to Darling and back. It was about four kilometres to his house, with a big hill in between. When Harry reached the top of the hill he stopped, sat down and watched the lights of Rasp, and soaked the night in. Earlier this afternoon, he didn't even know this girl. Now, he was infatuated.

04

Bridget

Bridget Coleman was born to Dennis and Rachel Coleman, and raised in Rasp. She was born in November 1959, and lived in a different school catchment area than Harry, so went to the same school as Webby, not the high school that Harry, Steve and Max attended. Because of this Harry, had never met Bridget or crossed paths with her. She would have been in the same year as Harry, but left school after Year 10, two years before he did. Perhaps this is why Harry used to think that Bridget was much more mature and worldly than he was. When Harry met Bridget, she had been working for almost three years and Harry less than one.

Bridget also seemed a little rebellious. She didn't enjoy living at home and had moved out when she was 17. Dennis was a kind-hearted, softly spoken man and did not stand in Bridget's way. He put trust in Bridget's decisions and decided that if she was working, she should be able to make her own decisions about her life. Dennis worked on one of the mines in Rasp and was well remunerated. In the '70s, mine workers enjoyed many benefits, such as medical and dental packages for their family. Harry used to think that most of Rasp sucked off the mine, then complained if the mine wouldn't compensate them for something. As a result of mine dental cover, Bridget had a beautiful smile, thought Harry.

Bridget had an older sister and younger brother, and Harry thought they were all a little wayward and independent. Bridget looked up to her sister and Harry used to think she took cues from her and her grandmother, who also seemed very intelligent and self-sufficient.

Bridget's sister had lived in Adelaide for many years and was very opinionated. Her brother was a bit of a rat bag, thought Harry. He was three years younger than Bridget and rode a large-capacity motor bike, oblivious to most road rules. He and Harry never got on, and Harry thought it was because the brother was matey with Bridget's ex-boyfriend. Harry thought that Bridget's mother was a lovely, kind, homely person – he figured that's where Bridget got her caring nature from.

Bridget worked at a building and office supply company in the main street of Rasp. Webby worked in office supply and Bridget in building material supply. Bridget was charged with quotes for bulk supply and responsible for some of the larger regular customers. She was good at maths and a very good communicator, with an amiable personality.

Bridget was a fan of alternative music, Harry thought. She wasn't interested in the latest pop hits. She preferred Santana, and Chicago, and blues rock, which Harry thought of as very mature. He wondered if she started listening to music earlier than him, or if it was because she was more mature than him, or if he was just a lazy listener who liked the usual ELO and Pink Floyd. Bridget was patient with Harry: he soon learned to like all the music she would listen to and they often played records at her flat.

Harry never questioned why Bridget had moved in with her boyfriend, or why she had moved out before he met her, but he reckoned that the ex-boyfriend wasn't on the same intellectual level as Bridget, and maybe they didn't have a lot in common. Harry also deduced that he was probably an angry person, and that the Bridget he came to know would not accept that.

Clothes were never important to Bridget. Harry thought she was always well-dressed, but she never seemed to follow fashion closely. Harry was just happy that she was a very feminine girl who liked girly stuff and reading. She wasn't interested in sport, but did have a shapely, toned body with larger-than-average breasts. On weekends, she would often wear tight blue jeans with a simple T-shirt, sometimes long-sleeved, depending on the weather. She enjoyed wearing sandals, which she claimed help keep her feet cool. Bridget explained to Harry that she suffered from mild hyperhidrosis, which caused her hands and feet to sometimes sweat more profusely than they should. At work she would wear simple skirts and a blouse, with a tailored jacket in winter.

Harry was amazed that a young woman who left school when she was 17 had such intelligence. Bridget was always grammatically correct and had a wide vocabulary, which impressed him, and she was always ready with an opinion.

When Harry met Bridget, he was overawed by her casual style and maturity and wondered why he hadn't crossed paths with her before in such a small country town.

05

That hurt

August 1978

Harry saw Bridget every night for a week after their first encounter. At lunchtime, he would walk to her office just to say 'Hi'. And every night after being with her, sometime after midnight, he would run home along deserted streets.

Bridget spoiled him with kind remarks and gestures, and Harry thought that soon he would be able to say 'my girlfriend' about someone he truly cared for. He hadn't had feelings like this before, even though he had had a number of girlfriends during and after school. She was different, and Harry thought his feelings could be love.

His relationship with Webby was fine. Harry had talked to him on the Monday and told him that Bridget would be more than a one-night stand – and that even at this early stage he was keen to see if he could build a relationship with her. Webby said he thought they would be good together – but that Harry should be wary of her old boyfriend, who was three years older than them. 'He is a gorilla and he'll kill you Flash,' Webby said.

Harry told Webby that he had asked Bridget about the relationship, and that she'd said it was over and that she was now living by herself. She said she had first moved out of the house they had shared, then told him she didn't want to be with him anymore and asked that he return the key to her new flat. Webby reckoned that *to Bridget* it was over, but that the old boyfriend didn't want it to be over, and was an angry jealous bloke. Harry didn't grasp the gravity of what Webby was saying. He'd never been in such a situation before and so wasn't worried by Webby's warning.

Harry spent the whole of the following weekend at Bridget's flat. They walked together, bought take away and just talked the whole weekend – and of course, made love frequently. On the Sunday afternoon, Harry was dozing length-ways on Bridget's lounge, facing away from the kitchen and door to her flat; Bridget was in the kitchen making a snack.

Suddenly, he felt a powerful blow to the side of his head. He wasn't sure what had happened. Had something fallen on him? Then he heard Bridget scream, 'NO, NO, get out!' Harry struggled to get to his feet as another blow caught him. He could now see Bridget trying to get between him and another man, but he couldn't see very well, as one eye was filled with blood from the first hit above his eye.

Groggy, Harry knew he had to get away from the bloke. He was concerned for Bridget, but the man wasn't hitting her – he was aiming his aggression at Harry. Harry fended off more blows and tried to retaliate as he got past his attacker to the door. He got out the door to the landing and was considering how he would get down the steep stairs in his current state when he received another blow to the back of his head, which sent him rolling down the stairs.

He tried to get up at the bottom of the stairs, but his ankle had been twisted or broken, it seemed. As he saw the man coming down the stairs, followed by Bridget, yelling and crying, he made the ankle work enough to hobble out the door onto the street. Outside, he limped and turned right around the first corner. He then crossed the road and turned left up the lane towards the rear entrance to his bank and stopped for a few seconds to catch his breath. His ankle was on fire and very painful to put weight on. There were living quarters at the rear of the bank premises and he thought if he could get there, he would be safe. He hopped and limped the 300 metres and banged hard on the back door of the bank. The bloke hadn't followed him and someone opened the door.

Harry rang Webby from the bank quarters and asked him to come and help. Webby was there within minutes. 'I knew this would happen,' Webby said. He took Harry to the hospital saying 'I told you so' most of the way, but he was worried for his friend. Harry needed four stitches above his left eye. They X-rayed his ankle, which was sprained, not broken. After he had been examined by a doctor, they sent him on his way with crutches, which he was told to use until he was able to walk on his ankle.

Webby drove Harry home, promising him that he would check on Bridget somehow, then let him know how she was. Harry's mother was more concerned than his father. He told his mother he got in a blue at the pub. He didn't want her to know about Bridget. Harry's father took a look and said, 'You'll be right mate – I hope you got him with a few shots.' Harry's dad had played rugby league for many years; he was used to knocks and could look after himself. His father didn't know that Harry had been caught completely off guard and was groggy from the first blow to his head. Harry didn't try to explain that to his father.

Webby reported back to Harry later that night. He had picked up Steve and Max as reinforcements before he went to Bridget's flat. Max was very concerned about what Webby had told him. They had learned during the week that Flash was seeing Bridget, but this news shocked them.

'Harry's been bashed,' explained Webby to them both as he picked them up. Steve nervously laughed and said, 'He will play with fire.' But Webby knew that Steve was the one friend that would help you in a blue: he does not back down. They circled the block in Webby's Torana looking for the bloke or evidence that he was still there. They could see a light on in the flat, but couldn't see a car likely to be his.

Webby decided that he would be the best one to knock on Bridget's door. He at least knew the bloke and the bloke knew that Webby worked with Bridget, so he had a defence of sorts. He would say he just needed to talk to Bridget about a work matter – to get into the office for parts for a photocopier. The plan was for Steve and Max to be close by, but out of sight.

Webby parked the car and left it unlocked with the keys in the ignition so that they could make a fast getaway if needed. He knocked hard on the street-level door so that it could be heard upstairs. He heard a noise at the window above and looked up. Bridget was at the open window. 'It's only me. Can I talk to you? Are you alright?' Webby said in a sort of loud but soft voice to try not to attract attention.

'I'll come down' she replied, and Webby could hear her footsteps coming down the steep stairway. The door opened and he was relieved to see she was alone.

'Where is he?' he asked, referring to the ex-boyfriend.

'I don't know – he's gone,' cried Bridget. 'John, is Harry okay?' Webby could see she was shaken by what had happened and was still crying. Her eyes were red and tears were streaming down her face.

'I took him to the hospital, but he'll be okay,' Webby replied. 'He has some stitches and they say he has a badly sprained ankle. He's home now, but he wanted me to check on you. He wanted me to make sure you are okay. What can I do to help you?'

She started crying again. 'Will he still want to be with me now?' she sobbed, before assuring Webby she would be fine and that they could talk in the morning. Webby waited while she closed the street door and listened while she climbed the stairs and closed her top door.

'Fuck – what a mess,' said Steve. 'Do you think Flash will see her again?' They all knew that Harry would get himself in strife over a girl at some point. It was just a matter of when. He was always flirting with and talking to girls. But it was the severity of what had happened that worried them.

It was dark as Webby dropped them off before heading to see Harry and tell him about Bridget. Webby was still worried that Harry might not be safe.

06

Can James Bond fix it?

August 1978

Harry went to work the next day with his crutches and immediately got attention from all and sundry. He had been working at the bank for only a short time and didn't want to take any time off work. In any case, he knew that word would get around. Rasp was a small town.

The sub-accountant Barney called Harry into his office for a chat. 'Well, well, boy, are you alright?' Barney asked. He was in his late 30s, a down-to-earth, rumble-tumble sort of guy who Harry could talk to. Barney had responsibility for about 40 staff and had seen and heard just about everything before.

'Do you want any help?'

'No thanks,' replied Harry. It dented his pride a little that he had been in a fight in front of Bridget and got whipped. He consoled himself by remembering that he was punched and injured before he even knew what was happening. He was groggy and couldn't see properly, but did retaliate as best he could and had got out of a really bad situation.

'You know what happened Barney?' Harry asked.

'Yeh, I know, and most of the staff know. I'll tell the big boss that you fell off a motorbike so he won't know what happened – and I know you don't want help, but I've got a mate coming to see me in a minute and I want you to talk to him.'

Barney's mate was a detective sergeant of police. The station was across the road from the bank and Barney used to play rugby league with him.

'So, you don't want to press charges against the bloke who did this to you?' the copper enquired. Harry told him the story and said that he didn't want the girl involved to be caught up in any police action. The sergeant said he understood, but that Harry may not be fully aware of what he was getting into.

'She told you she didn't have a relationship with this fellow anymore? Are you sure about that?'

'That's what she said to me,' Harry responded. 'She said she had moved out of their shared house and then she had told him their relationship was over.'

Harry wasn't sure if the copper didn't believe him – or Bridget. Alarm bells rang: Webby had raised his eyebrows when Bridget had said 'I don't have a boyfriend'. If she did still have a boyfriend, she should have said that to me, thought Harry. I still would have made love to her, but I would have been much more careful.

'I tell you what I think Harry,' said the sergeant. 'Even if he was still her boyfriend and he had cause to hit you, he's gone about it in the wrong way. You were hit in the side of the head without any notice while you were relaxed. You could have suffered a more serious injury or even worse. They put people in jail for doing that. Your case is made more complicated by the involvement of the girl, but I can't have blokes – and I take it he's about three years older than you – "king hitting" other blokes in my town.

'I'll tell you what I am going to do. I'm not going to charge him with assault because you have asked me not to, but I could if I wanted to. I am going to visit this bloke in the next few days and have a chat with him. Rest assured he won't bother you or her again, but go and see the girl and make sure her story checks out, son. I can't have any of Barney's crew in strife,' the sergeant said with a concerned smile.

Harry was ropeable as he left Barney's office. Had Bridget duped him? Did she still have a relationship with this guy? Had she really told him it was over? At the same time, he was disheartened that he may not see her again. Work was a blur that day as the whole past week went through his mind. She was so genuine, he thought, and they had spent the whole week together. He wanted to believe her, and he resolved to find out if she was truthful to him, but he was so sore he could hardly get about. Harry decided that if he hadn't heard from Bridget by Wednesday, he would go and see her.

Webby called on Harry at his house on Monday night to tell Harry he had tried to talk to Bridget at work about everything, but she just welled up and went into the bathroom.

'Every time I see her, she's crying or about to cry,' Webby said. 'I just can't get near her.'

Harry said he reckoned he would be feeling a bit better by Wednesday night. 'Can you pick me up on Wednesday night?' he asked. 'I'll go and see her.'

'I'll do it, but I don't think it's a good idea Flash. I was right that he would get you and I don't want it to happen again. You can hardly move about,' Webby replied.

Harry told Webby about the copper and what he had said. 'Mate, if she said she told him to fuck off then I would believe her … but I'm not sure,' Webby said in his most concerned voice. 'And how can you be sure the copper has seen him yet?'

'I don't know mate, we'll just have to chance it,' Harry said.

Webby picked Harry up on Wednesday night, wearing a beanie and a dark windcheater. 'I have a great idea,' he said. 'We sneak up the lane behind the flat where there is a fire stair you can climb up – that goes to a small landing right near her bedroom window. First, we sit outside to make sure no one else is there, then you climb up, tap on the window and talk to her.'

'It's not fucking *Mission Impossible* mate – it's "talk to a girl",' Harry countered. 'This is how all our troubles start – with your stupid plans.'

'What if he's watching her front door, you go in, he follows you – next minute, mincemeat Flash?' retaliated Webby.

'Okay, I'll do it,' Harry said. 'And by the way, who do you think you are in that get-up? James-fucking-Bond?' They laughed hard and long like they always did when doing something stupid – it was a relief for both of them.

They sat in Webby's car up the street a little way from Bridget's front door and watched for about half an hour. The town was quiet and no one was about, apart from those going to and from a nearby club. They could see the lounge light on but couldn't see anything else from street level. They then went up the lane and parked behind the building. The bedroom light was on as well.

'How's your ankle?' Webby asked, as Harry got out of the car. Harry had strapped it and could hobble on it. The rear fence was about 2 metres tall, but the gate was only loosely chained. Harry noisily unchained the gate, went in the yard and found the ladder right where Webby said it would be. The plan was, if the guy was there and went for Harry, Webby would jump on the horn and make as much noise as he could.

Harry painfully made his way up the ladder then looked through the window carefully, so as not to be seen. He couldn't see anyone; he could see the bedroom, but only part of the lounge room. Music was playing from the stereo.

Then Harry thought, What if she is still in a relationship with that bloke and she tells him about this – he will kill me! Suddenly, Bridget appeared – she was hanging something in her cupboard. She must be ironing, thought Harry. he knocked gently on the window.

Bridget turned quickly, rushed to the window and parted the curtain. Harry made sure he could be seen. She quickly unlocked and slid open the old timber window. Its sill was low enough to step through and she did, embracing Harry on the small landing and crying. Harry now didn't have to say anything or ask her anything. He knew she had told him the truth about the bloke.

'I am so, so, sorry Harry. I want you in my life so much,' sobbed Bridget. 'I didn't know he would come to my place. I did tell him

I didn't want to see him again, and I have told him again to leave me alone. Please believe me.'

Harry did believe her and told her so. He told her what the police had said and what he had been feeling since that night – and they waved to James Bond sitting down below in his car. Harry knew that night that Bridget would be feeling the same relief as he was. They both felt the same way about each other.

Harry never crossed paths with the ex-boyfriend again, but one Saturday morning about four months later he came out of Bridget's flat to find his beloved Monaro had four flat tyres. Someone had stuck a match in each valve. Harry guessed who it had been, but thought it a small price to pay.

07

The camping trip

8 September 1978

It was Friday, and the boys were packing the cars and loading their bikes. This was the weekend for their planned trip to 'Poonawalla', north of Darling. Steve and Harry had said their goodbyes to Debbie and Bridget. Both were a little reluctant to be away for the weekend; Steve because he would miss out on sex and Harry because he was building a relationship.

Webby, Max, Steve and Harry would meet Ryan and his mate in Darling, about 200 kilometres away, then they would all head north to the station. Steve and Max would take Steve's Ford, and Harry and Webby would be in Harry's Monaro. They had so much shit, thought Harry – bikes, petrol, a barbeque, food, drinks, swags and the huge tent. The list was endless, but that was part of the fun.

It was around 4:30pm. Even if everything went to plan, they wouldn't get there until about 8:30pm, then they would set up, cook and – best case – get to bed after midnight, thought Harry.

They were taking four bikes and Ryan would bring two, so there would be six bikes in total, ripping around the countryside.

Harry had been born in Darling and knew the area well. The soil ranged from a dark clay near the river to a rich red loam. The vegetation was different to that found in the rocky country around Rasp. Around Darling, there were more trees and open grassland, which was ideal for wool sheep. Harry's father had also been born in Darling, and to Harry it felt like coming home as they passed through the town towards the property, located on red country – ideal for riding dirt bikes.

Webby was tired of listening to Harry's limited selection of eight-track cassettes, so they talked a lot about the previous few weeks. Webby was supportive of Harry and Bridget's relationship and took some pleasure in being able to talk to Harry about Bridget. Webby hadn't seen the ex-boyfriend come into their workplace since the fracas and reckoned that the copper may have put the wind up the gorilla, which he was pleased about. He also reckoned that Flash had made the right decision not to press charges, because it all might now go away.

Ryan and his mate, Red Kennedy, met them in Darling, where they refuelled and headed north on a dirt road. Steve was in the lead, with Harry and Ryan following. They weren't breaking speed records, but they were awfully close. Stevie loved to 'hit it on the dirt', as he would say. Harry wasn't about to let him get too far away, and Ryan only had two speeds – fast or faster.

Webby got out his cassette player and put in a Hot Chocolate tape. He reached back into the esky and grabbed them both a can of beer. Up ahead, Stevie had pulled to the side of the road where he thought the track into the property was, and was standing on the bonnet of his car pissing on the windscreen to clear it of bugs. Webby and Harry pulled up in a cloud of dust with the cassette player blaring out *Everyone's a Winner*. Soon everyone had a beer and Harry knew the weekend had just commenced.

That night was a blur. Max was on the barbeque, Ryan was handing out the beers like there was no tomorrow, and Webby and Harry were erecting the big tent. Stevie always lit the fire when they were out bush, and this time was no exception. He dragged in huge logs of timber, which would burn all night. Max and Harry reckoned he was a pyromaniac in another life. Ryan and Red unloaded all the bikes, camp chairs and food supplies. The barbeque was basic – sausages and lamb chops with tomato sauce – but after a long day, it was the best food ever.

The beers were flowing and there was much laughter and banter, in a good-natured way. Webby asked Stevie who would be rooting his missus tonight. The best Stevie could come up with was, 'At least I have a regular root!' And the discussions continued around the themes of which bikes were best, what girls were hot and who had girlfriends, and who did they think were dickheads.

Webby's cassette player played all their favourites – *You Took the Words Right Out of My Mouth*, *Warm Ride* and *Baker Street*, and of course hits by Hot Chocolate and Electric Light Orchestra. All the guys had known each other for years and got along famously. Lubricated by alcohol, the night went into the next morning, until one by one the boys drifted to the tent and their sleeping bags. Not everyone made it that far though. Ryan and Red were asleep in their fireside chairs in the morning when Harry roused himself awake.

The plan for the day was to ride to an old, large, round concrete tank. Harry knew there was an old homestead near the tank: a good excuse for the long ride. The bush tracks were narrow and the guys usually rode two at a time, side by side.

Harry and Max knew each other's style and would always ride together if they could. Webby paired up with Steve, and Ryan and Red rode together. Harry and Max led, followed by Ryan and Red, then Webby and Steve. Steve and Webby weren't quick riders and the others had already pulled up at the old tank when they got there.

It was a warm day for September; they all stripped down to their underpants and climbed up and in the tank. It was the coldest swim imaginable, and didn't last long, but everyone was refreshed after no shower the previous night. Years later, the boys still talk about the old tank and how cold it was, and Stevie still has a photo of them all in the tank hanging on his wall.

Harry was out first and said he would do a bit of a 'reccy' to try to find the old homestead while everyone was getting their gear on. Harry left, sending a rooster tail of dirt behind.

He was 'sending it' Red commented. 'He loves to rev it,' confirmed Max. Harry was riding fast. He was in good spirits; life was very good, he thought as he rode away. A new girlfriend, out bush with my mates, back home tomorrow. How good is this, he said to himself inside his helmet. Harry would often ride and think and talk to himself as he rode. 'Watch this bend Harry' or 'give it to her' would come out of his mouth as he rode quickly. The boys could hear him go through the gears as the noise of his two stroke Suzuki slowly disappeared.

Harry had been gone about 10 minutes and the boys were getting restless. 'He should be back by now,' said Ryan. Ryan knew the area as well as Harry, and knew the old homestead was only a few kilometres away. 'Fuck waiting,' Red said. 'You know the way Ryan, let's go.'

Ryan was now leading and saw as he came around a bend a gutter across the road that had eroded from running water. All riders know dirt bikes go fast, but they don't stop very well, and Ryan had trouble washing off enough speed so his suspension could cope with the gutter.

The rear wheel chattered as he jumped on the rear brake. The front tyres do the best job of slowing a bike, but you need to be careful, or the front end will 'wash out', particularly on a bend. The front tyre bit in enough for him to manage the gutter without falling, but only just. The other guys were only seconds behind him, but Ryan managed to turn and wave everybody down before the bend. Red was the closest to Ryan, but with the warning was able to apply the front brakes hard before the corner and not hit the massive gutter. Ryan rode up the track further and slowed everyone. As he did, Red ran up: 'I've found Harry – he must have hit the gutter. He's in a bad way.'

Everyone had now pulled up as Ryan and Red ran to the bend and gutter. In his panic to stop and miss the gutter, Ryan hadn't noticed the skid marks that led to the gutter just after the bend. The tracks suggested Harry's bike had hit the gutter, Ryan now noticed.

Fuck, Ryan thought. The front wheel would have dug into the gutter then the back of the bike would have flipped forward and over the front wheel. Ryan now saw the bike on its side in a bush about 30 metres off the track. About 10 metres further on was Harry, lying on his back.

Red had found him on his face and turned him over, but couldn't get a response – which is when he ran to get Ryan.

Max, Steve and Webby could now see Ryan and Red on their knees leaning over what appeared to be Harry. Max saw the bike's front forks and handle bars were bent. The petrol tank was lying on the ground a bit further off the track. 'Shit, he must have hit hard,' Max said to Steve as they ran to see what was going on.

Harry was motionless on his back. 'He won't talk to me, but he's breathing,' said Ryan. 'Fuck!' said Webby, 'he's only just got over his sprained ankle.'

'Fuck the ankle!' shouted Steve, 'What do we do?'

Max took charge while Ryan did his best to look after Harry. Ryan took off his jumper, rolled it up and put it under Harry's head, then checked his legs and arms for broken bones, all while talking to him. He was relieved that Harry was breathing.

'Come on mate,' said Ryan calmly, 'Wake up for me.' Ryan and Harry used 'mate' as a nickname for each other when they were growing up and Ryan was using it now as a term of endearment.

Meanwhile, Max had made some decisions – he, Steve and Webby would ride back to camp and get Steve's car. It was a four-door and they could open the rear door and slide Harry in. He and Steve would then set off for the hospital in Darling.

We can't do anything else, thought Max. Red's already moved him, so I don't think we can do any further damage. Webby stayed back at the camp and began packing.

Ryan was very worried when the boys returned in Steve's car, because Harry was yet to stir. His breathing was steady at least, and they couldn't find any other injuries. He had now been unconscious for over an hour, 'But he had made murmuring noises,' Ryan told Max and Steve. Max reiterated the plan to drive Harry to Darling hospital and they all agreed.

'Steve and I will get him to Darling as quickly as we can,' Max said. Max thought he would drive, as he was a better driver than Steve, who could monitor Harry on the back seat.

Webby, Ryan and Red would pack the camp and wait for Steve to return from the hospital and help with the bikes; they would need Steve's car to come back and get one of the trailers and take some of the other gear. 'I will stay in Darling with Harry,' Max advised.

They lifted Harry very carefully, trying to remember what they had been taught in school about first aid and how to be careful of spinal injuries. Harry murmured, but they didn't know if that was a good sign or not. Harry was tall and took up all the back seat of Steve's car. Steve laid back the front passenger seat so he could lean over and monitor Harry with a hand on his chest. They all knew that breathing was the most important thing to be concerned about.

They were all tense and worried. Ryan was shaken and emotional, which is why Max wanted to leave him at camp. 'We need to think clearly,' Max told Ryan. 'You guys can come back and get his bike later,' Max yelled from the car window as he and Steve left for Darling.

Max drove back along the bush track quickly but carefully so as not to disturb Harry. As they got near the camp, Steve yelled to Max, 'He opened his eyes! He shut them again but he opened them. Wait a minute – he's trying to say something!'

'Are you okay Harry?' Steve asked. 'I haven't had a headache like this since you and Sandra got married,' mumbled Harry. 'Do you feel okay mate?' Steve asked again. 'Bloody sore head,' Harry said as he tried to raise himself up on his arms. 'Fuck,' said Steve, 'I think he's going to be okay, but he's talking shit.'

Max pulled up at the camp. Webby ran over to the car to see how Harry was as Ryan and Red pulled up behind them on their bikes, and hurried over. Steve had the back door of the Ford open and was leaning in towards Harry. 'He's talking boys. It doesn't make much sense but he's talking.'

Harry had propped himself up a little on his elbows and was looking surprisingly well. He even gave them a grin. They all started grinning and laughing and making taunts at Harry, but Max knew he wasn't out of the woods. They needed to get him to the Darling hospital as soon as possible to have him checked. Max thought the hospital may even call the flying doctor to Darling and take him back to Rasp, where the hospital had more sophisticated equipment to properly examine him. At least, at the moment, his condition was good.

As planned, Max and Steve continued on to the Darling hospital, where Harry was admitted. There was no full-time doctor on duty in Darling: emergency patients were examined by an experienced nurse who organised the flying doctor plane to evacuate the patient if necessary.

The nurse told Max and Steve that Harry would be flown to Rasp that night so they could give him a CT scan. This was necessary to ensure there was no bleeding on the brain. He had told the nurse he had a bad headache.

'What did he say to you when he woke?' she asked, 'Was it coherent?'

Max looked at Steve and said, 'He said he had a bad headache and that he hadn't had a headache like that since I got married – but I'm not married, nurse.' The nurse made a note, then asked if they would like to use a phone to contact Harry's parents.

'The plane will be here in about an hour,' she said. 'You can talk to him before he goes, but only for a moment.'

Max telephoned Harry's mother and gave her the news, then contacted Bridget. 'Yeh, he seems ok, but they want to do a brain scan, apparently,' he told Bridget. 'He doesn't seem to have any broken bones, but the nurse is concerned he may have a small brain bleed, because he wasn't totally coherent. He should be in Rasp in about two to three hours. We'll pack up and come home as well.'

Max had done a good job. He didn't alarm Mrs Barnes or Bridget, but was matter-of-fact about what had happened and Harry's current condition. He didn't tell them how frightened they had all been when they found Harry, and how awful he looked laying there unconscious.

'Fuck that was scary,' said Steve as they left the hospital.

'What did he actually say to you Stevie – you said he was talking shit?' asked Max. Steve retold Max what he had said.

'What, he said when you and *Sandra* got married?' Max clarified.

'That's exactly what he said Heady,' Steve confirmed.

'Maybe he was just confused. Debbie, Sandra – who knows,' opined Max.

'Well, I reckon it was strange and I'm going to talk to him about it when I see him,' replied Steve.

Harry's dirt bike crash at Poonawalla happened on Saturday, 9 September 1978 at around 11.30 am.

08

Rasp Hospital

9 September 1978

When Harry arrived by ambulance to Rasp Hospital, his father and mother were waiting, as was Bridget. Bridget waited in the background as Geoff and Tania greeted Harry and asked him how he felt. Harry was on a stretcher but was conscious and seemed aware of his surroundings. His mother clutched his hand for a moment when they were transferring him to the emergency department.

A doctor had already been briefed by the Darling nurse and was directing staff. He organised X-rays to check for bone damage as well as a CT scan of his brain and abdomen to check for bleeding. His vitals did not show he was suffering any internal damage, but the doctor had been informed he may have been unconscious for around an hour, and this concerned him.

Harry noticed Bridget in the background as he was being wheeled into the hospital and asked his mother if she could get Bridget to come over to his stretcher. Tania didn't know Bridget, but she followed

Harry's gaze to a young woman dressed in jeans and a long-sleeved T-shirt with a windcheater tied around her waist. Tania motioned to her to come closer as Harry was being taken down a corridor. Bridget, with tears in her eyes, took Harry's hand and gave it a gentle squeeze.

'How did you know, Bridge?' said Harry quietly.

'Max rang me from Darling,' she said. 'Are you alright?'

'I think so.' Suddenly, Harry was taken through some double doors and Geoff, Tania and Bridget were left outside. The doctor told Harry he would talk to them when he had done his tests.

Bridget, a quiet but confident young woman, introduced herself to Geoff and Tania. 'Harry probably hasn't told you about me, but my name is Bridget.' Harry was like that with his relationships. He rarely told his parents about relationships he had. He used to think there was little point, as the girl may not be around for too long. He knew his father wouldn't be interested – and he just didn't want his mother to know too many details about his life. Harry was seeking the right time to tell his mother about Bridget because he wanted to be with her for a long time. That opportunity was taken away from Harry. Even though Bridget had not said she was Harry's girlfriend, it was obvious.

Geoff and Tania stayed in the waiting room while Bridget went for a stroll – she wasn't keen to be interrogated by Harry's parents. In any case, she knew it would be a while before the doctor completed all his observations. She didn't escape fully, though, because when she came back, Tania asked her polite questions – such as how long had she known Harry, and where she worked.

After a couple of hours, the doctor came out to give them an update. All their tests showed that Harry would be fine. There were no broken bones and most importantly, no damage to his brain. He complained of a headache, but the doctor told them he had taken a significant knock, and he considered that to be a normal side effect of the brain moving within the skull as a result of the accident.

They were then allowed to see him. Bridget stood on one side of the bed and took Harry's hand. His mother and father stood on the other side and talked to Harry about his crash and how he felt. The visit only lasted a few minutes before they were ushered away. The plan was to observe Harry for 48 hours, then he could be discharged. Harry asked Bridget if she could come and see him tomorrow and Harry's mother said she would see him tomorrow as well.

That night, Harry had dreams centred around him being older. He could see himself in different cars, different houses, and in different towns talking to people he didn't know but seemed friendly with. The dreams seemed like movie shorts. Harry could see things happening, then there would be another 'movie short' and he was doing something else.

The predominant dream was about a young woman. She had long dark hair, long legs and was so kind and thoughtful towards Harry. He saw them dating and going places. He was driving a dark brown Holden. He couldn't understand or see when or how they met, but she was a constant. Harry saw and felt them making love. It seemed she was a part of his life – yet he didn't know this girl. She seemed to be hiding something at first and seemed uncomfortable with her life, but Harry changed that.

Harry also saw himself in an unhappy place. The dream showed him a long way from home with no close friends around. No Ben or Webby to lean on. He was desperately lonely and scared for his safety.

When Harry woke, he contemplated that maybe his mind was telling him that that's what it could be like when you are older, as in 'Aren't you glad you didn't die when you crashed – you have your whole life ahead of you!' But why wasn't Bridget in his movies as his lover – and why was he so lonely in one of his dreams? He felt confused. Everyone has dreams, he thought, but mine were so lifelike.

That day, he had what he later called 'visions'. If he dozed or wasn't concentrating, or sometimes if someone mentioned something familiar, he would see things. Some visions were of everyday things. Dinners, parties, being with friends – Max, Webby and Ben, and Stevie with a woman whom Stevie called 'Sandra'. All the dreams and visions were haphazard – shifting from one scene to another. Harry had no control over what visions would come into his head. They were so random, yet so real.

It was now Sunday afternoon and his concentration on his dreams was broken by Max, Webby and Steve. Harry was parked in a bed with a monitor on his heart and needed regular visits from a nurse, but she allowed the boys in for a short visit. 'No skylarking,' she said. Harry was as pleased to see them as they were to see him, propped up in bed.

The boys had retrieved Harry's bike and got home late on Saturday night. 'You got lucky,' said Webby, 'You didn't have to pack up all that shit we had.'

'Lucky you have a job as well,' said Stevie, 'because your bike's rooted!' They wanted to know what happened.

'He's just a shit rider,' laughed Stevie.

'I just remember going hard on the front brakes and thinking, "I'm too late." I must have gone too hard on the front brakes … That's about all I remember,' Harry said, adding 'Did you get a root last night Stevie?'

They all laughed. 'Do you know what you said to me when you came to?' Steve asked. Harry looked blank. 'You said that the last time you had such a headache was after Sandra and I got married! Who the fuck is Sandra?'

For a moment Harry was blindside by the comment, but he told Stevie he had no idea why he had said that. 'Debbie, Sandra – as if you care bud,' covered Harry. In an instant he saw Stevie getting married and could see someone toasting Steve and Sandra. 'I got nothing mate,' lied Harry. He didn't want his mates to think he was crazy. *What's happening to me?* he thought.

Bridget visited, which made Harry very happy. She cares about me, he thought. Harry held her hand tightly and didn't let it go the whole time she was with him. He promised her he would be out on Monday, he felt so well. He was concerned about the dreams and visions he was having, but thought that they may be a side effect of a head injury. He wasn't going to talk to the doctor about it or they may keep him in the darn place.

Harry's parents also visited and after they had gone, and it was quiet, he had a most disturbing vision about his father. Geoff was in hospital in a coma. His head was bandaged and there was all manner of machines hooked up to him. Harry and his mother were being spoken to by the doctor, who was talking about significant head trauma. The doctor said that Geoff may not have sustained such an injury if he had been wearing a protective helmet. The vision then ended.

Harry was frightened. What if my visions come true? he thought. What if *that* vision comes true?

Harry was released on Monday and went to work on Wednesday 12 September. As he crossed the street to the bank, he saw in the distance the huge slag heap that crisscrossed Rasp and had a sudden vision of it covered in white, like snow – but then he saw himself and everyone else in the bank mopping the floors. Someone in his vision said the hail covered the slag heap and looked like snow. 'The gutters are blocked by hail,' they said 'which is why the water is coming through the roof.' In the vision, Harry noticed the date board the bank kept on the front counter: it said Friday 14 September. He could see cars with hail dents all over them and some with smashed windscreens. The vision ended as quickly as it started. Something is wrong with me, thought Harry.

Well, there is nothing wrong with me physically, thought Harry, after he visited Bridget on Wednesday night. They hadn't been together since the previous Thursday night, and Harry modestly believed his performance was fantastic. That contention was supported by Bridget's flushed cheeks as they lay together. 'Hey Bridge, I think there's going to be a huge storm on Friday,' ventured Harry.

'What would make you say that?'

'Oh, I can't do a thing with my hair,' Harry said, laughing.

Bridget chuckled as well. 'You are an idiot,' she said.

Harry had the same vision during the day that he had on the way to work and thought, What if my visions are about the future, and I am right? Bridget will only laugh at me if I am wrong. I might tell the boys as well.

'Bridge, tomorrow tell Webby he better leave his car at home on Friday, or it'll be destroyed by hail,' Harry said. 'Okay Alan Wilkie,' replied Bridget teasingly, invoking the nation's best-known weatherman, 'I'll tell him, silly.' One of the things Bridget liked about Harry was his all-embracing nature, and his desire to do silly stuff sometimes. *Life will never be dull with Harry*, she thought.

Even though it was late, Harry drove past Max's place on his way home from Bridget's. Stevie's car was there, so he called in. They were down in Max's shed. Steve was helping Max replace the exhaust on his car. They had just about finished as Harry walked in the garage. 'Flasha!' said Steve, 'I thought you would be on the nest; I will be in about 10 minutes' time.'

'No mate, I've still got a headache,' replied Harry.

'Yeh bullshit,' said Steve.

'Hey boys,' called Harry, 'I've been reading the tea leaves and I reckon you should leave your cars home on Friday, because it's going to hail cats and dogs.'

'It only says a chance of storms,' Max said.

'I have to tell you boys, I had a dream about it,' Harry said in a light-hearted way. 'See you naysayers on Friday – the Monaro will be staying at home boys. Don't say I didn't warn you.'

'Told you he's crazy,' Steve said as Harry left.

* * *

That Friday, Rasp endured its biggest storm in over 50 years. Trees were shredded, businesses and homes flooded, iron roofs badly damaged and hundreds of cars destroyed beyond repair.

Gutters along the streets became blocked by hail stones and as a result, many of the streets flooded. That Friday when Steve arrived at work, he parked in the shadow of one of the huge mine machinery shops.

Nah, Flash won't be right about a storm – the sun is out, he thought. But … just in case, my car will be safer here.

Max's car was still in pieces, so he rode his pushbike to work, and Webby – well, he and Bridget laughed at Harry's prediction, but his car was parked at the rear of their office behind Bridget's flat and was protected by the two-storey building.

Each of his friends had a different opinion of Harry's prediction, but Steve went and saw Harry that night at his home before Harry and Bridget went out. Harry was getting ready to go out and was busy. 'You talk and I'll listen Stevie,' said Harry.

Steve had a bee in his bonnet. He wanted to know why Harry had warned about the storm – how he knew. Also, he wasn't satisfied with Harry's explanation of 'Sandra'.

Harry had been thinking the same thing all day as well. He was incredulous and worried: one of his visions had come true. Worried because that meant other visions may come true as well. Harry had been having more dreams and visions during the day, and each time he had one of these episodes the situation was clearer.

He had seen the girl with long dark hair many times now. Her name was Lucy and she lived in a town somewhere near the large regional city of Gidgee. The name of her town was vague. He could see the town and thought he knew where on the edge of town Lucy lived – on a farm – but the name of the town eluded him.

He had also again seen Steve and Sandra getting married. It definitely wasn't Debbie. Debbie was blonde and Sandra a little shorter with dark hair. Another bloke called Bill also appeared in his dreams. Bill was offering Harry financial advice, and they were discussing investments. In his dreams, Harry respected and looked up to Bill as a business mentor.

Harry just couldn't put any of it into a sequence. His dreams were more detailed, but haphazard. They were not premonitions, because he only dreamed about or viewed things that he was involved in – or that someone had told him about. He did not have distant premonitions far from his experiences. That would be witchery, thought Harry. I only see things that affect me.

The first part of Steve's question was easy. Why had Harry warned his friends about the storm? Harry didn't want to obfuscate, and just jumped right in with his explanation. He trusted Steve and needed to tell someone what he had been experiencing.

'Well, I kind of thought that I knew it would happen,' said Harry, 'and I wanted to put it out in the open and back myself.' Steve seemed perplexed. 'I've been having dreams Steve. Ever since my accident, I have visions and dreams and they seem to be about the future. Not everyone's future, but the future as it relates to me.'

'What the fuck!' exclaimed Steve, 'You can see into the future? I think that knock on the head has affected you, Harry.'

'No, I can't see into the future, I see my future,' Harry clarified.

'But you told me about my future – that I marry a girl called Sandra,' replied Steve.

'I am sorry Steve, I wish I hadn't told you about that, but it's too late now, isn't it? Those words tumbled out when I regained consciousness. I was at your wedding and it obviously had an impact on me and is a lasting memory for me. It's a memory of mine that I share with you. Well, it's not a memory yet, but it will be.'

This only served to further confuse Steve. Harry was being careful not to tell Steve about all the visions he had had, but he wanted to be honest with him. He truly felt uncomfortable about telling Steve who he was going to marry – but then again, would he be right? Harry was struggling to determine if he was seeing the future or if the dreams were just that – dreams.

Harry wanted to put his credibility on the line. If he said it out loud, he couldn't take it back. He was daring himself to believe. The most pervasive of his dreams was that of the girl with long dark hair. He dreamed about her every night, and each time he learned more, and their relationship became clearer. He was obsessed with this dream and wanted to know even more.

Steve startled Harry back from his thoughts: 'Flash, we need to figure out if everything you see in your visions will come true – and what about the storm you said would happen,' he said.

'I was walking to work on Wednesday and suddenly I saw the slag heap covered in what looked like snow,' Harry said, 'and then I saw in my mind that it was a hail storm and that it would be on the Friday.'

'So, it was a vision and had nothing to do with a weather forecast you saw or heard about. Totally from your vision?' Steve asked.

'Yep,' confirmed Harry.

'Fuck mate,' Steve said, 'I can't believe this. This only happened after your accident, right?'

Harry could only nod his head. Life last Friday was so good, remembered Harry. He was on top of the world then, and now he didn't know if he was Arthur or Martha. But Harry was determined it wouldn't change his life. He was going to carry on as if nothing had happened. He was determined not to change a thing – to carry on as if things were normal.

'Hopefully the dreams will just go away one day Stevie,' sighed Harry.

'In the interim, how can you figure out if the dreams are just that or if they come true?' asked Steve.

'I don't know mate. If you have an idea, let me know – but please Stevie, don't tell anyone about what we just discussed. Promise?'

'What about Max?' Steve demanded.

'You can tell him, only! But don't talk to Webby about this – he'll tell Bridget. Okay?' With that the conversation was over. But Harry knew Stevie would want to revisit the 'Sandra' matter again.

Bridget didn't really care about Harry's prediction of the storm. When he picked her up that night, she greeted him with a smile and a kiss, 'Hi my Alan Wilkie,' she said, laughing, and that was the extent of their conversation about the storm. Harry didn't want to talk about it, and Bridget was just happy to have Harry back in one piece.

09

Harry needs to know the truth

Harry was still close to Webby, but he didn't tell him about his dreams and visions. He was concerned that Webby might share their discussion with Bridget inadvertently. Harry was confident that Webby wouldn't deliberately disclose their private discussions with Bridget, but they worked in the same office, and he was concerned that something may slip out.

That was why he told Steve he wasn't to share their conversation with anyone but Max. It was now the weekend and he would have to enlighten Max.

It was starting to warm up in Rasp and a small group of car owners had converged on the main street. It was a warm Saturday evening and the sun had just gone down. It was common for young guys to take their freshly polished cars down the main street on a Saturday night, to show them off and meet girls.

Harry pulled up in his Monaro near Max and Steve. They both greeted Harry as they jumped in his car. 'What's happening Flash?'

asked a concerned Max. Harry was well aware that Steve would have talked to Max about their discussion: now he was about to get the third degree from Max.

'Mate, you know if you need help, we are here for you,' Max said quietly. 'Yeh, I know Heady,' replied Harry. 'But there's not much you can do. I think my visions will peter out one day. I'm not letting them affect me, just getting on with life; Bridget is really special and I don't want to mess that up.'

'Stevie told me about the Sandra comment when we were back in Darling,' Max said, 'and now I understand why you said it. But do you reckon all your visions will come true? I mean, you warned us about the storm, but one summer doesn't make a swallow,' said Max.

Max wasn't being nasty – he was being his matter-of-fact self, and Harry knew that. He's trying to discern fact from fiction and make me feel better, thought Harry.

Harry had kept most of his visions a secret. He hadn't told either friend about the girl he now knew as Lucy, and thought he would never tell them about her. He didn't tell them about the vision he had had of his father's near death; he didn't tell them about his mate Bill, whom he would obviously meet sometime in the future; he didn't tell them that he would spend years in Sydney in banking, analysing companies and making stock recommendations for entrepreneurs who made huge amounts of money; and he didn't tell them that he and Lucy would be financially comfortable in later life, and married with children.

In fact, he had only told them about Sandra and the storm.

Harry hadn't made up his mind – if he was protecting them, or if he wasn't sure his visions and dreams would come true. He thought it was the former. He didn't want them trying to work with any predetermined outcome. I don't want to be responsible for that, he thought.

He kept returning to the real question: were all his dreams true, or would they come true?

He had dreamed of Lucy again the night before. In the first 'movie short' he was on a farm, which he gathered was Lucy's home. He had driven the short distance from town to visit her. It was a cropping farm, but they also ran a few sheep and pigs. It was apparent to Harry that

Lucy's father was not enamoured with him, but that Lucy didn't care. Harry could see that he and Lucy were young. The dream seemed to show that they were, at the very least, boyfriend and girlfriend.

Then the scene shifted to a much older Harry. It was Christmas time and he and Lucy were celebrating with three young children, and Lucy's mother and father were there. Then came another scene where Lucy was crying and telling Harry, 'Dad's been in a very bad accident. His arm was caught in the tractor and he may lose it.'

'Heady, you could be right,' Harry said. 'Maybe my dreams won't come true, but they seem so real.'

'So, mate, other than the storm vision, have any other visions or dreams come true? asked Max.

'No,' answered Harry.

'Do you see anything about my future,' asked Max.

'No,' lied Harry.

'What does Sandra look like?' Max continued.

'I don't know,' he lied again. Sandra was not very tall with a Rubenesque body and shoulder-length dark hair. She smiled a lot, laughed out loud and would tell everyone what she thought. Harry had learned all of this from his dreams, but he didn't want Steve to know any of it. He'll find her on his own, thought Harry.

The boys didn't grill Harry anymore, but talked about cars and what people they knew were up to. Stevie also said that Heady was interested in a skinny hairdresser that Flash had yet to meet, and Max tried to shut the conversation down. 'I only talked to her for a bit,' said Max, 'You bastards.'

Harry left to go and see Bridget, and Steve to see Debbie. 'Her name is Debbie,' Steve shouted to Harry as he walked away with a big smile on his face. On the drive to Bridget's, Harry decided that he had to find out about his dreams, and that he would tackle his most common dream first. He would find Lucy. Then he would know one way or the other.

Am I crazy, or can I see the future? he thought. This wasn't about finding love and losing his relationship with Bridget, because he loved Bridge. Not knowing was eating him. He was losing his confidence and was being careful around his mates and family. I want to be more honest with myself and others, he kidded himself. Would he tell every-one he could see the future if he found out he could?

Bridget had a fundraising event on the night of Friday 23 September. She was raising money via the Miss Australia quest. She would be busy with her friends and not expect him to be there at a function, which was mainly for women. They would normally catch up on Saturday night after he spent the day riding bikes with his mates; Harry calculated that if he left to find Lucy on Friday, immediately after work, and drove most of the night, he could get to Gidgee in the early hours of Saturday, find Lucy and be home about six on Saturday night.

He wouldn't tell Max or Steve – and definitely not Webby. He would only be away for around 24 hours. Hope I don't break down or hit a kangaroo, he thought. Kangaroos are plentiful in western New South Wales. They stray onto the roads at night and are often struck by cars, causing considerable damage.

Harry left work early. Barney said light-heartedly, 'No punch-ups or bike-riding this weekend. I want you fit and healthy next week boy!' The Monaro was already fuelled and Harry snuck out of town. He hoped no one he knew would see him leave and ask questions of anyone.

Harry had been having more dreams about Lucy. He didn't know the name of the town where she lived, but he somehow knew that if he got to Gidgee, he would recognise where to go. He didn't know why, but he could see himself driving from Gidgee to where Lucy lived in his dreams. Gidgee was around 850 kilometres east-south-east of Rasp, in the Riverina district. The major town in the area, it was a service centre for farms and a hub for government services, with a population of around 45,000.

He now knew that he and Lucy would have three children – and he knew their names, and he knew her best friend. Heaps of detail, he thought. But the destination and why he goes there, or how he meets Lucy in the future remained a mystery to him.

It was a very long and lonely drive to Gidgee from Rasp. There were long distances between towns, but the roads were straight; Harry had his foot down and the Monaro's engine was 'singing'. The quicker he got there, the quicker he would know, he thought. His excitement kept him awake when the roads became quiet late into the night as he pressed on.

Rasp was an isolated town and Harry and his mates were used to driving long distances. He had travelled this way only once with his parents on a family trip. Harry's father had a sister who lived in Gidgee, but the road seemed especially familiar. His visions hadn't shown him the way, but somehow, he knew where to turn and what towns he needed to transit through to get to Gidgee.

It's like I'm on autopilot, thought Harry. After around 850 gruelling kilometres, he approached Gidgee from the west. About 20 kilometres from the town, he saw a sign pointing south-west off the main highway. The sign said 'Little Creek, 86 kilometres'.

Harry knew. 'That's it,' he mouthed, as he turned the Monaro down the narrow road.

10

Lucy Martin

September 1978

Lucy's mother usually woke her up. She wasn't a morning person –
or a night person, for that matter. She often stayed up late but didn't
usually go out to parties. When she stayed up late, it was usually in her
room. She would read or tune in to her favourite radio station, listening to music talk-back. Other listeners would ring in, request songs
and explain where they were partying, and what they were doing. Little
Creek was too small to have a radio station, so she listened to a station
in Gidgee, about 100 kilometres from her farm.

Lucy was born in 1963. Her father and mother were farmers. Her
father, Mick, had drawn a soldier settler's block of around 2000 acres
and they had farmed it since 1965. Mick was old-school. He didn't
borrow from a bank. Everything he had, he paid for in cash. Lucy
thought that maybe he could borrow and upgrade some of his
equipment, but she never had that discussion with her father. She didn't
think it was her place and she wasn't so sure Mick would listen in any

case. She loved her father very much and respected him for the hard work he did. He didn't smoke and didn't go to the local pub. He was a religious man and was always kind to anyone he thought may be in need. His pastime was old-time dancing and Lucy would indulge him by regularly accompanying him to dances in nearby small towns. This was a joy to Mick, as his daughter was tall, graceful and pretty with long dark hair and dark eyes. He was proud of her.

Lucy's mother Mavis was also a frugal, God-fearing person – although more like a religious zealot, Lucy thought. She often cited Bible verses and tried very hard to lead a Christian lifestyle. She wasn't materialistic and was satisfied that she could provide good food and a welcoming home for her children. She didn't like to go to dances with Mick. She was a little hard of hearing, which made conversation difficult for her, and she didn't enjoy getting dressed up, so she was pleased that Lucy accompanied Mick. She would wait up at home until they returned and then talk to them about their evening: her enjoyment was to see that Lucy and Mick had a good time.

Lucy inherited her parents' kindness and compassion towards other people but was sceptical of religion. She sometimes thought that her mother put religion before her family and wasn't comfortable with that.

Lucy was the youngest of three. She had a brother and a sister, both more than 10 years older. Her sister Janice was very rebellious and had left home around the age of 17. She wasn't yet married but lived with a guy in Perth, Western Australia. Lucy often thought that that was about as far away as Janice could go – and maybe that's why she went there! Mavis often said that Janice was very stubborn, but that they shouldn't have let her go so far away. Mick said, 'She is head-strong and won't be swayed, so we should just let her go.'

Lucy was privately critical of her parents and their relationship with their children. She thought if her mother had given Janice more love, things would have been better – she might still be living at home.

Lucy's brother Dan was 13 years older than Lucy and married to a local girl, Heather. He had four boys with another on the way. They lived in Little Creek. Dan was not particularly ambitious and worked for the district water board. He was happy to work nine-to-five and have Friday night beers at the Club. He got married when he was quite young – in fact, Mick and Mavis had to provide formal permission for him to be married. Dan's wife Heather was a year older than him. She loved watching Elvis movies with Lucy when Lucy visited to help with the boys. Lucy loved being involved with her nephews and doing housework with Heather.

Because Lucy was now an only child living at home, her parents doted on her. Lucy wasn't spoilt, but if she needed something, Mick would make sure she got it. Mavis would make sure that Lucy got up in time for school, and her clothes would always be neatly pressed, ready to go. Lucy was in Year 10 at school and intended to leave at the end of the year, but hadn't yet discussed that with her parents.

Lucy had a very large bedroom in the old farmhouse. It was originally a sitting room, but when Mick acquired Little Creek South, he set it up as a bedroom for Janice. When Janice left home, Lucy moved in. The room had two sets of French doors that opened out onto a timber veranda. Lucy slept in a double bed with a built-in shelf and light and had a simple wardrobe with a matching bedroom dresser with a mirror.

On this particular morning, Lucy was sitting in front of her bedroom mirror brushing her hair. She wondered what it would be like with short hair – she was often late and that would save time in the morning – but she was too cautious to have her hair cut. She knew her Achilles heel was her inability to make decisions, a trait she blamed her mother for. Lucy vacillated about lots of things – including her hair.

Mavis came into her room. 'If you don't hurry, you'll be late for netball,' she said. 'You know your father can't take you this morning – he's got pigs to send away.'

Lucy loved playing netball. She felt she was good at it and wasn't embarrassed to try really hard. She had a competitive spirit, a slim athletic build and long legs that helped her excel at sport. Mavis didn't often go and watch Lucy play, which irked Lucy a little. Lucy thought that her mother was happy at home, but maybe if she took more of an interest, Janice would still be home, and maybe she could also share her joy of netball with her mother.

'I know mum. I'm hurrying.' Mavis told her she would have to ride her motorbike into town, which Lucy already knew. 'I know mum.' Lucy thought that maybe she should rebel like her sister, but didn't want to leave the safety of home.

Mavis knew that Lucy would ride the short distance into town to Alice's place, then get a ride with her and other players to the game in Coolabah. Lucy had a bright yellow Suzuki agricultural motor bike that she sometimes rode to town. She used to putter into town and covertly make her way to her friend Alice's backyard. Mavis watched her daughter hop on the bike and ride towards town and was happy that Lucy would have a good time, and that she would hear all about it later that day.

Little Creek

11

September 1978

Harry wasn't sure whether it was the cold or his excitement that finally woke him.

He had driven most of the night and quickly slipped into a deep slumber when he pulled up. He didn't have a pillow with him, but rolled up a spare pair of jeans he had on the back seat and used that as a pillow. He was in the passenger seat so he could stretch out a little, but wasn't comfortable. He was half sleeping and half awake, thinking he should have taken his Golden Breed windcheater with him – with that warmth he would still be sleeping. But then he remembered why he was there and was immediately excited and apprehensive at once. Still in a light slumber, he then thought he would have looked good in his favourite windcheater; it was fire-engine red with the small Golden Breed insignia on the left side of his chest, and it fitted just right. It made his shoulders look broad and would have teamed well with the light blue jeans he had on.

He could hear a small engine in the distance, which irritated him, and contributed to him waking up. Last night he had driven close to 1000 kilometres and somehow found his way to Little Creek. His visions showed that he needed to drive through the small town to the first gravel road on his right, about a kilometre out of town. When he saw the gravel road, he immediately knew this was the farm he was looking for.

He had crept into Little Creek at around 2.30 am. The final 80 kilometres or so of the road to little Creek was bitumen, but also narrow, with a gravel verge. He had been vigilantly looking all night for kangaroos: he didn't want his beloved Monaro damaged. He slowed for the last T-intersection before turning right into the town. On his left were the four large wheat silos he remembered from his visions. He went across the railway line that led to the silos, his car creaking as he crossed. Because it was very dark, he could see very little of the landscape surrounding the town, but knew it was typical wheat-belt country. Undulating, loamy soil best suited to cereal cropping, sheep and, in improved paddocks, cattle fattening and breeding. This time of year, the crops would be mature and green, if there was adequate rain. It was the last week of September now and the farmers didn't really need a lot of rain. He knew that in drier years in this area, crops were prone to failure or low yields.

Little Creek seemed deserted as he drove slowly, turning left, then right, into the main street. It felt like he had been here before. There were a few streetlights but nothing open at such a late hour. The town was very small, and he guessed at a population of around 900. In the main street he saw two large pubs, both on corners. They were both two-storeyed with wandering balconies, just like he had seen in his visions. He wondered why such a small town needed two pubs, then answered himself: in country towns they are the fabric of the town. People meet and party there, and the pubs support local sport. There was also a small general store with an iron veranda protruding out over the footpath. It was small, but he knew that it was owned by Mr and Mrs Hoare. His visions were becoming clearer and more detailed. This is why I'm here, he thought.

Across the road from the general store was a café – a country town café where you could get a milkshake, a cup of tea and a toasted sandwich. The café was next to the biggest pub, The Little Creek Hotel. Then there was the Australian Rural Bank bank branch. He slowed and studied it carefully, because he worked at the Rural branch in Rasp. It was a very small building – probably with four or five staff, he thought. He liked country towns and wondered if he would like working there.

But all he had were visions of the girl he was searching for and the town. He hadn't had any vision of working there, so he dismissed these thoughts. After all, his visions were now very detailed: surely he would have seen himself there if that was to be. The only other commercial buildings in the main street were a stock and station agency, next to the bank, a post office and a Ford dealership. The post office and stock agent buildings were made of stone and brick, but the Ford dealership was a large iron building. Instinctively, he knew where to turn and what roads to take. It was surreal: he knew that in the future he would come to visit this town – or perhaps live there?

The engine noise was getting louder and at last he opened his eyes. He had pulled about 20 metres off the main bitumen road, about 300 metres past the bridge that led from town, which he had crossed last night, and onto the gravel road leading into the farm. He was close to the entrance of the farm. There was a grid on the gravel road to stop stock from getting out and he knew that the road went straight on for about two kilometres to the farmhouse. He didn't want to block the grid, but wanted to park close enough so that he would be able to see if anyone came through. He had had many visions about the girl who lived there and thought he would be able to recognise her easily. For some reason, his visions about her father were that he was not friendly towards him. He didn't want to test the relationship with her father at this time, so he made sure that the grid was kept clear.

The sun came streaming through the driver's side window and made it difficult to see, but he could hear the engine more clearly now and recognised it as a motorbike. Then, as he squinted into the sun, he could see a small trail of dust behind a motorbike coming down the gravel driveway from the farm towards him. He leaned forward towards the side window and cupped his hand in front of his eyes so he blocked the sun and could see. The bike wasn't travelling very fast, and he thought it sounded like an agricultural bike, not the type of fast trail bike he would ride.

He got out of his car leaned his bottom on the bonnet. It was even colder outside. He again thought he should have bought his windcheater with him, not only to keep himself warm but also to impress the girl if he was able to meet her. He was dressed in what he left Rasp in – a white T-shirt with 'Australian Rural Bank' written across the back, blue jeans and white runners. He knew the T-shirt looked cool and he would just have to do without the windcheater.

He squinted and saw it was a girl riding the motorbike. He knew it was a girl because she wasn't wearing a helmet, and he could see her long hair waving about as she rode. At the thought of this his chest rose, he lost his breath and he became very nervous. It was like when you are a teenager and you see a girl without any clothes on before you become intimate. So nervous with anticipation it can take your breath away. He steadied himself by thinking, It's probably not her – it could be her sister.

But he didn't know if she had a sister, and he had been here all night and seen no one come in. This girl must live here!

He stared as she rode towards him. It felt like half an hour but in reality, it was only minutes. She had a navy coat on over a light blue jumper and what looked like caramel-brown-coloured jeans. Her jeans are probably corduroy, he then thought – a popular choice among girls of her age. It was 1978 and given his visions he thought that she would be around 15 years old – about three-and-a-half years younger than him. He thought that she was riding slowly because it was cold – or was it that she was being careful on the gravel? It would be easy for the front wheel to slip sideways if it hit a large stone, and then she would be off. She seemed competent enough to use the bike as transport, he thought, but it seemed to him that she wouldn't ride wildly for fun like he did.

As she slowed for the grid, he could see she had a pretty face and what he considered a shapely body. She had long dark hair, dark eyes and long legs. He had so many emotions going through his mind about what to say, what to do, how long he could talk to her, and, lastly, whether she would believe his story.

He wondered if he should tell her what he had seen in his visions. She might think I'm a lunatic, he thought. But he had come all this way and didn't want to back out now. All my visions and dreams to date since that day have been right, he thought. The Rasp hailstorm; Little Creek and where she lives. It must be true.

12

The grid meeting

September 1978

He stood up straight as she reached the grid. She didn't smile at him. She's probably wondering what I'm doing here, he thought – Who is he? Is he safe? Is he a lunatic?

So many thoughts were running through his head. She would be the first stranger he had tried to talk to about what he had seen – and about the future.

She kept her bike running for a moment, apparently assessing him, then turned the key to the 'off' position as he moved towards her.

'Hi, is your name Lucy?' he asked.

'Yes,' she said. Harry wasn't sure what his face showed, but he was astounded. Holy shit, my dreams are true, thought Harry. His whole world changed in an instant. He had found the girl he had dreamed about. It was almost unbelievable, but he continued as best he could on jelly legs.

'Well, you obviously don't know me, but I wanted to talk to you for a bit.'

Lucy eyed him carefully and seemed very reserved. 'How do you know my name?' she asked. 'Do you know some of my friends?'

There was a pause. Harry looked at her longingly, hoping that she would give him a chance to explain himself and then not think he was weird.

Lucy thought, How does this guy know who I am? Then on another level altogether she mused, He *is* handsome.

From where she sat, he looked to be about 6 feet tall and slim, with long blonde hair, long legs, some freckles on his face and what look like hazel-coloured eyes. And, she thought, he looks good in that T-shirt – but he must be cold.

Harry was thinking, She is so beautiful – I hope she believes me, or believes *in* me.

'Umm, I know of a friend of yours – Alice?'

'You know Alice?'

'Well, I sort of know of her.'

Lucy was getting the upper hand in this conversation and Harry was rattled.

She smiled as she questioned him, 'You sort of know of her?' She was beginning to think, even though he's handsome, he's a weirdo.

'Wow, this is getting really hard,' Harry said out loud. 'Promise me that you won't ride off if I seem a little weird. I've driven a very long way to see you,' he said. She smiled a little because he seemed nice. He seemed smart and he was from out of town. She thought that most of the boys in Little Creek were boring and not adventurous or ambitious, like her brother.

'Okay I promise.'

Harry started to explain hesitantly. 'I sometimes can see the future,' he said.

Now she *knew* he was a good-looking weirdo, and was a little disappointed, but there was something about him. Not his clothes or his bright blue car or his broad shoulders and skinny hips. When she looked into his eyes, she could see that he was sincere, and he seemed worldly.

Lucy was generally a good judge of character, and for some reason she wanted to believe this guy, and wanted to believe in him. She had a lot on her plate, including wrestling with what she wanted to do when she left school later that year. She disliked school; the only thing she enjoyed about it was athletics, and even though she had won running races in some regional carnivals, she knew there was no future in that. She wanted to leave school at the end of the year and maybe join the army; she thought she might like to drive trucks. She was a feminine type of girl, who liked having nice fingernails and long hair, so truck-driving in the army did seem out-of-kilter. Maybe it was just that she wanted to be independent, get out of Little Creek and do something different – and maybe cut her hair!

But what could she say to this guy she didn't know who had just said to her that he can sometimes see the future? 'Tell me some more,' she said. 'Why do you want to talk to me?'

'Phew,' Harry said, out loud. 'Because you are part of my future.'

Now it was Lucy who was rattled. She now really wanted to know what this guy had to say, but she knew she wouldn't believe what he was about to tell her. 'How am I a part of your future, and why do you want to tell me this? Isn't it bad luck to know the future?'

Harry knew he was going to have to blurt it out. What an idiot he was. He shouldn't have come here to try to talk to her. He had decided to come and visit her to see if his visions of her were correct, but now he was afraid that his mere knowledge of her might change the future. He had been very careful of not changing things because he wanted the future to be exactly the same when he reached it or got back there. He didn't understand what had happened to him and was fearful that he would never be the same. Was he the same guy as he had always been, but with this ability to see parts of the future, or was he now someone else? It was like a dream, but it was real, and he was trying to navigate it the best way he could.

At that moment, he realised why he had come to see her. He was lonely and afraid, and he just wanted to be with her. His visions of the future showed him that she loved and supported him in all kinds of ways, and he felt bulletproof when he was with her and had her support. But at the moment, he was all alone and talking to a stranger.

'We get married,' he said in a loud but pleading sort of way. His voice waivered and to Lucy he suddenly seemed vulnerable. 'I'm sorry, I don't know how to talk to you about this. We have children together and I don't want to jeopardise that. I don't want to ruin our future. I am here because I want you to wait for me. I don't want my visions to change. I don't want to miss being with you. What if you find someone else?'

Lucy was still sitting on her motorbike and felt his torrent of words rock her. He was so convincing that for a moment she believed every word he had said, but reality told her that his words could not be real. How could a young guy know all that? If he could see the future, surely he would be famous. People would flock to see him and ask questions, she thought.

As if he could also read her mind Harry said, 'I don't know everything, but I do know about you and me, and I just need you and only you to believe me.'

Once again Lucy wanted to believe him, but she resisted and looked at her watch. 'I'm running late,' she said, 'I need to go.'

'Please wait,' he said. 'I'll tell you something so you can believe me. Something that you will learn soon. Alice will have a son early next year and she will call him Jon, without the "h"!'

Lucy was again rocked. She and Alice were very close, particularly since Alice's mum had passed away. It was now late September, and next year was only months away. Surely Alice would have confided in her if she was pregnant. She couldn't be pregnant! Alice was only a little over a year older than she was and they were both still at school. *Oh my God*, Lucy then thought: Hang on, here I am believing a guy I don't even know who is telling me about the future – this is crazy.

'I have to go,' she said again. Harry tried to retrieve the situation. 'Wait – I want to write something down for you.' He ran to his car, opened the door and got a pen and paper from the glove box.

On the paper, he wrote in dot point form:

- *Little Creek has huge rains in December and there is a flood.*
- *You get a job at the local bank.*
- *The next time you see me I'll be in a dark brown 1976 Holden.*

- *You and I get married.*
- *We have three beautiful children – two boys and a girl.*

He hadn't seen much more than this in his visions about their relationship. He didn't know how they met or where, and he didn't know what year they would meet. But he had seen what he had thought was deep into the future. He was older, and he and Lucy were together. It seemed like it was Christmas and they were with their children. Two boys and a girl. Sometime in the future, Lucy had told him Jon's birth date. The thing with his visions was that he only saw in them what he would witness in the future, or what he would be told.

He handed her the note and wanted to hug her, but he knew he shouldn't. She took the note, turned and put it in her sports bag with her netball uniform. She turned back and he was half smiling at her as if he was pleading with her to believe him. She smiled back and wanted to embrace him, but he didn't move towards her. She felt something that she didn't understand. Did she care for this guy she had only known for 10 minutes, or did she feel sorry for him? Either way, he got to her emotionally, which isn't easy to do to Lucy Martin.

He knew he couldn't stay around Little Creek for long, because he wasn't meant to be there. He was only there because of his visions and he didn't want to risk their future. He wanted to cement their future, but thought he hadn't done a very good job. He wanted to say goodbye and I love you, but he couldn't. He knew he would love her dearly in the future, but now it would seem glib.

Lucy couldn't take her eyes off him as she turned the key and kick-started her motorbike. Even if his predictions don't come true, she thought, I'll remember him forever. She had only been with him for minutes but was taken with his demeanour, looks and the way he carried himself, and reckoned he would be fun to be with. He was different to all the boys in Little Creek – a genuine, fantastic weirdo, she thought.

'I'll be thinking of you,' she said. 'I hope we meet again.' She was genuine. Imagine, she thought, if everything he said came true. It would be a dream, but dreams don't always come true.

'I will see you again,' Harry said, confidently this time. 'Oh – I nearly forgot. If you meet a guy at one of your dances, be careful of him. He's not what you think. Don't get involved with him.'

She turned onto the main road with tears in her eyes. She had been emotionally impacted by Harry. If it were true, he had just told her about her future. If not, she had just met a really nice guy with a problem. Maybe I could help him, she thought, as she neared Alice's house.

Shit, she thought, I don't know his name or where he is from. She turned the bike quickly across double lines and went as fast as she could back towards the farm road, but as she approached the bridge, she could see his big blue car disappearing into the distance.

'WAIT!' she yelled as loudly as she could, 'WAIT!' But she was talking to no one. It was an emotional relief to yell at him. It made her feel better. Why had he come along and made her feel this way? It wasn't fair, she thought.

She stopped, put both feet flat on the bitumen, and cried, without quite knowing why. Was she unhappy about school or not knowing what she was going to do when she left school? Was she crying because at present she felt she had no purpose in her life? Or was she crying because he had gone and left her with a million thoughts and no answers?

'YOU ARE NOT FAIR! I HATE YOU!' she shouted. She sobbed loudly about what she thought was her meaningless life – and about being left behind by someone she didn't even know.

Harry, meanwhile, felt he hadn't performed well at the meeting. I should have been more composed, he thought. Why didn't I rehearse what I was going to say? Imagine if you met someone for the first time and they said, 'Oh, by the way, you and I are going to get married sometime in the future, and we'll have three children!'

But he reminded himself that he didn't have the full picture. His visions were becoming clearer and less confused, but he didn't know everything. Maybe, he thought, I should have Googled 'How to talk to someone about the future?'

Hang on, he thought – I know about computers and the World Wide Web, but I don't think it's been invented yet, or has it? He knew from school that they were working on super computers in the USA. But in his visions, he has a computer and he looks stuff up using something called 'Google'! In the future the military probably use it to spy and send messages, he thought.

The issue with his visions, he thought, was that there is no timeline: I just see things. He got lucky with the vision about Alice's son. He didn't witness the birth or anything like that, but had a vision in which Lucy tells him when Jon was born. Lucy also tells him, at a point in the future, about the big rains in December 1978, and that the creek that ran beside her parents' farm, Little Creek South, almost took their house.

But when would he meet with Lucy again? When would he be in Little Creek again – and why? These uncertainties made his life difficult, he thought. I might have been asking Lucy to wait for 15 years, and that's scary.

One thing he was happy with was that Lucy didn't ask him his name or where he was from. He decided early that if he told her this, she might come and visit him, and that could really stuff things up. My relationship with Bridge will have to run its course, he thought. If Lucy visited him and the present changed – then automatically wouldn't the future change?

Anyway, she didn't ask and he didn't have to try to explain – or worse, lie to her – so he was comfortable with that, but could understand that Lucy may become very frustrated by the lack of that information. He reckoned that around about now she would be chastising herself for not getting his name. Then he wondered, had she looked at my number plates? (His personalised plates – HB 2420. Sometimes his mates called him 'Pencil' because of the HB. He didn't like that as he thought it could infer his penis was small – as in 'Pencil Dick'. His real nickname was Flash and he liked it.)

Nonetheless, he thought that if Lucy had seen and remembered the plates, she could track him down – then again, girls don't usually remember plates like blokes. Blokes will see a plate with the numbers 454 and know that the car has, say, a 454-cubic-inch Chevrolet motor.

But there was so much going on at the grid, he doubted she had noticed, which was a relief. There was something else he was going to tell her that he had seen, but couldn't remember right now. It will come to me later, he thought.

When Harry drove to Little Creek, he had come in from the east, driving through the town to get to Little Creek South Farm. He had travelled around 1000 kilometres in about 10 hours. Now he was heading west to go back to Rasp; it would only be around 850 kilometres.

His vision of Little Creek had been vague, but he knew that if he got to Gidgee, east of Little Creek, he would follow his nose and get there and learn where he was going – which is exactly what had happened. He had found Little Creek, and now that he knew where it was, could take a more direct route home, which would take around nine hours. He had left around 3 pm on Friday after getting off work early, and it was now 8 am Saturday, so he should be home around 5pm.

Bridget had had her fundraiser on Friday night, and then he usually rode his motorbike with his mates on Saturday – so she wouldn't be expecting to see him until Saturday night in any case.

It took some time for Harry to process what had just happened. He had found Lucy and he had also confirmed that his visions and dreams would come true. There was no other explanation. Then his thoughts turned to home. By visiting Lucy, was he being unfaithful to Bridget? This thought hurt him and he needed to think about it a bit more. He wondered: If I marry Lucy, what happens to me and Bridget?

He loved Bridget and was not only shocked by his meeting with Lucy, but concerned about his relationship with Bridget. He didn't have an answer to what happened to him and Bridget yet, but comforted himself by thinking, 'I don't make the future, I just watch it.'

Harry sang along to Electric Light Orchestra's *Telephone Line*, blasting from his eight-track. Harry hadn't clicked yet, but eight-track cassette technology was superseded in the early 1980s by the smaller cassette tape, which was also then superseded by USB and Bluetooth technology.

Harry, at this point, was none the wiser, and happy in the present day listening to his eight-track tapes, which were huge – about 10 centimetres by 12 centimetres, and two centimetres thick. Bulky for the car, Harry only had two or three, and his mates used to chide him for listening to the same music over and over – but he didn't care. He liked ELO, Meat Loaf and Jimmy Buffett, and knew all the words to most songs. He was making very good progress along the quiet road at well over the speed limit, thinking about the song lyrics:

Hello, how are you?

Have you been alright through all those lonely, lonely, lonely, lonely, lonely nights?

Suddenly, he remembered a vision.

'Fuck – transportable phones!' he said out loud. 'No, no – *mobile phones!*' he corrected himself. People use small telephones to call each other and even view each other and send each other stuff, he recalled. That will be amazing, he thought. He wasn't sure what he was going to do with this information, but was astounded at what he knew. He'd seen that in another life, he had a mobile telephone and he wondered when it would become available. It's shit not knowing everything, he thought.

He had seen in his dreams that he could contact anyone by using a very small handheld telephone and wondered about this technology. In 1978, communication was much more difficult. People needed to be near a landline to receive a call. Imagine if I could just call my mates from wherever I am and make arrangements, Harry thought, or just call Bridget at any time. Life would be so much easier.

Alice

13

September 1978

Alice Blackwell lived in Little Creek with her father and two brothers. She had nine siblings, but seven of the others had left home, so now there was only four in the house.

Alice's mother passed away about three years earlier from cancer. Alice and Lucy had gone to school camp together and when they returned, she had passed. Alice's father was waiting on the train station platform with the terrible news. Lucy was upset because the Blackwell's place was like a second home to her, and Mrs Blackwell had been like a second mum.

Mrs Blackwell was different to Mavis. She had a very soft nature and people would gravitate to her when they needed an emotional cuddle. She was short in stature but had a very big heart. She also had a very big family – and enough love to give them all a very good start in life.

Mrs Blackwell would always call Lucy, 'L', as in 'Are you staying for dinner L?' The more kids and people she had around her the better, it seemed.

Following Mrs Blackwell's death, Alice became the mother of the house at the tender age of 13. The family had a 'corner shop' attached to their house and Alice would organise and run the shop and manage the house for her father Fred. Fred was liked by all and sundry around town, but he was lazy or seemed to have lost interest when his wife passed away. He didn't seem concerned that Alice had to grow up very quickly to look after the house, cook meals and run the shop.

Lucy would often help Alice in the shop or in the house, and together they would happily drive 50 kilometres each way to a neighbouring town to get stock for the shop.

Alice was the opposite to Lucy in many ways – short, solidly built, with short curly hair. She was also more outgoing than Lucy; she had a wonderful friendly disposition and would talk to anyone. She always had a mischievous smile that people would warm to. She wasn't an academic by any means, but was very streetwise and could sum people up in an instant.

Alice was usually late, like Lucy, but this morning it seemed Lucy was especially late! They were both travelling with the Mangan family to Coolabah to play netball. It was a semi-final and Mr Mangan would already be waiting, thought Alice. They lived just up the street and when Lucy arrived it would be a minute walk, but she wasn't here yet. She thought about ringing her, but knew that Mavis would say she's on the way.

Lucy has been a bit lost lately, thought Alice, and not really interested at school. Lucy had told Alice that she would be leaving at the end of the year. Alice was also going to leave, but she had her reason. It seemed Lucy had no plans, but was determined to leave anyway. Alice told her that even if she wanted to join the army, she would need decent grades, which just annoyed Lucy. Alice wondered if Lucy might even leave Little Creek and go to Perth to be with her sister. Not a bad idea, thought Alice, because there would be more jobs there than in Little Creek. She loved her friend, but was concerned about the future, for both of them.

She went out the side gate and looked up the road towards the farm turn-off. She could see a figure on a motorbike in the distance and thought it looked like Lucy, but the rider was facing the wrong way and wasn't moving.

She knew Lucy would come into town on her motorbike, even though she didn't have a licence. She often did it on Saturdays for netball when her father couldn't drive her. Mavis didn't drive. She had a licence but hadn't driven for years.

It seemed as if Lucy – if it was Lucy – had her head down on the handlebars. Maybe she'd dropped something and was looking for it, thought Alice. 'Hurry up,' she said in a low voice to no one.

Then she saw the person lift their head, followed by smoke from the exhaust as the bike started. Good, thought Alice, she's coming. The bike turned and moved towards Alice. It was Lucy; she must have found what she was looking for and now we can go, surmised Alice.

Lucy rode up the road and turned into Alice's back yard as Alice approached her. 'Where have you been?' Alice asked, then saw Lucy's eyes. Her eyes were red and it was clear that she had been crying. She got off the bike and they hugged each other very warmly. They both needed it.

Earlier, Alice had decided she needed to tell Lucy a secret she had been keeping – but Lucy looked like an emotional wreck.

Mr Mangan beeped his horn and the girls knew he was tired of waiting. They looked in each other's eyes: they both seemed to understand that what they wanted to talk to each other about could wait, and that they needed to run to the Mangan's. They grabbed each other and ran hand in hand up the street to the car.

The 70-odd kilometre trip to Coolabah was quiet. Mr Mangan was driving, his wife was in the front passenger seat and their daughter Julie was in the back with Lucy and Alice. Julie was in the year below Lucy and Alice, and although they were comfortable with her company and played netball with her, they were not close to her. Julie enjoyed different pastimes, and was also very smart: top of her year in most subjects. By contrast, Lucy and Alice didn't really want to be at school at all.

The Mangans always went to the netball with Julie and were happy to cart along some of the other girls and help the netball coach, Karen Davis. Ms Davis was also a school teacher at Little Creek Secondary

School and enjoyed the extracurricular activity. She had played A-grade netball at university and was well qualified to coach a small regional team.

Lucy was consumed with thoughts of her strange encounter, and wanting to talk to Alice about it privately. She was recounting her conversation with the boy and thought he may have said his name. Did he say 'Damien', or 'Ross'? She knew she couldn't remember because in fact, he didn't say his name. She was 'grasping at straws', as her mother would say. Then, she wondered, did he deliberately not tell me his name, or was he so caught up in telling me about what he thought he knew that he forgot to tell me?

'Hmmm,' she mouthed quietly. Worse still I didn't even ask where he was from: 'Hmmm' again. My social skills really suck, she thought. However, she placated herself by remembering how much information she had to digest! No wonder I didn't get his name or where he came from. In a period of about 10 minutes, I was married, I had three children, my best friend had a baby – and whatever else he wrote on that note.

'Hmmm.' She thought, am I infatuated already with Mr White T-shirt Man or was it that I just want to learn more? Imagine me – Mrs White T-Shirt Man – I could do worse! The first thing I am going to do when I see him again is go crook at him for treating me badly. Just wait until I see him again! But when will that be? Next month, next year – in five years?! He'd better hope I wait.

Hang on a second … Here I am talking about what is going to happen. He is probably unhinged, she thought. But maybe I can fix him! Stop it, she said to herself. Stop thinking about him. When I tell Alice, she'll say, 'Yeah, I bet that's Dingo Fred from Blah Blah. He does that to lots of girls. Gets them excited thinking about things that are never going to happen – then they let down their guard and next minute he has a new girlfriend.'

Yeah, thought Lucy, but I'll counter with, 'He is cute though!'

Meanwhile, Alice was thinking: Lucy is on a cloud all by herself. But why had she been crying, sitting in the middle of the road? I need to talk to that girl. What could be going on that had caused her to be so upset? She is out at Little Creek South all by herself, and Mavis panders to her, thought Alice. Can't be too bad. Boy troubles? Nope, she isn't keen on anyone in Little Creek at the moment.

Then Alice's thoughts turned to herself. What am I going to do? she thought anxiously. My belly has already started to show; well, I can notice it. I have to tell Dad – and he'll be so mad at me. He will yell, then my brothers will know, and they'll talk to everyone about it, and some people will say cruel things about me behind my back. I just wanted to meet a nice boy, fall in love, get married and have a baby. *In that order.* Now I'll be a single mum with no future in Little Creek; I am so scared. I'll listen to Lucy's problems and calm her down tonight, then tell her about the mess I am in.

* * *

Ms Davis was usually a calm, relaxed teacher and coach.

'But really girls,' she said, exasperated, at half time. 'The score is 17 to 31. This is the major semi-final and some of you appear uninterested. Lucy, you need to watch their GS more closely. The GA is feinting to her right, then passing to the shooter on her left every time. I know you are trying, but there is no cohesion out there today! Alice why aren't you talking more? I want to hear your chatter. I want you to organise everyone. It's as if you two aren't here today. Earth to Lucy and Alice – come in Apollo 11!'

Coming from Ms Davis, this was quite a spray. Lucy and Alice were her key players and today Ms Davis thought they were playing poorly and seemed completely uninterested. She would cosy up to the girls later, and all would be forgiven. She got along very well with all the girls but was worried about Alice and Lucy. Did they have a disagreement about something? she thought. It's strange that they are both playing poorly.

Ms Davis appealed to the team's sense of pride at three-quarter time when they only trailed by six. Lucy and Alice had clicked in the third quarter and Julie and the other girls' performance also lifted when they sensed the enthusiasm of Lucy and Alice. Now the coach wanted their fieriness to come out. She wanted them to play clean but be prepared to fight for every point and deny the other team access to points.

'You know, girls, that all the other grades are here watching, as well as all the football fans and players. Rarely do people get an opportunity to do something fantastic with their friends. But you do. Also think about when was the last time you did something for the last time? You know there will come a time in your life when you nurse a baby – or perhaps *your* baby for the last time – they grow up and they are too big for you to hold. We should all cherish moments like that because they are not forever and this team is not forever.

'Some of us won't be here next year,' she concluded emotionally, 'So go out there and play for each other. Play for memories.' It was only country netball, but Ms Davis always wanted her girls to give their best and she could see now that they were ready, with 15 minutes to play.

Alice went back on the court, tears welling. Her face was ruddy from exertion; she didn't care if anyone noticed that she was emotional. Lucy watched closely as Alice went to the centre of the court and knew that Coolabah was in for a very torrid 15 minutes. Lucy, too, had an ache in her heart and wanted to cry again, but was too stoic to do it in front of everybody – maybe she had a little Mavis in her after all, she thought. This morning had touched her deeply, and then when Ms Davis mentioned holding a baby for the last time …

Coolabah won by a single point.

There would be no more netball for Little Creek that year. Coolabah would beat Eucalypt Bend in the final. But the reputation of Little Creek netball team was intact in the regional netball league and in Little Creek itself.

14

Back in Rasp

September 1978

Harry had done really well; he was back in Rasp around 4.15pm. He had a mixture of thoughts running through his head. He was elated that his dreams were actually a window into his future. He was not crazy, and for this he was relieved. Lucy was real and that meant any other visions he had would be real as well, he thought. But should he tell Max and Steve – or his mum? And – fuck – what about Dad's accident?

He knew he couldn't talk to Bridget about this. He would love to talk to her about it and she would offer advice and help and be so understanding. She would be entranced, he thought. They would often sit and have cerebral conversations about national and world issues or their thoughts on business leaders or just other people. Harry really enjoyed those conversations and knew that Bridget would want to understand why and how this had happened to him. But given Lucy, and what he had just done and learned in the past 24 hours, this was no longer an option.

As well as being relieved, Harry was frightened. He wasn't sure he wanted to see the future. He wondered how and why his visions were happening. He was frightened about his future with Bridget, because he didn't want to lose her – but now he was captivated by Lucy.

Fuck, what a mess, he thought. But he had a plan – something he would go on to use for most of his life: Don't worry about things you can't control, just continue on your chosen path until something actually diverts you.

Bridget was in a great mood when he went to see her. Her charity night was such fun and they had raised a good amount of money. She spent most of the night telling Harry about the games they had played and who did what. Bridget's best friend Sally came home from university to be there and had played guitar requests. 'Such fun,' Bridget reiterated.

Harry knew that Bridget was smart enough to enrol in university. They hadn't discussed why she didn't enrol. Harry thought her previous relationship may have affected what she wanted to do, but couldn't really understand why. If she had gone to uni, I wouldn't have met her, thought Harry. Maybe she leaves me to go to university? Harry was so tired, he drifted off to sleep after they had made love and didn't wake until the morning. This was the first time he had stayed with Bridget overnight, and he felt a little guilty about impinging on her life and enjoying her body so much. He wasn't using her – he loved her, he reasoned, and he reminded himself that he would not break his relationship with Bridget. There must be a reason why Bridget and I aren't together in the future and I marry Lucy.

Harry was home for dinner on Sunday evening with his mother and father. As usual, Harry dried the dishes as his mother washed. Harry's father had gone into the lounge to watch television when Harry ventured, 'Mum, I need to talk to you about something.'

Growing up, Harry didn't often talk to his mother about personal issues. They didn't have that type of close relationship. He knew his mother would be there if he needed her, but he could never bring himself to divulge information about his private life to her.

'Yes, we do need to talk. You didn't tell me about Bridget,' said Tania. 'Is she your girlfriend? Do you want to bring her to dinner one night?'

'Yes, she is my girlfriend, and I'll bring her over one day to meet you and Dad,' replied Harry. 'But, Mum – it's about Dad.' Tania stopped her washing up and looked directly at Harry. 'What about Dad?' she asked.

Harry had decided he wouldn't tell his mother about his visions or dreams. If he did, there would be so many questions, and Harry reckoned his mum would have him seeing every medical doctor in Rasp, plus a few psychologists. She would think the knock to the head had sent him crazy. Instead, Harry started, 'Does dad wear protective equipment at work?'

'I guess so,' Tania replied. 'Why?'

'Well, I saw this documentary on television the other night and it said that if you get a hit on the head while wearing a protective helmet, you have at least a 50 per cent chance of avoiding serious injury,' lied Harry.

Tania stopped washing up and again looked directly at Harry. Their relationship may not have been very close, but Tania was Harry's mother and she thought Harry was either hiding something from her or alluding to something.

'Harry, why are you telling me this?'

'I guess I was just thinking of Dad when I saw the program and hoped that he would be wearing protective equipment.'

Tania was still staring at Harry. 'Harry, I really don't know why we are talking about this. Do you need to tell me something?' Harry's head was bowed. He couldn't look at her and tears were welling up.

'No Mum.' Harry was thinking about his vision of his father, critically ill in an intensive care ward. It was likely that his father would be left with a lifelong impediment. He may even die. Harry hadn't seen what would eventuate.

Tania wasn't finished. 'Have you been feeling well since your accident Harry? You've had a tough month, what with that hotel fight, then a new girlfriend and then your motorbike crash?'

Darn, thought Harry, no wonder I don't tell her stuff – this is too hard.

'Yeah, mum, I'm OK.' He looked at her with tears in his eyes. 'I just don't want Dad to get hurt at work. Can you please make him wear a protective helmet when he is lifting bores with lots of equipment around him?' Which is exactly what Harry had seen in his dreams, when his fathers' workmates and the doctor in Adelaide had told him about the accident.

Harry walked away decisively to gather himself. Tania followed as Harry went up the hallway to his room.

'Why are we talking about this Harry?!'

Harry turned and looked his mother in the eyes. 'Mum, can you just do it for me, please? Tell Dad to always wear a helmet. I don't know – go crook at him like you do, just make sure he does it! Please. You only have to think about what happened to me when I crashed my bike. If I didn't have a helmet on, I may not be here now.'

Harry went into his room and closed the door behind him as Tania stood in the hallway trying to understand her son and his sudden concern for his father.

I'll talk to Harry about his emotional state when he is feeling better, she thought. She was perplexed by Harry's reaction and her maternal instinct told her that Harry was not being completely honest with her. What did Harry know that she didn't? Did someone tell Harry that Geoff could be injured if he kept doing what he was doing? she wondered. But now was not the time.

Harry had raised a very good point, however; Harry had worn his helmet, and it may have saved him from a more serious injury. She would tell Geoff to promise her he would always wear a helmet when around bore equipment, and she would also check with his supervisor when she next saw him, telling him, 'I don't care how bloody hot it is, make Geoff wear a helmet.'

Harry had become emotional when he talked with his mother, but he thought he covered well when he reminded her about his accident. If she asks me again what's going on, I'll just say I was thinking about how lucky I was when I crashed, and I transposed those feelings to Dad. Dad's occupation is dangerous, she can't argue against that.

In his room, in that moment, Harry had a vision. The world seemed to stop turning and all he could see was Lucy in a very emotional state telling him that her father, Mick, had been hospitalised, had lost an arm, and was fighting for his life. He had this vision once before and thought that it may have been prompted again because he had been thinking of his father's accident.

That's what I forgot to warn Lucy about when I saw her at the grid! Harry had no sense of when this event would happen, apart from knowing it would occur when they are a couple.

Harry couldn't bring himself to tell his mother that he had seen his father's accident in a vision – but he could tell Lucy. Lucy already knew he could see the future. He would warn her about Mick's accident, she would accept this information and hopefully be able to use it to ensure Mick avoids the accident. He resolved that as soon as he saw Lucy again, he would tell her about Mick. So he wouldn't forget, he took his leather Monaro key tag and using a small pocket knife engraved Mick's name in the leather. I look at that tag every day and will never forget now, he thought. I don't want to see Lucy that upset ever.

15

Revelations

September 1978

Lucy rang her mother from Alice's and asked if she could sleep over that night. Lucy had stayed at Alice's many times and Mavis knew she was safe there. Fred put sausages on the barbecue and the two girls talked about the netball semi. They chatted about the 'cow' on the other side and her nasty behaviour, and what they could do when they played them again. They didn't talk about their comeback. It was by the by. Both knew they shouldn't have been down by 14 points at half time, and didn't want to admit why.

Fred gave them sausages on bread with tomato sauce, smiled and heaped praise on them for their 'heroics', as he called it. They ate their dinner on the step with a soft drink each and were happy to end their day in this simple way, in the cool of the evening.

Fred had borrowed a VHS from the town library – *Smokey and the Bandit*. The girls had seen shorts of it at the cinema and didn't want to watch it, but understood that Fred did. They let him down gently by telling him they were really tired and just wanted to go to bed and talk. The last bit was right – they couldn't wait to be alone and talk.

They snuck outside and sat on the swings in Alice's backyard.

'Let's have a smoke,' Lucy suggested, but Alice declined. They occasionally 'half smoked'. They didn't really inhale, just took a drag and exhaled the smoke. They thought it was a cool thing to do and a bit rebellious, but it seemed tonight Alice wasn't in the mood, so they just talked about the netball and Ms Davis. They agreed she was really nice and was just trying to help when she berated them. Problem solved, they went back inside, had a shower and got ready for bed.

They each had a single bed pushed together in Alice's room. It was cool and they had loads of blankets and too many pillows. Soon enough they had had enough of skylarking and Alice asked about the bike incident this morning. Alice was very matter-of-fact about things when it came to relationships; who she liked and who she didn't like and all those personal things. 'Why were you parked in the middle of the road on your bike, facing out of town, with your head resting on the handlebars? Then when I saw you, you had been crying,' coaxed Alice.

Lucy looked everywhere but at Alice. She looked at her nails, her pyjama top, the floor, the ceiling – everywhere.

'Come on Luce,' Alice said again gently. Lucy was working up the courage to talk about it. She could tell the story to make Mr T-Shirt Man sound like a weirdo, or tell it so he seemed a little lost and vulnerable, or tell it as if she believed all that he had said. She couldn't pick which one, because at the moment she had a foot in each camp.

We've shared a lot over the years, thought Lucy, particularly the loss of Alice's mum, so I am just going to tell her. I didn't do anything wrong, she told herself. This thing was thrust on me. I'm not weird.

'Yep, I was crying on my bike,' confessed Lucy.

'Why?' asked Alice.

'Uhmmmm,' exhaled Lucy while she delayed her response. 'I met a guy today. He was waiting for me at the grid when I was riding to town.'

'You met a guy and 10 minutes later you're crying about him?' questioned Alice. 'You really do have a problem with boys!'

'It wasn't like that! I didn't know him, but he said he knew me and he knew stuff about me!' exclaimed Lucy.

'Some guys are dogs,' decreed Alice. 'I'll bet Mrs Rogers the local gossip has been saying stuff about you. She is always saying I'm easy and like chasing men. I hate her.'

'I think he was a bit of a weirdo,' explained Lucy. 'He knew my name, and he knew where I lived, and he said he knew about my future.'

Now this is getting really strange, thought Alice. Lucy continued and dropped the bombshell. 'He said that in the future he and I would get married and … we would have children together.'

'Sounds more like he wants to have children with you now,' Alice said, half-joking. 'I bet he knows you from somewhere and wants to get in your knickers.'

'No. It didn't seem like that, and I knew you would say that.'

Alice could see that Lucy was getting upset and changed tack. 'I'm sorry. Tell me more.'

'Well don't make fun of me – I didn't ask for him to be sitting there in his big blue car,' said Lucy. 'He just seemed so genuine, and I wanted to believe him. But I was very good Alice – I kept my cool and questioned him about what he said. But I didn't have a lot of time because I was running late.'

'I know you were late,' interrupted Alice. 'But you were crying because … ?'

'Well, I can't get anything right. I just wanted to listen and take in what he said, and I wanted to watch him. It was like I knew him, but I didn't. If I was out and he asked me to dance I would have swooned,' said Lucy.

'Oooh, swooned,' said Alice. 'What did he look like?'

Lucy told her all about his confidence and his looks and what she liked about him.

'What was his name then?' asked Alice.

Lucy lowered her head again and looked at her nails, 'I don't know.'

'What the fuck?' said Alice. 'You didn't ask him his name?'

'Well, I was so interested in what he was saying and I was trying to get my head around it, and I was also thinking, "Would I marry this guy?" and then he wrote things on a piece of paper for me. It was fucking weird and emotional and' – 'hang on, he wrote something down for you.'

'What did he write? Show me the bit of paper,' said Alice.

Lucy grabbed her sports bag and immediately went for the small inside zip pocket. When she got changed in Coolabah, she carefully stowed the note so she wouldn't lose it. It was in the pocket with her purse and earrings that she had taken out prior to the game. There it was. Just plain white paper with faint blue lines where White T-Shirt Man had written his dot points.

Alice and Lucy quickly changed positions and lay on their chests side by side so they could share and read the note together. Written in black pen, it read:

- *Little Creek has huge rains in December and there is a flood.*
- *You get a job at the local bank.*
- *The next time you see me I'll be in a dark brown 1976 Holden.*
- *You and I get married.*
- *We have three beautiful children – two boys and a girl.*

'Oh my God,' said Alice quickly, 'this is so exciting. A mystery man.'

'He's not a mystery man, he's Mr White T-Shirt man,' said Lucy. 'I call him that because I don't know his name.' They laughed hard at that, and Alice jumped up, rummaged through her drawers, found a white T-shirt, put it on over her pyjamas and strutted around trying to flex her muscles. They laughed and squealed.

Alice then returned to her question. 'So, why were you crying?'

Lucy looked her in the eyes and said, 'Well I liked him and I don't want to wait for him. I want good things to happen to me now. I don't want to wait 10 years to be happy. And besides that, I got cranky when I realised I didn't even know his name, so I turned back to talk to him again and I could see his car leaving in the distance, and he didn't see me. He left me here in this shitty town, and I don't like school and I don't know what to do when I leave school.'

Lucy had tears rolling down her cheeks; Alice put her arm around her friend and tried to console her. 'You're a good netball player and you are going to get a job in the bank,' Alice said mischievously. Lucy started to sob and laugh at the same time and they giggled again, both knowing Alice was just trying to cheer her up.

They sat up on the bed with their legs crossed under them while Lucy held the note in one hand. Alice said, 'Let's try to figure out who this guy is. Are you positive you've never seen him before?'

'Alice, if I had met him before I would have remembered and would have let him know I liked him. I would have said, my bedroom is on the right-hand side of the veranda at Little Creek South,' Lucy said, smiling.

'Okay so he's not from Boree or Coolabah or Eucalypt Bend?' ventured Alice.

'No, never seen him before.'

'But he's got a big blue car, right?'

'Yep.'

'And what sort of car was it?'

'Umm … it was blue.'

'Fuck Luce!'

'Well, I'm not good at cars. Boys say "Look at my nice car" and I go, "Great, it's red",' said Lucy, laughing.

'Well, was it an old car or new car?'

'Maybe old, but not too old.'

Alice had a look of despair, so Lucy continued.

'It had a black stripe on it and the blue was sort-of a shiny blue, not a dull or flat sort of blue. Wait, wait – it only had two doors! I know because when he went to the car, I noticed he opened a very large door. Oh, and on the T-shirt there was some sort of logo on the back, in red I think.'

'Okay,' said Alice sarcastically, 'With all that information we should be able to track him down. Maybe we can do it before the year 2000!'

'Come on Alice, you are supposed to help me,' said Lucy.

'Well, I would if you had some information. You said he left to the west, towards Barnbale, right?' asked Alice with raised eyebrows.

'Yep, and he said he knows you,' returned Lucy.

'He knows me!' exclaimed Alice.

'Oh well that's not exactly what he said – he said to me, "Well I sort of know her." That's exactly what he said,' Lucy explained.

'You know what Luce; I reckon I know a guy who looks like that from Rennie,' said Alice.

'Is he a farmer?' asked Lucy.

'Yes.'

'Then it's' not him' replied Lucy confidently.

Alice asked why it couldn't be him.

'Well for a start he didn't dress like a farmer,' Lucy said. 'You know, six inches of leather belt not in the loop hanging loosely at the front, checked shirt with rolled-up sleeves, R.M. Williams boots. Farmers dress like farmers, but Mr White T-Shirt Man dressed like … I don't know, surfie-casual style: runners, T-shirt, bell-bottomed slim-waisted jeans. He's not a farmer. Anyway I'm not marrying a bloody farmer who has to wait for his father to die before he's in charge of the property, blah blah blah.'

Lucy had a point, thought Alice, but just because he's not from around here doesn't mean I don't know him. I'll think about it. Maybe he's a friend of Jake Smith who wants to take advantage of Lucy, like Jake did to me. You can't trust men.

'So, Luce, we've got bugger all to go on, but I'll believe whatever you want me to believe,' said Alice consolingly. 'Are you going to wait for him and keep your pretty body for him?' giggled Alice.

'Well, what about the other things he predicted?' reminded Lucy.

They read the note again. Alice said, 'December isn't far away, so we can see if he is right about the rain and flood. Not sure you'll get a job in the bank though. There are only four people working there: the manager, Mr Small, then there's Helen Pratt, then there's Bond, James Bond – the young guy from away who is a bit dorky – and then Marion Delhunty, the local girl who isn't going anywhere.'

The conversation lulled and Alice said, 'I've got something to talk to you about too, Luce.' Alice was going to use tonight to tell Lucy that she was pregnant. No one else knew, not even the child's father. She needed support from someone, and she wanted to share it with Lucy before it became obvious. But Lucy interrupted with a wry smile.

'There was one more thing he said to me that I haven't told you about, because I didn't want to ask you this – but Mr White T-Shirt Man said that you are going to have a baby next year, and I know that's not right, is it? So he must be a dud.'

Alice's face must have told Lucy something. Alice had her deadly serious face on, and with that Lucy fell silent. 'He can't have said that,' said Alice. 'No one knows.'

And with that, Alice had told Lucy her big secret. Once again, they were both confused, emotional and elated all at once. Lucy was excited for Alice but dreading the news of the baby becoming common knowledge. Alice would be in trouble with her father and people around town would gossip about them both.

Shit, I am excited, but how can I support Alice? thought Lucy. One thing I am not going to do is heap more of Mr White T-Shirt Man on her: 'It's a boy and he is called Jon, without the "h",' Mr White T-Shirt Man had said.

Alice told Lucy she didn't know the sex of her baby and she really didn't want to talk about the father. Suffice to say he was Jake Smith who lived not far from Little Creek. Alice had met him when he was in town playing football. He worked in the New South Wales Roads Authority office in Barnbale.

Lucy knew of him and thought of him as a loser. She didn't say that to Alice, but he had a panel van and she figured it would have just been about the sex for him. Alice didn't even want Jake to know about her pregnancy, so Lucy promised to let Alice do all the telling and would just support her in any way she could.

The baby was due in January. It was September now, so in four months she would know if it is a boy, and also know his name.

I'll wait and see if your predictions come true Mr White T-Shirt Man, Lucy told herself.

16

Arwon is Nowra spelled backwards

November 1978

October meant warmer weather was on the way for Rasp as the southern hemisphere moved towards summer and Christmas loomed. Harry's priorities since returning from Little Creek were Bridget and his motorbike.

Harry had been lavishing time on Bridget. He would spend most of his weekends at Bridget's flat and would see her most weeknights after work. He was becoming comfortable with Bridget. He didn't doubt her in any way. She had told him she loved him, and he had reciprocated many times, and was learning so much about her.

He knew she didn't like the bush or going out bush, but thought he would fix that – she hasn't been bush with *me* yet, thought Harry. He also found that they both didn't really enjoy crowds. They would rather be together or with close friends than go to a club or disco.

Harry thought Bridget's taste in music was more mature than his. He liked the Bee Gees, but she liked Santana or Chicago. They would often listen to her music at her flat. Harry didn't mind what or who he listened to, as long as he was with Bridge.

Bridget loved reading, but Harry was confused about her choice of novels. She was a very intelligent person, but would read what Harry called 'chick' books. The books were all boy-meets-girl, boy-loses-girl, boy-rediscovers-girl, but in different settings – cowboys, then office towers, then farm life.

She loved reading and that gave her something to do when Harry wasn't around. She was happy if he wanted to go off with his mates and she was happy when he spent time with her. She was a very understanding, undemanding girlfriend, thought Harry, and he loved their arrangement.

He often spent weekend nights at her flat now, and didn't feel guilty about it. Bridget enjoyed his company and his attention. She talked to Harry about doing an accounting degree course, and he encouraged her in this regard. Her work entailed quoting on building supplies to companies, and she seemed to enjoy the actuarial side of her work and was good at it. He would often visit her office, where she was likely to have her head in a book doing calculations with a pencil behind her ear and reading glasses on.

'Old four eyes at it again,' Harry would say, laughing from the front counter. She was good for him, he thought. She bolstered his confidence and disarmed him when he was worrying about something – 'It'll be alright, you could do it this way' sort of advice. Life was good again for Harry as he tried not to think about his dreams, which were still occurring.

Harry was saving to get his motorbike fixed, and his frugal lifestyle with Bridget allowed him to do that. He would occasionally buy her flowers, and they would sometimes go out for dinner, but they were really homebodies, intent on enjoying each other's company. He had saved over $350 and now only needed another $50 before he could order the parts to repair his bike. Max was going to help him with the rebuild to save on repair costs. Harry only earned around $100 a week and his mother asked for $15 a week for board, but he also had a second account with $200 socked away. He was going to use this to spoil Bridget, he thought. Given Harry's absence at home these days, his father called him a 'star boarder', but he still paid his board to his mother each week.

Tuesday 7 November 1978 was going to be a big day for Harry and Bridget. Bridget's birthday this year coincided with the annual Melbourne Cup race meeting. He had planned a romantic dinner at a local restaurant, Escargot, and had bought a bluebird friendship ring to give her on the night.

His workplace was also celebrating the Melbourne Cup. The female staff eschewed their usual uniforms to dress in beautiful racetrack attire. Some of the blokes would wear blazers or racing caps and the branch was festooned with balloons and streamers. Everyone chipped in and the girls organised roast chicken pieces and the blokes some oysters. It was Harry's first Melbourne Cup at work and he was keen to enjoy the day ahead of going out to dinner with Bridget.

Office sweepstakes were sold in the morning. Each staff member contributed $5 to draw a horse, with the promise that if your horse won the race, you won first prize of $60. A junior employee, Harry was having a busy morning running errands when he was interrupted by Elizabeth, who was selling the sweep tickets.

'Harry, how many tickets do you want?'

'Just one,' replied Harry. He was doing the last of Mr Hayden's cheque dishonours at his desk, and had a sudden vision. Visions didn't usually occur when he was at work, but time seemed to stand still as one of his 'movie shorts' flashed before him.

Harry could see he drew Arwon in the sweep and the horse had won and he won $60. He could see himself laughing and saying, 'Arwon is the town name of Nowra, where the horse comes from, spelled backwards,' as he pocketed his winnings.

Harry hadn't yet thought about using his 'powers' for financial advantage, but he saw an opportunity. What if I invested my money on Arwon? he pondered.

'Hey Barney, what odds would I get if I backed Arwon?' asked Harry.

Barney was a keen punter and consulted the newspaper on his desk. 'Maybe six or seven to one, but he won't win Boyo – Karu is going to shit it in. You could back So Called, he's the favourite and a good chance as well.'

Harry quickly dialled Steve's home number. It was early morning and Harry knew Stevie was on afternoon shift and wouldn't be going to work until 3pm, right when the race is usually run. 'Mrs Taylor, can I talk to Steve please? It's Harry.'

'Mate,' said Harry as he talked to Stevie, 'come and see me at work, it's important.' Harry knew that Stevie would be all over this like a rash. He figured that Steve wasn't as sceptical as Max about Harry's ability to see the future, and he was a bit of a risk-taker. In fact, Harry thought that Steve would think this a good test of Harry's powers. Steve would think, 'If he gets this right, I am a believer!'

Steve spotted Harry and came straight to the front counter. Steve would often visit Harry at the bank just to ogle the girls, and today he was rewarded with girls beautifully dressed.

'Want to swap jobs Flash?' asked Steve with a big grin. Harry knew what he was alluding to. 'Only if we swap pay packets,' replied Harry.

Harry then told him that he reckoned he knew who was going to win the Cup: Arwon.

'What are you an expert on horses now?' asked Steve. Harry winked at Steve and said, 'It just came to me.' He didn't need to say more: Steve was hooked. Harry handed him $350 and asked him to put it on for him at the betting agency.

'You should be able to get odds of six to one,' he told Steve.

'Fuck,' said Steve in a hushed tone, '$350 is about three weeks' pay for you.'

'Yeah, it's my bike money,' replied Harry. Because Harry was committing $350, Steve was in no doubt that the horse would win. 'I'll put $350 on it as well!' exclaimed Steve.

Because he wasn't working, Harry asked Steve to let Max know as well, and at lunch time he would walk down to Bridget's office and tell Webby and Bridget about his 'tip'.

'Come back and let me know our odds and what Max did?' asked Harry. 'And one last thing. I don't think we should tell anyone about this, Stevie. You could encourage Debbie, but that's it.'

'Safe with me,' replied Steve.

Bridget's workplace was celebrating as well when Harry visited during his lunch. Neither Webby nor Bridget knew about his visions, so he talked up his analytical skills and told them Arwon was going to win the Cup. Bridget laughed; Harry had never bet on horses before, she thought, but said she would put $5 on it. Webby was keen on the favourite, but said he'd have $10 on it. 'Have a bit more bud, I really reckon it's going to win,' urged Harry.

Stevie reported back in the early afternoon. 'Right, here's your ticket. If it wins, we collect almost $2500 each,' he said excitedly.

'What did Max say?' asked Harry. 'You know how tight he is Harry, and you know he doesn't really buy your vision stuff. I urged him and he reluctantly gave me $100. He will win $700 if it gets up.'

'Did you tell him we put $350 each on it?' asked Harry.

'Yep, which is why he gave me a $100.' Harry was a little disappointed with Max's commitment, but could understand. Maybe I should have told him he marries a skinny redhead and buys a red Commodore, thought Harry.

'Okay Stevie, let's see what happens at 3pm,' said Harry.

'I'll be in the cage on my way underground, but someone will have a radio,' replied Steve.

The race was close but Arwon won by what the commentator said was 'a half neck'. He was behind when they came into the straight but wore the field down. Harry was elated. Harry wondered if he had cheated, but justified himself by thinking about everything he had been through with his dreams and visions. Life owes me this, he thought. I am just living life, no more, no less.

'You are my wonder man,' said Bridget that night at their dinner at Escargot. 'Is there anything you can't do Harry Barnes?' Bridget had won $35. 'John won $60 I think.'

Later that night at Bridget's flat, not long after they fell asleep, there was a loud banging on the street entrance. Harry got up and ran quickly to the front window to see who it was. He thought, This'll be a mess if it's the old boyfriend. He looked out the window and was surprised to see Steve, who had just finished his afternoon shift. Harry poked his head out of the window.

'Flash, we did it! I can't fucking believe it!' shouted Steve.

Harry, grinning like a Cheshire cat, replied, 'Fuck off mate, I'll see you tomorrow.' They both laughed as they waved good night. I did do a good thing thought Harry, everyone is happy.

Harry was the talk of his circle of friends for the rest of the week, but only he, Steve and Max knew what had really happened. Harry was careful not to tell Barney or others at work how much he had risked or won. He told Barney he put $30 on the horse and won nearly $200, together with $60 from the sweep. Barney would go crook if he knew how much I actually put on the horse, thought Harry. If I was backing a horse normally, my limit would be $5.

Harry valued his hardworking reputation and didn't want people to think he was a gambler. But Steve was a nuisance about the win. 'Harry, just let me know who's going to win the AFL competition next year and I'll load up,' said Steve. Steve didn't really understand that Harry couldn't direct what he could see in the future – it either came to him or it didn't, and this seemed to be a one-off.

Max was happy to win $700 but was clearly annoyed that he didn't risk more. Was Max now a believer? wondered Harry. 'Heady, you are one of my best mates. Don't ask me how, but I do know that my visions come true,' he told Max.

'How do you know?' Max asked. Harry wanted to tell him, but didn't want to risk his future relationship with Lucy.

'How about I guess your new "friend's" name?' taunted Harry. Max had dated Emma only twice and was yet to tell the boys about her, and even Steve didn't know her name. All Steve knew was that she had red hair and was an apprentice hairdresser. Max was aware that none of his friends knew her or knew about her, because he was trying to keep the burgeoning relationship quiet.

'Okay, first look me in the eye and tell me no one has told you about her,' said Max.

'I promise,' replied Harry. 'No one has told me a thing. The only way I know of her is from my dreams.' Max continued to eyeball Harry.

'Okay then smartarse,' said Max in a kindly way. 'What's her name?'

'Emma Forrest,' said Harry without hesitation.

'Fucking hell Flash! I don't know how you know all this stuff! What else do you know?'

Berkshire Hathaway

November 1978

Steve was still pumped up when together with Max and Harry later that week.

'What's our next foray going to be Flash?' he probed. 'What do you see in your dreams?'

Harry hadn't seen any more sport in his visions, and didn't really know one end of a racehorse from the other, but he did know about finance, and his visions indicated he would work in the field for another 30 years or so.

'I reckon we should do something responsible with our money, and that is buy a few shares,' advised Harry. Steve knew absolutely nothing about shares or the share market, and Max reasoned it was only for savvy investors.

'What do you know about the share market?' asked Steve.

'Nothing at present, but apparently I get good at it later in life,' replied Harry.

Suddenly, Steve was hooked, because he knew this advice wasn't coming from present-day Harry, but from a vision or dream, which would come true.

'I'm in Flash,' responded Steve immediately. 'What's the plan?'

'First we all have to agree that this idea must be between us three only, okay? No girlfriend talk, no bragging to mates or even telling our parents,' Harry said.

Max, as usual, was hesitant. But he didn't want to be left behind. 'So, do we invest all that we have just won?' asked Max.

'Well, we take out our seed funding so I can fix my bike, and I reckon we invest the rest,' Harry said.

'What are we buying shares in Harry?' asked Max carefully. Harry looked around and could see no one else was listening. Was this insider trading? he wondered, but only for a second.

'Berkshire Hathaway,' said Harry softly.

'Berk what?' asked Steve.

'Don't fucking shout it Stevie, *Berkshire Hathaway*. I had a look the other day and they are selling for around $175 at the moment, so if we invest, say, $2200 each, which is our winnings of $2500 less most of our seed funding, we could buy 12 shares each, or in Heady's case, say three or four shares.'

'Twelve shares!' exclaimed Steve. 'That's not many; we won't make much.'

'Listen mate, I am not sure of the exact dates in my visions, but I have seen that in 2015, which is 37 years away, they will be worth around $250,000 each. Plus, I also saw that the Australian dollar will slip, so they could even be worth $300,000 each. Then, if we reinvest dividends, we could make, say, three or four mill. But I also saw myself trading in what I think was 2023, and the shares were worth over $500,000 each!' said Harry.

They all went silent for a moment until Steve asked, 'Do you understand all this Harry?'

'Not really Stevie, but it's in my dreams,' he replied.

'I'm in then,' said Steve enthusiastically. 'But do we have to keep them for 45 years?'

'Do what you want mate, but I know they just keep rising over time. That's what I see,' explained Harry.

'I'm in as well, but I'll put in $1100, not $700, so I'll have about half what you blokes will,' said Max.

Using his bank contacts, Harry arranged the investments. It was difficult, because they were a United States share, but Harry got it done, and locked in dividends being re-invested each year. Now sit and wait, he thought.

(18)

Can Bill help?

December 1978

Harry had seen Bill Keith many times in his dreams. It seemed to Harry that somehow, he would meet Bill when he was around 40, and that he would then become an important figure to Harry – someone he would often talk business with and be guided by. Bill would be like a mentor to Harry, and Harry would come to rely on his advice.

But Harry was struggling *now*, this December – with the now, and with the future. He didn't want to be like this forever. Some days, knowing things overwhelmed Harry and he felt sick in his stomach. He had no one to confide in or lean on and thought Bill may be able to guide him.

It was risky, Harry thought. What if I turn up on his doorstep and he thinks I'm a crackpot? Harry knew that Bill played golf regularly and thought that if he arranged a game with him, that could break the ice. He boldly put his name down to play golf with Bill, on a Saturday.

'Hi, Mr Keith, my name's Harry,' he offered that morning. 'Call me Bill,' was the response. Bill was about 25 years older than Harry, and his friendliness pleased Harry. Bill was a respected local businessman. He was well-dressed, tall – perhaps six foot two – wore wire-rimmed glasses and was around 40 years old with manicured greying hair.

Harry had a low handicap and was able to offer Bill some tips. They enjoyed each other's company tremendously. After the game, they learned a bit more about each other. Bill owned an accountancy firm and two supermarkets in Rasp, and was obviously financially comfortable.

Harry told Bill where he worked, learning that he worked with one of Bill's daughters, June. Bill was so enamoured with Harry, he asked Harry to come over to his house for dinner one night and bring his girlfriend. They enjoyed talking about golf, and Harry was keen to learn about accountancy, but Harry didn't want to involve Bridget, as he wanted to talk about how he was feeling and what he should do. He suggested instead lunch after golf the following Saturday.

Harry was very unsure about divulging his predicament to a stranger, but he had done it with Lucy, and now he was determined to seek help from Bill.

Bill chose the restaurant. It was quiet, with few diners for a late Saturday lunch. They spoke mainly about the golf round they had just had, and golf in general. Bill let Harry know that even though he had a higher handicap, he had two holes in one to his credit and Harry none. Harry retorted that he didn't always aim at the pins on par threes, particularly when they were what he called 'sucker pins'. Bill reckoned he always aimed at the pin and therein lay the difference.

They had a detailed conversation about the share market, which was not performing well in 1978, and Bill was surprised about Harry's knowledge of it and his views on where it would head. He thought his views were surprisingly mature for such a young man and listened carefully to Harry's analysis. All Harry's knowledge had been gleaned from his visions of his future roles in the bank, but he was careful not to tell Bill about the calamities that would befall the markets.

Instead, Harry would say, 'In my opinion' and 'I think'. In his future, Harry studied the market intensely and was well aware of its history. Bill reckoned that the market was about at its bottom and was prepared to re-invest. Harry knew that the market would not bottom until 1982 and then crash again in 1987, so urged caution.

'Okay Harry, when do you think the market will bottom and on what basis?' asked Bill, who was now keenly interested in the young man's opinion.

'Simple economics,' replied Harry. 'Inflation will continue to rise and governments around the world will need to put the brakes on to lower demand. Business profits will suffer and share prices will fall as a result, and I think that scenario is not far away now, maybe 1982?'

Bill was astounded by Harry's reply. He had never met a young man with such a grasp on economics.

'How do you know so much about economics Harry – and how come you aren't at university studying this stuff?'

'I just love banking and finance and read as much as I can,' Harry replied. 'It just sticks with me and I try to interpret it as best I can.' Some of this was true: he did love working in banking, but his interpretation of the markets had come from his dreams and visions.

'And what stocks will ride out the 1982 fall?' Bill asked. Harry relied on his knowledge of Berkshire Hathaway again.

'Funnily enough, I reckon it will be an investment house – Berkshire Hathaway, headed by a guy called Warren Buffett. Berkshire started out as a textile manufacturer but has been transformed by Buffett into basically an investment firm. He seems to get most things right from what I have read.'

Bill was now even more intrigued by Harry and decided he would go home and read everything he could about Berkshire Hathaway.

Harry knew the time had come to talk to Bill about the reason he had sought him out. He didn't want to revisit his story about dreams and visions with a stranger but was desperate for help. His relationship with his parents wouldn't allow Harry to have such a conversation, he couldn't share his problem with Bridget, and his mates were supportive but couldn't provide the kind of fatherly advice that Harry needed.

'Bill,' started Harry. 'I deliberately sought you out because I need some help. I don't want anything from you apart from friendship and advice, but what I'm about to tell you will cause you to think I'm not well,' cautioned Harry. 'Just promise me one thing: whether you believe me or not, I don't want you to share what I am going to tell you with anyone.'

Bill was again taken aback. 'If you don't want me to share, I won't buddy,' replied Bill in a soft voice.

Harry told Bill about his motorbike crash and what had happened to him since that day. 'I don't want to see the future – it just happens to me, at any time. I have like a vision in my mind, and then later it will return, and each time I get more detail. I can't deliberately look for anything in my future; the visions are just random. I also have dreams in much the same way. All of what I see relates to me. If I wasn't involved in an event happening or didn't see it, it won't come to me as a vision or dream.

'The reason I'm coming to you is because I have seen in the future that you and I become close friends. We meet in the late '90s, it seems. Not sure why we meet then, or how, but that's what happens.'

Bill was stunned and concerned – he wondered if Harry were mentally unwell.

'How do you know what you are seeing aren't just dreams but the future?' asked Bill.

'I wondered the same thing when it first happened, then I tested it. I predicted the big hailstorm we had in early September to some of my friends and I was right. I then went to visit a girl I had seen in my dreams, who I didn't know, and she turned out to be exactly who I had seen. Same name, same town – everything! And I even knew the name of the Melbourne Cup winner.'

Bill didn't know where to start. 'So, you *see* we become friends in the future, which is why you have come to me, but what do you want from me at this point?' he asked.

'I'm not really sure Bill, I just wanted to lean on someone. I want someone to talk to, and in the future, you always seem to have the right answers. It's starting to get me down. I can't be totally honest with anyone, including my girlfriend, and I can't talk to my parents about it. Lots of people would probably think being able to see the future would be fantastic, but I don't want to Bill – it shows me things I don't want to see, and makes me worry,' said a now emotional Harry.

'I could get you in to see a really good neurosurgeon, or a psychologist, buddy,' offered Bill, who wasn't convinced that Harry could see the future.

'I don't need that, Bill. I'm not suicidal or crackers. I know this is very difficult for you to believe – I mean a person who can see the future, wow! Can you just pretend that you believe me and tell me what you would do, if you were in my predicament?'

'Well, Harry, I think you are doing a good job already if what you tell me has happened. You firstly determined *if* the dreams come true, and then you have been cautious with what you know about the future. If I were to believe you, I would say that's an admirable job. You are obviously conflicted by what you *think* the future will be, and what your dreams show you the future will be, and that's why you are uncomfortable and maybe unhappy with what's happening, but you are on the right track, mate. Live in the moment and don't be distracted by what you see – but if you want to visit the very best doctors in Australia, I can organise that for you.'

As Harry had seen in the future, Bill's advice was basic but comforting. In the future, he often said what Harry was thinking, and if he didn't, Harry would reassess. 'Before I go Bill, I know you are not comfortable with this conversation, but thank you for listening – it's made me feel better. To convince you, remember, bet on Berkshire, the market will decline until about 1982, and the next time I see you, you'll have five holes in one, because my visions show me that when we play in the future you remind me of that all the time.'

Harry left and Bill shook his head. The meeting had confounded him. Harry was such a genuine young man and had his head on his shoulders, he thought. Bill was a pragmatic thinker and could not believe Harry's story, even though he wanted to. In the short hour or so that they were together, Harry had infected Bill with his story, which it seemed he truly believed.

It was December 1978 and Bill wouldn't meet Harry again until March 1998, nearly 20 years later, as Harry had predicted.

Bill arrived home and found his daughter June, in the kitchen. 'I just played golf with a young fellow you work with – Harry Barnes?'

'Oh yeah, I know Harry, he's been at the bank for about 12 months now. He's a nice guy,' replied June. 'He won money on Arwon in the Cup and was so happy about it.'

'Won money on the Melbourne Cup?'

'Yes, word got back to Barney that Harry had a big plunge on Arwon and it won. Harry didn't say anything about it, but you know Barney, he knows everything. Barney hasn't embarrassed Harry by asking him how much he won – he reckons Harry's been through enough in the past month or so. He crashed his bike heavily in Darling in September and was flown back to Rasp by the Royal Flying Doctor, but before that an older bloke, his girlfriend's ex, bashed Harry. He's all fine now though,' said June, 'everybody likes him and he's a good worker.'

Bill retired to his office. At least some of the story I got from Harry was true, he thought, and he did win on the Cup. The poor bugger has been through a bit lately.

Harry's story stayed with Bill over the next six months as he watched the share market move sideways. During that time, he investigated Berkshire Hathaway – its share price was resilient, as Harry said it would be.

In August 1979, June told Bill that Harry had been transferred – to Ber-Beri, she thought. Bill wondered how he was faring. Harry hadn't contacted him after that initial meeting, and Bill wondered why, but he would regularly ask June about him and her reports were always positive about his work. Each time he asked she would add that he still had the same girlfriend.

Bill didn't see Harry at the golf club again. It wasn't unusual for younger guys to drift in and out of the club as they followed other pursuits, such as cars, girls and bikes, he thought. Then when Harry moved, he was told that Harry was still a member and played only occasionally when visiting Rasp. Bill was true to his word and never told anyone about his encounter with Harry in 1978.

In 1982, there was a severe recession in Australia and the share market dived. Interest rates peaked and commodities plunged. Berkshire Hathaway's share price was around $500, and the US dollar to the Australian dollar was at parity, when Bill purchased 100 shares. When he died in 2016, his investment was worth more than $30 million dollars.

The Monaro

December 1978

Max was working underneath his car on a very hot Sunday afternoon when he heard someone come down the drive. Harry kicked one of Max's feet to get his attention. 'Hey Heady, it's me,' offered Harry. 'Can I talk to you for a bit?'

Max came out from under the car and got two Cokes from his garage fridge. Just as Stevie was reliable in a fracas, Max was a great friend when you needed emotional support. They had gone to school together and Harry knew that if he needed support, Max was the one to turn to. He was dependable, and a deep thinker. You would tell him something and he would say, 'Yeah, but what if we …'.

'I think I fucked up, Max,' confessed a worried Harry.

'What did you do mate?' Max asked.

Harry hadn't been totally honest with any of his friends since his accident. He hadn't lied to them – he just didn't tell them everything he had been up to, and he hadn't told anyone about his visit to

Little Creek, or his visions about Little Creek and Lucy. He was in a serious relationship with Bridget and he didn't want her to know about that trip – and he didn't want his mates to know what he had been up to. They would obviously think he was really unhinged, and he would get more questions about his health and about his ability to sometimes see things.

It was all so complicated and it was starting to wear on Harry. His life had been out of sorts since September when he crashed his motorbike, nearly four months ago. Things were going great with Bridget; they were friends and lovers – and she was his girlfriend. But his visions showed him Lucy and their marriage, and he wasn't sure how that would all eventuate. At the moment, he just wanted life to continue the way it was. If Lucy found him, *everything* would change. He knew his vision of a future with Lucy would come true because he had visited her and talked to her. She was real. He wasn't crazy. He knew that's why he went. He went to prove to himself that he wasn't going crazy.

'It's not what I did that worries me Max, it's what might happen.'

'Have you had another vision?'

'No, I haven't had a vision about this, I just think it might happen and I don't want it to happen, for reasons I don't want to talk about right now.'

'Well, mate, what do you want me to do for you?' asked Max.

'I want to transfer ownership of my Monaro to you. I don't want to sell it to you, I just want you to be recorded as the official owner of the car.'

'Flash, what have you done?'

'Mate, I haven't done anything illegal; I promise. I wouldn't put you in that position.'

Max knew Harry was a man of his word, and if he said he did or didn't do something it would be the truth, so he was comforted by what Harry had just said.

'But why Harry?' asked Max.

'Look, I will still pay all the insurance and registration costs and everything, and if the car gets a parking ticket or whatever, I will pay it, okay?' Harry paused. 'Max, I think that one day a girl with long dark hair will come looking for me, and I don't want her to find me.

The only thing that this girl knows about me is I own a blue HK GTS Monaro with a 186 engine in it – at least that's what I think she knows. She knows what I look like and my car. That's it. So, if in some way she is able to trace my car, and it's in your name, she won't find me – unless you tell her about me, that is. If she does come to Rasp, she will find you, and you will say, "I sold the car. I had it for ages and it's now in Adelaide." If she asks "Do you know a blonde guy who looks like me?" you say "No!" '

Max took in everything Harry had said and tried to process it. 'Did you get this girl pregnant or something like that in your car?'

'No, I didn't! I met her for about 10 minutes one day and now I am afraid she will find me,' Harry explained.

'Nothing untoward happened that I or you could get in trouble for?'

'Absolutely nothing like that.'

'I'll do it on a couple of conditions, Harry. One, sometime in the future, or when I see this girl, you tell me what happened to make you fear her. And two, we change the registration back to your name as soon as you can.'

'Max, you don't know how much I appreciate that,' Harry said. 'My brain is all over the place at the moment. It's like I worry about the present and the future as well … So the deal is, if or when this girl shows up at your place – yes, you used to own a Monaro but sold it; you didn't get the car off me and you don't know me. Don't tell her anything that could lead her to me. One last thing, please don't tell Bridget or anyone else about this arrangement.'

'Okay, but Harry – if she noticed your numberplate she may already have your address,' said Max. 'Yeah, I know,' said Harry, sounding resigned. 'I'm just hoping she didn't look at that. At the time she seemed to just be watching me, so I am hoping.'

With that the deal was done. Max or Harry would tell no one about their deal, not even Webby or Steve, but Max couldn't stop wondering about Harry's mental health. He thought that if Harry seemed to deteriorate more or get any weirder, he would involve Harry's mother and father. But at the moment, Max had a mission and would be ready if a young girl with long dark hair visited him.

⟨20⟩

It rains

September to December 1978

Lucy was full of news when she got home on Sunday afternoon, but she didn't tell her parents everything.

Mavis and Mick had already heard about the netball result and commiserated with her.

'Everyone is saying how well you all played,' said Mavis. 'They said that Coolabah was well in front at half time but you ended up just getting pipped 57 to 58.'

Mavis was not a person who enjoyed watching or playing sport, but she liked to take an interest in what Lucy was doing. 'They said Ms Davis gave you girls a good talking to at half time,' Mavis continued. 'She is a very good teacher and nice person. It would be good if you were in some of her classes next year.'

Lucy and Mavis were yet to have a conversation about schooling the following year.

Mick hadn't said much, but he asked after Fred. 'I think he is well,' said Lucy. Mick didn't wear his emotions on his sleeve, but Lucy knew that was her father's way of asking how Fred was coping without Mrs Blackwell.

'I saw you at the grid talking to someone on Saturday morning,' said Mick suddenly. 'I went to the silo to get feed and I thought I saw a car parked at the grid and you on your bike.'

Lucy hesitated for a moment. There were two things she was determined not to talk about: Mr White T-Shirt Man, and Alice's pregnancy. Lucy had promised Alice that she wouldn't tell anyone she was having a baby. Alice would probably go to one of her sisters first, and maybe they would talk to Fred together, she thought. Lucy remembered one night that Alice's eldest sister had talked to them about sex and about being careful and she wouldn't be pleased with Alice's predicament, but she sure would stick up for her, thought Lucy.

Meanwhile, telling Dad about Mr White T-Shirt Man was totally out of the question. Firstly, she thought, Mick would say he's a lunatic – or say 'I don't like you talking to boys you don't know.' 'Boys I don't know' is code for 'I don't like them', thought Lucy. The topic was definitely out of bounds.

'Yes, I did talk to a man at the grid,' said Lucy. 'It looked like he had slept there. He asked me if this was the road to Finley and what was the road like.'

'Did you know him?' inquired Mick.

'No,' replied Lucy.

'Make sure you are careful, Lucy, there are a lot of lunatics around. What sort of car was it?'

'I think it was a green Ford,' said Lucy to throw Mick off the scent. What if he comes back, thought Lucy? He might want to see me again and Dad will say, 'You're talking to a stranger and he's a lunatic.'

They talked about the Mangans, the trip to Coolabah, how the football went and who got injured. Did she see Dan and his boys there? What did Fred cook her and Alice for dinner?

They hadn't been together since Friday night and Lucy had their full attention. There was no dance on the previous Friday night, which was just as well because Lucy's weekend turned out to be very busy.

There was going to be a dance on Friday 17 November, and given that she didn't have any netball on the weekends now, Lucy told her father she might go with him.

Now she was on his good side, she asked about the crops.

'Well,' he replied, addressing Mavis and Lucy. 'I had an agronomist here on Friday and he thinks they look very good. The wheat will probably go around 3 tonne a hectare. In due course, they would like to make an offer on the wheat and barley. The protein looks like it will be good and prices also look good so we could do well this year.'

It would be good to see Dad's hard work rewarded, she thought. She knew a little about farming and knew that good prices and a good yield meant a very good return. She had asked this question deliberately because of the note in her sports bag. She thought, one swallow doesn't make a summer, but Alice is pregnant – tick, and if the rains come true – tick. Oh, and what will Alice call her baby?

She didn't want her father's hard work to be washed away, but she really wanted Mr White T-Shirt Man's predictions to be true.

'When do you think the crops will be ready for harvest, Dad?'

'Early December, I reckon.'

Shit, thought Lucy – the note said December rain. 'Okay … what's the weather forecast for December?' she asked.

'Last time I looked at the long-term forecast, it was going to be sunny all December. And it'll probably be stinking hot as usual,' her father responded confidently.

'You'll have to show me how you can tell when the crops are nearly ready,' Lucy said.

'I just break off some seed heads, rub them between my hands until the grains are released, then I bite down on them and if they are hard, they are ready,' he replied. Mick knew he had to consider the moisture content, but that's generally how he would check to see if the crops were ready. Lucy had seen her father rub the grains before, but wanted confirmation on how to do it so she could check on the crops, which would soon turn from a bright green to a yellow straw colour. She was going to start checking as soon as it was November!

Mavis thought Lucy seemed cheerier than when she left on Saturday morning. But something wasn't quite right, she thought. So, after Lucy had showered and gone to her room, Mavis went up to say good night. She knocked gently, went in and sat on the edge of Lucy's bed. Lucy was in bed reading a piece of paper, which she promptly folded and put in the middle of the book open on her lap.

'Is everything alright dear?' Mavis started.

'Yep, I'm just a little tired,' Lucy replied.

'Well, you have school tomorrow, so make sure you are ready. Not long until the end of the year now.'

Lucy didn't really want to have the conversation about school now because she wasn't armed with a plan. She also wasn't about to talk about her grid meeting, or about Alice, but she thought it nice of her mother to check in on her.

'I'm alright, Mum. Just a bit annoyed we didn't win the netball. I couldn't do a thing right until half time, and then we played well after Ms Davis talked to us.'

'Well, sometimes the truth hurts, but it is good for us, and if Ms Davis told you that you needed to pick up your game, she was just helping,' Mavis said.

With that, Mavis left Lucy alone with her thoughts. Lucy opened her book, *The Thorn Birds*, but she was more interested in the note from Mr White T-Shirt Man. Maybe she would hide it at the back of her knicker drawer with her keepsakes, she thought, but then folded it and put it back in her book, put the book in the drawer, got back into bed and fell asleep.

During the following week at school, Lucy connected with Alice. Alice had been talking with her eldest sister, so now three people knew her predicament. She said that her sister was coming to Little Creek on the weekend and they would tell Fred then. I'm not sleeping at Alice's next weekend, thought Lucy.

Alice's sister Beverly arrived on Friday evening and they spent that night talking. Beverly was annoyed that Alice was not taking a contraceptive pill, but she understood why. She was sure that their father Fred would not have had the same conversation with Alice that she might have otherwise had with her mother.

Beverly blamed herself a little. I should have followed up on my initial talk that I had with Alice and Lucy, she thought. Alice had told Beverly she didn't have a relationship with the father of her child. It had been a once only thing.

'He is a fair bit older,' said Alice, 'and I got carried away with the moment.'

'You shouldn't have put yourself in that position,' retorted Beverly.

'I never want to see him again,' said Alice. 'I don't even want him to know I am pregnant.'

'He'll find out,' replied Beverly. 'Well, I bet he doesn't come to Little Creek or contact me again, because he is living with a girl. Not sure if they are married or not,' said Alice.

Fuck, thought Beverly, Alice should have known better.

They told Fred the following morning. Beverly in her own way made sure Fred understood that their mum's passing would have affected Alice, and that she was not there to guide Alice, which Fred understood. Fred missed his wife and loved his daughter very much and these twin emotions caused him to be very compassionate with Alice. And so, it was done.

Fred thought, I will support Alice any way I can, and protect her from anyone in town who might be judgmental. He was going to be a grandfather again and he was looking forward to meeting the baby and having a baby in his house to spoil. He had softened since the passing of his wife.

Beverly and Alice went to Little Creek South on Sunday afternoon to talk with Lucy and share the news with Mick and Mavis Martin. Alice had told Beverly that she had already talked to Lucy about her pregnancy, but Beverly wanted to ensure the Martin family were brought into the fold and also to surreptitiously plant a seed with Mick, Mavis and Lucy that teenage pregnancy can happen.

Beverly was a mature married woman, but she had lived in Little Creek as a teenager and was wise to how something like this could happen. Beverly knew that contraception was a must for young women. There is no antidote to pregnancy. If an older man provides a much younger woman with some attention and flatters her, or even if something untoward happens, without contraception it is too late.

Lucy would be 16 in six months. Mavis and Lucy hadn't yet had a conversation about such things, but Lucy was wiser than her years suggested. In the last term of school, Mavis signed a permission note for Lucy to attend a sex education class but was not otherwise involved in her daughter's sex education. Mavis was a religious woman and, Lucy thought, blind to what really happens these days. At present, Lucy did not require or use the contraceptive pill. She knew, however, that she would need to make this decision herself without input from her mother.

Lucy and Mick went to the old-time dance on the Friday night, as discussed. It was in the community hall in Avondale, around 80 kilometres from Little Creek. Although Avondale was a very small town, the dance drew a lot of people from around the district. It was an opportunity to meet up before everyone became busy with harvest and then Christmas. Lucy looked beautiful in a long, apricot-coloured chiffon dancing dress. It had a scoop neckline with short flutter sleeves, and she kept her hair out trailing down her back.

Lucy had checked the crops on 16 November, the day before the dance. It had been very warm for the past two weeks and the wheat was a rich golden colour with no green evident.

She broke off some seed heads and did exactly what her father had told her over dinner a few weeks ago. She rubbed her hands together quickly and the seeds readily broke free. She then put them in her mouth and to her they seemed very hard. This was great, thought Lucy. If they started on or around 24 November, they should get the crops in before the rain starts – even if it rains in early December.

When it rains, the first issue is that harvesters cannot start because the ground is too moist, and the machinery is easily bogged. The second issue is that the crops get moisture in them and can't be harvested until they dry out and are acceptable to millers.

But Mr White T-Shirt Man had told Lucy this was to be a 'huge rain event and it floods', so the best course of action, she knew, would be to get the grain off the paddock. She had been watching long-term weather forecasts and noticed that some meteorologists were predicting a cold front in early December for the Little Creek district, and she could bring this into her conversation with her father as well. The forecasters were at this stage only predicting a slight chance of rain with the weather change, but if the cold front clashed with warm moist air, there would be a chance of medium rainfall.

Hmmm, thought Lucy, they are hedging their bets. Lucy decided that she would talk with her father about the harvest on their way home from the dance, when her father was always in a good mood.

The hall in Avondale was very small. There was trestle seating around the walls and a stage at the front. On one side there was a corridor leading to the ladies' bathroom and another doorway to the kitchen. Ladies were invited to bring a plate of nibbles, and later in the evening tea and coffee were served. The men's facilities were in a separate building outside the hall. No alcohol was served at the dances because it was an older demographic and most had to drive home afterwards.

Mick and Lucy had a very enjoyable night and left Avondale a little past midnight after helping the local ladies tidy the hall. It was nearly summer, the night was warm and they talked about who had been there and who they each danced with. Lucy talked about some of the ladies' dresses – good and bad. Not many attractive young women attended the dances and as a result, Lucy's card was usually full of dance requests. Mick danced with casual acquaintances and ladies he had become friends with at dances over the years. Mick was a serious man and didn't talk a great deal, but he would let his guard down when he was with his daughter, particularly when they were dancing.

'Dad, I tested the wheat yesterday,' ventured Lucy when they were driving home, 'and I don't know as much as you, but I reckon it's ready for harvest.'

Mick smiled in the dark of the car as he envisioned Lucy rubbing and bitting the wheat. 'What, do you think we should start?' said Mick. 'Yes, I think we should, because then I can wag the last few weeks of school and help you, and maybe you could pay me? You know I am going to see Janice in early January and I could use the money – plus,

I know you are not busy at the moment and then maybe you, mum and I could go to Ber-Beri and do some shopping before Christmas. We could get mum something really nice,' gushed Lucy, using her best persuasive powers. 'Better the grain in the silo than in the paddock. Less risk that way. Oh, and I accidently heard on the radio yesterday that a cold front is on the way in a week or so and there could be some rain.'

Mick had heard about the cold front as well, and Lucy's 'better in the silo than in the paddock' comment resonated. He thought he would check on the wheat tomorrow to see if Lucy was right. He had been busy with pigs for a few weeks now; he had a routine for harvest and hadn't considered changing his plans. But an early harvest and a trip to Ber-Beri with Mavis and Lucy would be nice before Christmas, he thought.

He knew Lucy was going to Perth in January to be at Janice's wedding. Mick and Mavis were not going; they had no one to look after the farm. It was too much to ask Dan, with his responsibility for four boys. Lucy, however, thought that her parents were being stubborn and resentful of Janice for running away from home – she already lived with the bloke, and Mick hadn't liked him when Janice bought him home for a visit.

Was Mick being more caring in his relationship with Lucy, or was Lucy a more loving daughter? Whatever the case, Lucy had persuaded Mick to reconsider his harvest plans.

They arrived home and regaled Mavis with what types of dances they did, and who they danced with. Mavis was full of questions about who was there and what everyone wore on such a warm night.

Preoccupied with the chat about harvesting, Mick had forgotten to ask Lucy on the drive home about the young man he had seen her dancing with, and thought to ask now. Mick said that the fellow had come up and talked to him. Apparently, he was the son of a lady Mick knew from dancing, and Mick thought he was being a gentleman by coming and introducing himself.

'Arthur Hall – seems like a good young bloke,' said Mick. Mick's words jolted Lucy. At the dance, she hadn't given the bloke a second thought. He was a good dancer, but that was it. He didn't stand out in any way and was a little anonymous. However, Mick's remark had made her remember what Mr White T-Shirt Man had said, 'At a dance you will meet a boy – stay away from him', or words to that effect. Mavis made them all a cup of tea and around 1.30 am they went to bed.

In bed, Lucy thought again about the warning given to her at the grid. I wonder if that's the guy Mr White T-Shirt Man was referring to? If he is right about the rain, I'll make sure I am careful around him, she determined.

Mick recounted his conversation with Lucy about the early harvesting to Mavis as they climbed into bed. She thought it was a good idea – particularly for them to be involved and working with Lucy – but noted that she had heard there was only a slight chance of rain in December. They both wondered how much longer Lucy would be at home with them. She would be 16 next year and was going to visit Janice, and could come home with ideas of being closer to her.

Mick was up at 5.30 the next morning to feed the pigs. He decided that once the sun had been fully up for an hour or so he would check the wheat with the moisture meter he had bought when he was last in Ber-Beri selling pigs.

After smoko, he headed to his largest paddock and first did his manual check. Lucy was right, he thought. He wondered why she made such and effort this year, but was pleased she was taking an interest. The crop looked good, but to make sure, he used his meter: it showed that the crops were ready for harvest. He decided they would start on Wednesday 22 November, and told Mavis and Lucy at dinner that evening.

Lucy was ecstatic but hid her excitement at the idea she may be helping her parents avoid a disastrous situation. She was not hoping for widespread damage to the Little Creek area, but more wondering if Mr White T-Shirt Man was right. If he was not right, the harvest would be done early and she would enjoy her time avoiding school and being with her parents, she thought. But if he *was* right …

It took the family plus a hired hand a week to get the job done. Lucy took the week off school and drove the tractor with the chaser bin behind it while her father worked throughout the day and most of the nights. Mick was determined to get the crop off and drove the header with lights ablaze well into the small hours.

The crop exceeded even the agronomists' expectations, and because of a hot finish, the quality was very good. Mick was now looking forward to taking his two girls on a shopping trip to Ber-Beri. He was delighted that Lucy had twisted his arm, which endeared her to him even more. Mick hoped that all farmers in the district would heed the weather warning for rain, which was now common on the hourly news. Thank God we started when we did, he thought. Even if our neighbours start now and work 24 hours a day, they won't get their crops off for weeks. It was the night of 30 November when the family finally finished their work and had the grain stored in silos.

On the 3 December it became unusually cold for the first month of summer and started to rain. Weather forecasters were now predicting that the cold front would collide with warm moist air from the north and that there would be heavy rain. It rained steadily the first day then that night it became calamitous. The house gutters were overwhelmed and during the night, Mick went to the pig shed to shovel sand around the bottom of the shed to stop water flowing through it, and make sure the pigs were safe.

Little Creek, which ran east–west from the township towards their farm, was about 100 metres from the homestead and rapidly rising. The water could not get away quickly enough, and in town the creek had backed up and broken its bank and was now near the back of the Little Creek Hotel in the main street. The creek rose so high that the bridge from the town went under, and some of Mick's paddocks were a metre under water.

There were varying reports about the amount of rain received, but the official report was 267 millilitres over the week. The main street of Little Creek was flooded and the caravan park disappeared under water. Tens of thousands of acres of crops were destroyed. Many farmers had hurriedly started harvesting when the initial weather reports, about three days prior to the deluge, suggested heavy rain. Getting heavy crops off in three days was, however, impossible and farmers suffered losses.

It was the middle of the night when the heavy rain started. Lucy was concerned for the whole district as it clattered heavily on her bedroom roof, but also frightened by the fact that Mr White T-Shirt Man was right: a stranger knew more about her future than she did.

Who is he, and what else does he know about me? she thought. She went and got *the* note out of her secret hiding place and re-read it. It was uncannily correct and this spooked Lucy. Mr White T-Shirt Man had known her best friend's name, he had known that Alice was pregnant, and now the rain was falling heavily. Shit, thought Lucy, what if Alice has a boy and she calls him Jon! What do I do then?

Who's Sandra?

27 January 1979

Harry learned so much about his future in the summer of 1978 and 1979. It was an agonising, frustrating, exciting time for him. Some days, he thought knowing his future was a curse, which is why he had been and sought advice from Bill. Most would think that it would be fun to see their future, but Harry now knew it was scary and exhausting. He couldn't talk to anyone about it, and it posed some vexing questions to him.

He loved Bridget but could see he was not going to spend his life with her, and this hurt more than anything. He constantly fought a battle in his mind about whether he was being fair to Bridget, but he didn't want to know the reason why they didn't end up together. Maybe it was something out of his control. Maybe it was something more sinister, which he hadn't seen. If I see in my visions something that suggests something tragic will happen to Bridget, I will warn her, even if it means I have to disclose my secret to her, he decided. I just don't want to bloody know, thought Harry often, as he battled his demons.

He had done his best to drip-feed Steve and Max as little information as he could. He had messed up unintentionally with Steve, and knew what damage could be done. Both he and Steve were wrestling with relationships that apparently would not last forever. Harry consoled himself by reasoning that he had blurted out the Sandra thing when he was only partly conscious, on the way to the Darling hospital.

Max was agnostic about the whole issue, thought Harry. He was concerned about the whole seeing-the-future thing. He thought that Harry's health was questionable, but he did sway when they backed the Melbourne Cup winner, and then when Harry told him about Emma Forrest. He even asked Harry one night about his future.

'Do I do okay in life?' was the broad-ranging question Max put to Harry when they were drunk.

'Mate,' said Harry, 'in my book, you fucking succeed Heady. You have a beautiful family and enjoy life.' That answer, more than anything, placated Max. Max was prone to worrying and for Harry to say he would succeed satisfied him. Max didn't ask about Emma Forrest because it seemed that he had already made up his mind thought Harry – she is the one.

Steve was more complicated than Max, and more difficult to satisfy. Steve wanted to know everything, especially after Arwon won. Steve was constantly inquisitive about his future and how they could capitalise on the information Harry had. Most of all he wanted to know about Debbie and Sandra.

Steve said more than once to Harry, 'Is there anything I can do or change that will keep Debbie and me together?' Harry already knew that there was someone else involved, but it wouldn't be fair to talk to Stevie about it. Harry had seen that Debbie still had a tie with her old boyfriend, and he made an assumption about what would happen.

Harry told Steve to perhaps just enjoy the sex while it is available. 'Go with the flow mate. Don't challenge life or it'll eat you up.'

Harry summed up what he had seen in his dreams that most affected him. Lucy and his future with her were the most important things he had seen, but he was deeply wounded by the apparent demise of his relationship with Bridget. He knew he would have three children with Lucy, and even knew their names and a little about their personalities.

He had seen himself succeed working in the more senior echelons of the bank. He worked in commercial lending and in the investment arm of the bank and was well rewarded. He had seen dark things, such as the death or near death of his father, which he still wasn't sure about, and he knew about a severe injury to Mick Martin.

There was a myriad of other visions that he thought he would carry with him for life and be aware of, but Bridget cut deeply and he sympathised with Steve. But how could he tell a mate that his girl sleeps with her old boyfriend and then it's over? He could, he thought, tell Steve that Sandra is a wonderful person liked by everyone, and they would have two children, as will Max and Emma, although that would be difficult for Steve to reconcile. Such a burden to carry, thought Harry.

The morning *it* happened was of no consequence to Harry. It was the last weekend of January 1979, a Saturday, the day after the Australia Day public holiday, and Harry had stayed all Friday and Friday night with Bridget.

He had planned to go riding bikes with 'the boys' on Saturday afternoon. Harry always woke first and stroked Bridget's back as she woke. This morning, he felt particularly well and told Bridget he had had a terrific sleep. 'Let's get up and go and have breakfast at the café,' he cheerfully encouraged.

'Why are you so chirpy this morning? Just let me sleep,' demanded Bridget. But he didn't. After breakfast, he dropped Bridget home and drove to see Steve to organise the ride. Debbie was just leaving and said 'Hi' to him and talked about what he was getting up to tonight.

'She is a good fuck, Flash,' said Steve when Debbie had left. 'I'll change that. She is a bit of a star fish but always ready. Too bad she won't be around forever.'

'What – are you and her breaking up?!' exclaimed Harry.

Steve eyed Harry suspiciously. 'Well, you know the whole Sandra thing,' replied Steve.

Harry looked quizzically at Steve, 'What Sandra thing?'

'Fuck me, are you on drugs Flash?' demanded Steve as they walked to his shed to check his bike.

'Mate I must have missed something – I don't know about the *Sandra thing*, and if you are so happy rooting Debbie, why are you ditching her?' asked Harry.

Steve looked directly at Harry. 'Fuck Flash, you told me I was going to break up with Debbie and marry Sandra. Get your brain in gear.'

'I told you what?!' exclaimed Harry. This was now getting frustrating for Steve. He was beginning to wonder about Harry's sanity. Max did say he was a little cuckoo, thought Steve – or is he having me on?

'If you hadn't predicted the storm, hadn't predicted the Arwon win, hadn't told me about Debbie and Sandra, and hadn't known about Emma and Max, I would never have believed your bullshit stories. Don't be a prick. You know what I'm talking about.'

But Harry didn't know what he was talking about. He just stood there, blankly watching Steve oiling his bike chain, confounded by what he was saying.

'Stevie, I really don't know what you are talking about,' Harry said. Steve put down the aerosol can of chain lube.

'Flash, are you alright mate? Do you remember the big investment we made in November?'

'No, what investment?'

Steve thought, I've got a problem here. He kicked over a milk crate and sat on it, offering one to Harry.

'Okay what *do* you remember?'

'What do you mean?'

'Well, you remember your bike crash when we went camping, right? And then you changed and told me you could see the future? Am I right?'

'I remember going camping – what crash?' Harry asked.

Fucking hell, thought Steve. 'Forget all that, let's go and visit Max in my car, eh,' said Steve brusquely. Steve wasn't about to get in a car with Harry driving. He didn't trust him one little bit at the moment. Max will say, 'I told you he is a bit bananas', thought Steve.

Max had just finished preparing his bike as Steve and Harry pulled up. 'You two ready?' he asked.

'No, we've got a big fucking problem,' shouted Steve.

'Heady, I don't have a problem,' argued Harry. 'I'm ready. I'm sure I already prepped my bike.'

'Harry is completely bananas!' exclaimed Steve.

'That's bullshit Steve, just because I can't remember what you want me to,' shouted Harry.

'Boys, what's going on?' asked Max.

'He came to my place about 15 minutes ago, talks to Debbie, then tells me he can't remember predicting the future, and he can't even remember the shares we bought in November after the Cup,' explained Steve.

'Bloody hell, I told you he wasn't right,' said Max. Steve was now getting cranky and Harry was perturbed that his mates were talking about him right in front of him. Max sniffed the tension in the air and told the boys to sit down and talk about it.

'Don't get cranky, Steve,' he ordered.

'I'm not cranky, I'm frustrated,' Steve replied.

'Well don't talk about me as if I'm not here,' pleaded Harry.

'Harry, we are only talking about you because we are worried about you,' explained Max. Max then told Harry all about the crash and what he had been doing since – how he had been having dreams or visions, and how some of them had already come true.

'What do you remember about the crash and what happened when we took you into Darling?' asked Max. Harry looked blankly at his two friends.

'My mind is a bit of a blank about all that,' confessed Harry. 'I remember going camping with you guys, and then I have been just seeing Bridget, and going to work – nothing exciting.'

'Did you rebuild your bike by yourself?' asked Max.

'What do you mean rebuild my bike?' asked Harry.

Max and Steve exchanged glances. 'Your bike was stuffed when you crashed, Harry. You hit a gutter at warp speed and bent the forks and ripped the front guard and tank off. It was a mess,' said Steve.

'Really?' Harry asked.

'Tell us if you remember anything from the past four months,' Max said. 'You crashed your bike on 9 September last year and now it's about the end of January. What do you remember?'

The problem for Harry was he didn't remember what he didn't know. The past four months of his life were a blank. He was filling in the blanks by saying 'I've been spending time with Bridget and going to work.'

'Ummm, as I said, I've been going to work and seeing Bridget and it was Christmas and stuff.'

'What did you give to Bridget for Christmas, Harry?' asked Max, who knew very well he had given her a gold bracelet.

'I can't really remember. I think it was jewellery,' lied Harry.

'Do you reckon we should take you to the hospital Harry?' asked Steve, whose demeanour had changed markedly from when he thought Harry was having a lend of him.

'What for Stevie? I am fine. So what if I can't remember what I gave Bridget for Christmas. I actually feel great. I said to Bridge this morning that was the best sleep ever last night, and you two want to whack me in the funny farm. Take me back to get my car Steve or I'll fucking walk, and if you guys say anything about this to Bridget, or Mum and Dad, I'll never talk to you again.'

'Harry if you think we are bullshitting, have a look at the rego papers for your Monaro, then come back and talk to me,' yelled Max as Harry huffed away with Steve in pursuit.

Steve drove Harry back to get his car and none of them went riding that day. Harry went back to Bridget's and told her that since Steve wanted to spend the day with Debbie, they had decided not to ride.

'Hey Bridge, do you still like the Christmas present I got you?' asked Harry.

'Of course I do silly, it's beautiful,' said Bridget, as she looked at her new bracelet. Harry was examining himself for the truth. Where had those past four months gone that the boys said he couldn't remember? I remember going to work and stuff, he thought. I don't remember any dreams or visions, or what shares I bought. Why would we each buy shares?

He was irritated about his conversation with Max and Steve. He went to his car and retrieved the registration papers from the glove box. There in black and white was the owner's name: 'Max Bruce'.

Harry was suddenly in turmoil. Why is my car in Max's name? Were my mates telling me the truth? Oh shit! What did I do during the past four months? What did I say to people? What did I say to Bridget?

'Are we okay?' he asked, smiling at Bridget as she read on the lounge. She came over, sat on his lap and put her arms around his neck.

'Of course we are okay, silly. What's up with you this morning?'

'Oh, it's nothing. I had a bit of a disagreement with Steve and Max – I better go and sort it out, if that's okay with you.'

When he arrived at Max's place, both boys were in the shed, and from the looks Harry received when he walked in, they were talking about him. 'Hey, I might have got it wrong when we were talking,' said Harry. 'You don't know what you don't know do you? You better fill me in about me,' Harry said, smiling.

Harry assured his mates that physically he felt well. He hadn't had any headaches, and slept really well last night, but couldn't understand what they were talking about. The three of them had a long chat that hot Saturday afternoon. Max told the story right from Harry's crash up until their recent drunken discussion about Max's future, and Steve added things that Harry had told him personally. They told him about his visions and dreams – the ones he had told them about – and how they had come true. They also told him about his predictions that were yet to come true, such as Debbie and their share plunge.

But the boys could only tell Harry what they knew – they didn't know everything that Harry knew or had been up to. They didn't know he had been to see his future wife Lucy, and now the only two people who knew about that were Lucy – and to the extent she believed the story, Alice.

Harry was oblivious to everything that had happened that summer.

'Hey, why is my Monaro in your name Max, tell me about that?' Harry asked.

'Can I tell you in front of Steve?' asked Max.

'Fuck me, he knows more about me than I do at the moment so why not?'

Steve was keen to learn about this as well and had been meaning to ask Max when Harry wasn't there, because Max had shouted that out to Harry as he left earlier.

'That's what made me come back and talk with you guys. The registration of my car is in your name, Max, and as soon as I saw that, I knew something was wrong.'

Max explained their pre-Christmas meeting, when Harry asked to transfer the registration of the car into his name. 'What, I'm hiding from a girl?' Harry asked. 'Why would I be hiding from a girl! I don't understand. Who is she Max?'

'You refused to tell me mate and now no one will ever know. You only told me that you had met her for about 10 minutes – she saw your Monaro and you were afraid she would come looking for you. You thought she may be smart enough to track the Monaro and find you. You told me you hadn't done anything wrong or illegal, that she wasn't pregnant and had long dark hair. That's it.'

Bloody hell, thought Harry. 'I don't understand,' he said. 'Please tell me if I did anything else strange. Do you think we should change the car registration back to my name?'

Max thought quickly and decided that they had only made the change in December and now it was January. A month is hardly enough time for someone to track Harry, and he wanted to protect Harry in his present fragile state. 'No, let's wait a bit Bud, it won't hurt if we leave it,' Max suggested.

With the exception of the shares they had bought, the boys thought their brush with the future was over. They couldn't understand why Harry's ability to see the future had gone, and why he couldn't remember those past four months.

'Mate, did you get on the grog or do anything unusual last night?' asked Max.

'No, I had a bloody good sleep and was really nice to Bridget,' smiled Harry.

Steve told Harry he had been hoping that he could tell him who won this year's AFL competition so he could make a fortune, but that was now out the window. They had all laughed at that suggestion, but Steve repeated that when they purchased the shares, Harry had said they could be worth up to about $250,000 each in around 30 years.

'One last thing boys – does Bridget know anything about what's been happening?' asked Harry.

'No mate, all along you told us not to say anything to Webby or Bridget. Not sure why, but if you told *us* not to say anything to them, it seems that *you* wouldn't have said anything to them either,' replied Max.

Harry left Max's, his mind churning through everything the boys had said. He couldn't believe that he would have been able to see the future, but there were the car registration papers as evidence, as well as the shares, and surely his mates would be telling him the truth.

For a moment, he thought that it may have been fun predicting what was going to happen, then dismissed that thought. He counted himself lucky he hadn't told Bridget.

(22)

Janice gets married

January 1979

For a month in January, Lucy didn't think too much about her grid meeting, or for that matter Mr White T-Shirt Man. Her sister was to be married and she was in Perth to be her bridesmaid and support her. She had a wonderful, if not a lonely, Christmas, with her parents at the farm, Little Creek South, then left for Perth. Janice was getting married on 20 January 1979 and wanted her sister to be with her.

Mick and Mavis had a tempestuous relationship with Janice. Janice was 10 years older than Lucy and had left home when she was just 17, and Lucy seven. Mavis always used to say that Janice was very stubborn and rarely did as she was told. When Janice told them she was quitting school and leaving town, Mick had quietened Mavis by simply saying, 'If she wants to go, we should let her. We can't stop her.'

In later years, Lucy would think that her parents had failed with Janice. While Lucy enjoyed a better relationship with her parents, she thought it should still have been better. Mavis was not a warm person, unlike her fraternal grandmother, Lucy would often think. Lucy would have liked to confide in her mother about personal things, but couldn't. She never had a 'birds and bees' discussion with her mother, and her mother didn't talk to her about contraception, and Lucy didn't think she could run to her mother for a protective, reassuring hug.

Mick and Mavis weren't going to Janice's wedding. They had told Lucy they couldn't go because they had no one to mind the farm for them, but Lucy wondered. Even if they didn't like Janice's fiancé, Chris Goodwin, they should have made an effort for Janice. Were they punishing Janice for her cold exit from the family home? wondered Lucy. Lucy knew there were people in Little Creek that Mick could rely on to help him with the farm if he went away, but that was never mentioned. Mick and Mavis felt the love of God, but they never truly put their children first and passed on this love. Mick had paid for Lucy's airfares and later would send some money to Janice to help with the wedding costs, but to Lucy and Janice it seemed a cold way of showing they cared.

Lucy enjoyed the hustle and bustle of Perth compared to Little Creek, but wondered if she would tire of it after a while. While in Perth, she did imagine what it would be like to live far away from Little Creek and enjoy anonymity. Everyone in Little Creek always seemed to know everyone else's business, and seemed to delight in knowing about others' personal lives – and Lucy didn't like that. Lucy despised the talk around Alice's pregnancy. Most of it was lies and nasty, she thought. Janice thought that Lucy would easily get a job in Perth, and didn't discourage her from thinking about joining her.

Shopping at a mall with Janice, Lucy heard her name called, and turned to see Arthur Hall. Apparently, he was holidaying with his sister in Perth. Lucy was surprised and a little annoyed to see a familiar face in Perth, after thinking she was anonymous, and later wondered if Arthur had somehow planned to be there and bump into her. She wondered, suspiciously, if her father had told him she was in Perth – she already held concerns about Arthur's jealous nature, but she waived that thought away, because to date she had little involvement with him.

Arthur asked Lucy to a dance in Perth, and she went with him and his sister. She enjoyed watching them dance together more than she enjoyed dancing with Arthur, but he seemed intent on building a relationship with Lucy, and once again she thought about Mr White T-Shirt Man's warning. Lucy only saw Arthur on one other occasion in Perth, having agreed to go sightseeing with him. Lucy didn't ask Arthur to become involved in her world over in Perth. He wasn't invited to the wedding and left for home before her.

Lucy went home at the end of January, as originally agreed with Mick and Mavis. She did think about aborting the trip home and ignoring her parents, but it wasn't in her make up to be like Janice and make a clean break from everything and everyone in Little Creek, including her parents. I will go home and see little Jon and consider my future, she thought, as she flew home. Maybe Mr White T-Shirt Man will be there waiting …

Jon is born

January 1979

Alice was going to be a young mother, so the local GP referred her to an experienced obstetrician in the nearby city of Ber-Beri, a large country city on the Murray River, around 110 kilometres south of Little Creek. The obstetrician advised Alice to be at the hospital on 28 January, a couple of days before her due date, so she could safely have the baby under his watch. Alice was happy with these arrangements. Regional hospitals such as Little Creek's do not have the facilities of larger cities. Somewhat frightened at the prospect of giving birth, she was comforted by the doctor's arrangements.

Lucy arrived home on 25 January. She had been in Perth for nearly a month, and had considered staying with her sister for longer, but wanted to be close to Alice when she had her baby. Mavis also wanted Lucy to come home and used a trip to see Mick's ageing mother as an excuse to get her home. 'Your father and I thought it may be nice for us all to visit your grandmother,' Mavis had told Lucy over the phone.

Lucy knew this was a ploy to get her home. She thought that she might go back to Perth after Alice had her baby, if she didn't go back to school.

Lucy bought lots of gifts home for the new baby. Mr White T-Shirt Man had said it would be a boy, and with this in mind she had mostly bought things in blue. She had, however, also bought some pinks and yellows, just to be sure. Lucy often joked with Alice, saying 'I reckon it'll be a boy.'

Lucy didn't dare tell Alice that she had been told at the grid it was going to be a boy and his name was to be Jon. Alice had enough things to worry about and Lucy didn't want to burden her with more of her stories. In any case, she still wasn't sure what Alice thought about Mr White T-Shirt Man and his predictions. When Lucy told Alice that Mr White T-Shirt Man had told her she was pregnant, Alice had said that he probably knew someone who knew. He may have known the father or a friend of the father, she said, but that didn't gel with the fact that Alice hadn't told anyone prior to Lucy. Alice knew that her baby's father would know of her pregnancy by now, because everyone in town knew and word would have got to him. This misalignment was put to one side by Alice and Lucy didn't want to argue with her about it.

Lucy had thought about it often and wanted Alice to believe in Mr White T-Shirt Man, so she could believe in him, and maybe then they could then be excited together, or so she thought. They had talked about the weather event and Alice had stewed on this as well. Alice wondered if Mr White T-Shirt Man looked at long-term weather forecasts.

'You know, like the ones the famous Lennox Walker used to publish,' she had said. The rain event was tough for Alice to reconcile. She satisfied herself by saying he guessed. 'He knew when the harvest would be and guessed about it being interrupted by bad weather.' So while Lucy was crediting Mr White T-Shirt Man's predictions, Alice was not convinced that someone could see the future.

As well as everything that was going on in Alice's world, her scepticism was a contributing factor in Lucy not telling her about Jon. Lucy had decided that she would tell Alice that she knew Jon's name, before Alice could tell her after his birth. The two girls had had a number of discussions about names before Lucy went to Perth, and when Lucy returned home Alice had told Lucy she had a boy's name and a girl's name picked out. She also said that Lucy would be the first to know the baby's name, once it was born.

In the 1970s, it was not uncommon to not know the sex of a baby before birth. In later years, most mothers wanted to know the sex as soon as they could, but in the 1970s, the practice was to wait. The doctor would usually say, 'I can't really tell.'

Alice didn't want her baby to have a name that was common in her family. She had decided that the baby was all hers: I want my baby to have a name I like – something a little different. The more people suggested names, the more stubborn Alice became.

Apart from *being* pregnant, Alice's pregnancy was trouble-free. She had not had morning sickness, and her blood pressure had been stable the whole time. The doctor had told her that as far as he could tell, her baby was healthy and would be an average size at birth. His last examination confirmed the due date of 30 January 1979. Alice would turn 17 in February.

Lucy told Alice all about her trip to Perth. Staying with her sister and sister's fiancé, Lucy felt more grown up than when she was home. Janice treated her like an adult and they allowed her to accompany them to clubs and pubs in Perth. With make up, Lucy could pass for an eighteen-year-old, and she enjoyed the freedom of not having to ask Mavis where and when she could go. People's attitudes in a large city were also different, she thought, and she had enjoyed the faster pace of the city and the hustle and bustle of catching trains and buses and struggling to be on time.

Lucy believed she could live away from her mother and father. Of course, Janice wasn't perfect. Janice is more stubborn than me, Lucy thought, and she lacks my compassion. I could get a job here, thought Lucy, and my own little apartment when I saved up a little.

But Lucy wondered how this change might fit into Mr White T-Shirt Man's 'grand plan'. He hadn't said anything about Perth, or about Janice – he just asked me to wait for him, whatever that means, Lucy thought. Do I have to put my life on hold?

'You are not fair,' Lucy said out loud, though this time she didn't shout it out like she had when she was crying on her bike watching him disappear. She also left out the 'I hate you.' Lucy was still as confused and frustrated as she was when she left for Perth. But now she was home and just wanted to meet and hold little Jon.

Fred and Beverly took Alice to Ber-Beri. Mavis and Mick agreed they would wait until Alice had had her baby before they all went on their trip to see Mick's mother. Lucy was happy with this. They planned to head to Ber-Beri as soon as they had heard from Beverly, who would let them know about the baby.

Lucy whiled away the days waiting for the baby to arrive by unpacking and visiting her nephews in Little Creek. She had brought home gifts for everyone and just wanted to reconnect with her family. She and Dan weren't particularly close, with an age difference of more than 10 years, but she enjoyed being with Dan's boys and his wife.

But she was, she thought, a little lost. School would be going back soon and this troubled her. She would be 16 in May and then she would have options, she thought. She was now resigned to going back to school. She knew 15 was too young to get a job, and at 15 Mick would certainly make her stay at school. She thought she might ring the army careers people and ask them how old she had to be to join, but suspected it was probably 18 – she would therefore need to fill in two years waiting.

At dinner on her second night home, Mick told Lucy he had had a visitor while Lucy was in Perth. 'You remember that nice young fellow, Arthur – who you danced with in Avondale? Well, he came and saw Mum and I.'

Apparently, Arthur had told them he was passing through Little Creek and thought he would visit. 'He told us he saw you in Perth and was disappointed that you were still away.' He had also endeared himself to Mick and Mavis by helping Mick with some jobs and staying for dinner.

Lucy didn't know whether she was flattered or if she should be concerned. He stayed and had dinner? She thought that a bit odd, a 19-year-old making conversation with two older people he doesn't even know.

Mick, however, seemed taken with Arthur. 'He said he'll be at the next dance in February,' said Mick, 'in Coreen. I think we should go.'

'That must have been nice,' was about all Lucy could muster in response to the news of Arthur's visit. She wasn't that keen – but obviously they were. Lucy thought, you know how it is – if your parents like him there must be something wrong with him. If they don't like him, he is usually the one you want. She didn't really respond to Mick's comment about the dance. She would sleep on it.

* * *

Alice's due date, 30 January, arrived. Lucy woke early, anxious and excited, and waited all day in the house. She dared not go out unless Beverly rang. She wanted to answer the phone and get the news first-hand. She wanted to squeal excitedly and then let Mick, Mavis and her sister know. The telephone didn't ring all day. Maybe Jon isn't ready she thought, because she was in no doubt Beverly would ring as soon as she could.

Then, at about 9.30 that night when Lucy was in the shower, her mother knocked at the door, opened it a little, and told her Beverly was on the phone. Lucy jumped from the shower, wrapped a towel around herself without even drying and demanded accusingly of Mavis, 'She didn't tell you anything did she?!'

'No,' Mavis said. 'She wanted to talk to you.' Lucy ran to the phone and Beverly told her Alice had had a baby boy and that they were both well. 'No name yet. She wants to tell you first. You can come and visit in the morning.'

Lucy hardly slept that night. She was a little jealous that Alice had had a baby. She didn't think about all the negatives – she just couldn't wait to get her hands on him and let Alice know she was so proud of her.

She also thought about Mr White T-Shirt Man and his prediction of the pregnancy and a boy, and was again spooked like she was when it started to rain in December.

Mick, Mavis and Lucy left early the next morning, at Lucy's urging. The previous night, Lucy had decided that she would write a note to Alice explaining what Mr White T-Shirt Man had said at the grid. She wrote the note because she didn't want to burst Alice's excitement bubble. Alice was going to be excited to tell Lucy her baby's name and share her experience with her, and Lucy didn't want the occasion to be spoilt. She did, however, want Alice to believe in Mr White T-Shirt Man, and this was her opportunity to show Alice how real it had been for her.

So, on a white sheet of paper torn from one of her school exercise books, Lucy wrote:

Alice, I am so excited for you and your baby boy. I love you and will also love your boy, and I hope that you will let me share in his life with you.

I know it will be tough for you juggling your life and building a life for your son, and I just want to be there and help you.

But I have to tell you something and I don't want you to be upset about it. I don't want to spoil the excitement you feel now, but I am telling you this because I need your support. I have no one else to talk to about what I am going through. I understand that you think the boy at the grid was crazy, and just a guy who wanted to get into my pants, but he did know you were having a baby, and he did predict the flood and now I am scared that he will get something else right. Please, please, don't hate me Alice, but the boy at the grid told me you would have a boy and that you would name him Jon, without the 'h'. Please Alice, I just love you and I need you, and I want to be there for you.

The population of Ber-Beri was around 50,000 and the hospital was very big. The maternity section had been recently rebuilt and was the most modern part of the hospital. Alice was in a room of her own with yellow curtains with flowers on them.

When Lucy and her parents went in, Alice was feeding the baby. He had taken to breast-feeding very easily, and they both seemed content lying in bed together, thought Lucy immediately. Lucy ran to Alice and hugged both her and the baby together. Lucy had tears running down her face when she released them and looked at the baby boy.

'He is just gorgeous,' said Lucy. 'I am so proud of you.'

Alice smiled like only she could. Mavis came to her bed and cooed about the baby. 'You will be very busy,' Mavis said in a matter-of-fact way. Mavis asked if she had picked out a name yet and Lucy quickly interrupted.

'Mum, Alice said she was going to tell me first and then I can tell you, but I want to know first when you aren't here.' With that, Mick and Mavis decided they would go to the hospital cafeteria to allow the girls some privacy

As soon as they left, Lucy said quickly, 'Alice, please don't tell me his name yet, I want you to read this note I wrote … Can I hold him while you read it?'

Alice nodded. She wondered what the note was about. She expected Lucy would say that she wants to help and do whatever she can for Alice and her baby. Lucy had drawn flowers at the top and bottom of the note in pen. Daisy flowers like you draw at school, and at the bottom were love hearts and XXs for kisses.

Alice smiled as she read the first couple of lines, then the smile faded and lines of concentration appeared on her forehead. She put the note down and looked at Lucy with tears in her eyes. Lucy, again, had tears running down her cheeks and they looked hard at each other for some time.

'My son's name is Jon,' said Alice, her voice breaking. 'I haven't told a single person, not even Beverly. You not only know his name, but how I am going to spell it. I can't believe it, Luce. I don't have any words to describe how I am feeling … and I am sorry if I didn't believe you about the grid meeting. I do believe in you and what you said he said, but I don't know how this boy knows so much. I know you are going to help me and I will support you, Luce. Let's work this all out together.'

'I am not going to tell anyone about our secret, Alice,' Lucy replied. 'I am not going to say I knew Jon's name or tell anyone else about White T-Shirt Man.' And with that, the friction that had been between the two girls for the past month or so disappeared.

They giggled, cuddled Jon and talked about getting him home. Lucy gave Alice her gifts, and Alice said laughing, 'If you knew he was going to be a boy, why did you buy some girl stuff?!'

Lucy had one last present behind her back, which she handed to Alice. Alice opened it: inside was a baby blue jump suit with 'Jon' embroidered on the front. From that moment on, Alice knew that Lucy believed everything the boy at the grid had said.

Can they find Mr White T-Shirt Man?

June 1979

It was the middle of her second term in Year 11, around June 1979, when Lucy became restless and bored with life. Last year and early this year was so exciting for her, but now everything seemed ho-hum.

That boy Arthur kept calling, but she wasn't really interested in him – or in anything for that matter. It seemed like her life was a dream that was meandering through a boring landscape. Arthur was like her father in attitude, but not particularly smart, she thought. He just seems to lack vigour and ambition. He doesn't want to be adventurous or try anything different. Mum and Dad like him, but I don't. Ooo – he knows about farming and he's a good worker, blah blah blah. He's kind of convenient, like a petrol station – just there. Not like an Asian restaurant where you can get something spicy or sweet. I don't want a food just to satiate myself; I don't want to just exist. Why can't my life be like an interesting art gallery, which stimulates the mind with colour and style? Why can't my life challenge me? she thought.

She blamed all her problems on Mr White T-Shirt Man. If only he hadn't come along and told her she would be married to him – and that this would happen, and that would happen. He seemed so interesting and so driven, but when would he come back into her life? This year? Next year? In five years? She didn't know, and what she didn't know was hurting her.

She complained to Alice, 'How long do I have to wait?'

'Why did he say he had come to see you, Luce?' Alice asked.

'He just said that he wanted me to wait for him, but I don't know what that means, Alice. Does it mean I put my life on hold? I don't have a boyfriend – I don't move from Little Creek. I just don't know what to do!'

'Well, it seems to me that being *you* is what causes you to be together. So if I were you, I would just follow my instincts. Don't do it because of the grid man, do it because *you* want to – or don't do it if *you* don't want to.'

'You know Alice, when he left and I turned to see him again, I yelled at him. I told him he "wasn't fair", and you know, I am right about that. He isn't fair. Who knows what he is doing right now? Is he thinking of me? Does he have a girlfriend now? Where is he working and why does he eventually come to Little Creek? Or *does* he come to Little Creek – maybe I meet him somewhere else? Wait a second, if he knew to come to Little Creek, he knows I live here and he will come back here. Fuck; I don't know how this all works. What does being able to see the future really mean?'

The one bright spot in both their lives at the moment was Jon. He was a cute, cuddly baby and well behaved. He was nearly six months old and Alice was accustomed to his routine and now had some time for herself.

'You know what you could do Luce,' said Alice, 'you could go and find him.' Lucy had never considered that but immediately thought she should have come up with the idea. Instead of me waiting for him, I find him. Alice is onto something here, she thought.

'That's a great idea Alice!' Lucy exclaimed. 'Why didn't I think of that? We could find him and I could take my time and talk to him, and I could find out if he was worth waiting for. That is a fantastic idea, Alice. Why didn't I think of that?' she repeated. 'How great would that be? I turn up on his doorstep and turn his life upside down. Let's do it together. You and I could go on a road trip and take Jon. I am sure Fred would lend you his car. Tell him we just want a couple of days to ourselves.'

Lucy was very excited now but hadn't thought of one thing. How would they find Mr White T-Shirt Man? Alice must have been thinking the same thing and broke Lucy's excitement by smiling broadly, 'I'm not just a pretty face you know Luce. Just one problem with the plan … how do we find grid man?'

The seed had been planted, however, and Lucy was going to hang onto the idea. She wasn't going to be deterred by such a small matter as *how*. She wouldn't be bored anymore and would add some purpose to her shitty life. I'll show him what's *fair*, she thought.

Lucy wrestled with the idea all that evening, and the next day at school, before going to Alice's and asking for help. 'So, Miss Smarty pants, you're not just a pretty face – how do we do it?'

'I would almost bet that you didn't get his numberplate, did you?' asked Alice. Alice knew the answer to the numberplate question but then asked Lucy to think about the *colour* of the number plate.

Alice was feeding Jon and told Lucy, 'Grab a bit of paper and write this stuff down.' Lucy obeyed. 'Okay, what information do we have?'

'Well,' replied Lucy, 'he's about six feet tall …'.

'No egghead, I know all that! What do we know that can lead us to him? Let's write that down.'

'Like what?' asked Lucy, who was concentrating on the outcome, not how to get there.

'How about we list what you know,' said Alice. With some cajoling, Lucy wrote:

When he left, he headed towards Barnbale.

Alice made her add:

He headed west.

He said he had driven a very long way.

'That's good,' encouraged Alice. 'What else? What type of car was he in?'

'A big blue car,' replied Lucy.

'Yeah, but what sort of car was it?' said Alice searchingly.

'Oh, I don't know, I'm not good with cars. It was BRIGHT BLUE!'

'It's your life Lucy, not mine. If we are going to find him, we need lots of information. There are 14 million people in Australia – and let's say half are women. That means we are looking for one bloke in 7 million! But okay, at present we have a blue car and he went west.'

'I will work on the list, Alice. Don't underestimate me,' and with that, Lucy said goodbye and left.

(25)

What car is that?

June 1979

Lucy went straight to the school library and found every book she could on cars. She gazed at the pictures. There weren't many books on cars in the school library, and there wasn't a town library. The school did have a subscription to a car magazine, however. She pored over as many issues as she could, but without any luck.

Lucy realised the magazine was full of contemporary cars – new cars. His car did look good, but it wasn't new, she thought. There was something that made her think it was an older car – not really old, just not new.

Lucy's advantage, it seemed, was that in the '70s, the Australian car market was small and limited to only a few local manufacturers. The market was dominated by Holden, Ford and Valiant, who all assembled their cars in Australia. Imported vehicles were primarily from Japan (mainly Datsun) and there were some European marques. From the late 1960s to the late '70s, the local manufacturers produced what were colloquially called 'muscle cars'. These cars were usually brightly coloured and had stripes as well as blistered mudguards or 'wings' adorning the rear boot. European and Japanese vehicles did not compete in this segment to a great degree. However, Lucy was not a car aficionado: she needed to talk to someone who understood cars.

That night she went to see her sister-in-law and Dan. Lucy knew that Dan loved cars. He was always putting himself in hock for a new car, and he was 12 years older than Lucy so would know older cars as well. Dan was 29, and had had cars since he was 18, thought Lucy, surely, he'll be able to help.

'Hey Dan, can you help me find out what type of car I saw the other day?'

'What car?' said Dan matter-of-factly. 'Well, not a car anyone in town owns. I saw a car parked near our grid the other day and it looked really nice, but I don't know what it was.'

Dan became interested at the thought of an exotic car passing through town. 'What was the car doing there?' Dan asked.

'I don't know, I think he must have had a kip there. I saw it and looked, and he drove off.'

Dan put his paper down and started quizzing Lucy. 'Was it a Holden or Ford, or a Jap car?' Lucy shrugged. Dan was now interested and wanted to solve this.

'Okay, we have to start right from the basics,' he said, then took her through seemingly endless questions.

'Big or small, Lucy?'

'Pretty big.'

'Okay, let's rule out Jap cars,' he said with authority. 'How many doors?'

That was a very good question, thought Lucy: she remembered Mr White T-Shirt Man had gone back to the car to get a pen and paper. He had opened the passenger-side door and it was long: there was no back door.

She was quite proud of herself: 'Two!'

'That narrows the field a lot. Did it look expensive?'

'What do you mean?' asked Lucy. It was like pulling teeth, thought Dan, but he persisted.

'Do you think it was a European car, like a Ferrari or BMW or Lamborghini or Mercedes Benz?' Lucy thought about Mr White T-Shirt Man and how old he was and with that in mind replied, 'I don't think so.'

Dan was narrowing the field down and reckoned it must have been a Ford, Holden or Valiant. Maybe a Charger, he thought. Big car, two doors.

'Did the car have stripes on it? If so, what colour was the car and the stripes?'

'It was a bright blue and it had a black stripe on the bonnet.' Dan thought that they were now making progress and he went and got his stash of car magazines. Two doors, bright colour, not an exotic, stripes. I'll bet it's a muscle car, he thought – maybe a Charger. They are such cool-looking cars, he mused.

He came back with a stack of magazines and opened one of them to a picture of an orange Valiant Charger with black stripes on it.

'I know it's not the right colour, but I bet that's it,' he said triumphantly.

'No,' replied Lucy, 'that's not it.'

'Why don't you think that's it?' asked Dan.

'Because it hasn't got slits in the mudguard in front of the door. I noticed them when he opened the door. There were like slits or slots in the mudguard,' Lucy said with authority.

'You didn't tell me it had those before,' said Dan.

'Well, I didn't know that was important,' replied Lucy.

'So they were definitely ahead of the doors, not behind the doors?' asked Dan, because he knew Holdens had racing slots in front of the door, and two-door Fords had a kind of vent aft of the doors.

'In front,' replied Lucy emphatically.

Dan now knew it was a Holden Monaro, but from the information he had, wasn't able to pick the model. However, he did know that the earlier models came in a bright electric blue colour that Holden simply called 'Bright Blue'. It was a metalflake colour they paired with black racing stripes. He found a picture of the earliest Monaro in that colour. It was a 1968 HK Monaro. He showed it to Lucy.

'THAT'S IT!' shouted Lucy. Dan couldn't believe she was so excited about a car. She knew nothing about cars and wasn't even interested in them, he thought.

'If you really like the look of that car, you should come to Ber-Beri next weekend,' said Dan. You can come with Heather and me and help with the kids. It's an all-Holdens car show. I am sure there will be some Monaros there, although the HKs are getting rarer – they are 10 years old and people tend to crash them.'

Lucy agreed that it would be great to go with them. Later in bed, she went back to her list:

- *He went west towards Barnbale.*
- *He owns a 1968 HK Holden Monaro – bright blue in colour.*
- *He drove a long way to see me, he said.*

Nearly got him, thought Lucy before she turned her light out.

Armed with questions, Lucy eagerly awaited Sunday, when she, Dan, Heather and the boys would go to Ber-Beri. She had been thinking about it and wondering how many HK Monaros Holden had made. A least a thousand maybe, she thought. Then I wonder how many they made in blue – surely that would narrow it down considerably.

The showground at Ber-Beri was filled with cars when they arrived. Luckily for them it was a nice sunny day and there were hundreds of cars. Lucy immediately began looking for Monaros – bright blue ones – but there were endless rows of cars and Dan was taking his time. She couldn't wait, so told Dan and Heather she was going for a quick look by herself. It didn't take long before she found several Monaros grouped together. She quickly found one in blue and stood admiring it. Now that she could see it in real life, she knew absolutely that it was the same car that Mr White T-Shirt Man drove!

The owner saw Lucy standing looking and came and said 'G'day'. He was in his 30s, guessed Lucy. He had owned the car since new and told her it was set to be recognised as a classic Australian muscle car in the future. It was only 10 years old now, but he reckoned that because they weren't making Monaros of any kind anymore, the two-door was set to become an icon – after all, a Monaro had won Australia's big annual race at Bathurst. He was intrigued about why a 16-year-old girl was interested. Lucy fibbed a little and told the man that one day she wanted to buy one because she just loved the shape, and she loved that colour blue.

'How much would a Monaro like yours cost?' she asked. 'Oh, they are not expensive yet, but they will be,' he replied. 'Mine is a 327 and it would be at the top of the tree in terms of cost, but the lesser models with a six-cylinder engine may only cost around $2000.'

Lucy was surprised. 'There is more than one model?' she asked quizzically.

'There sure is,' he replied. He went on to tell her that there were, 'ordinary Monaros – they don't have stripes – and then there are GTS Monaros, and they all have stripes. But within the GTS nomenclature there are different engine capacities, and this can make them more or less expensive if you are a collector.'

Shit, thought Lucy. More than one model, different engines – I'll never figure this out. 'So, your car is a GTS, because it has the stripe, right?' she asked. 'Correct' he answered. 'And all GTS have a stripe, despite their different engine capacities?' she affirmed. 'Correct,' he said again.

She knew then that Mr White T-Shirt Man owned a HK GTS Monaro made in 1968. I am narrowing it down, she thought.

'Well, how do I tell one GTS Monaro from another?' she asked.

'You just look at the badge right here on the front mudguard in front of the wheel. The badge will tell you what engine the car has. For example, my badge has 327 written on top of a "V". That tells you that the engine is a V8 with an engine capacity of 327 cubic inches,' he informed her.

Lucy racked her brain and tried to remember what badge was on Mr White T-Shirt Man's car. She recalled seeing some sort of badge on the side, because she had noticed what Dan had told her were cooling slots near the front wheel – and yes, she recalled there was a badge there.

'Have a look at these,' the man said as he went to the back of his car and opened the boot. Inside was a black carpeted board and on it were all the different types of badges that had graced Monaros over their lifespan.

'I have them grouped into model types,' he said. 'These are HKs, these are HTs and HGs – right up to the last model made.'

Lucy focused on the HK badges. There, towards the end of that row, was a badge that said '186' with an 'S' on it.

'That's a nice badge,' said Lucy. The badge had struck a chord with her. *I think* that's the same badge that was on Mr White T-Shirt Man's car, she thought excitedly.

'Yep, that badge is off a Monaro with a six-cylinder engine in it,' advised the man. 'Those badges are not that rare; I have a few at home. I'll sell it to you for $5.' Lucy also thought about the man's previous comments regarding the price of the six-cylinder engine cars. That car at around $2000 would most likely be affordable for a young guy, so that adds up.

Lucy thought that $5 was a bargain for the badge. She paid the man and got down to tin tacks. This guy knows a lot, and I am going to take advantage of that, she thought.

'So how many HKs were made?' she asked using the Holden vernacular. 'Apparently they made around 15,500,' he replied, 'and around half those were 186s – say 8000 of them.' Lucy's jaw must have dropped, or she must have looked surprised. He continued, 'But you have to remember of those 8000 that you like, there were six different colours.' He went on to name all the colours: 'Ermine White, Warwick Yellow, Bright Blue, Silver, Inca Gold and Red. So, you have to divide that 8000 based on colour popularity.'

Lucy was right back where she was when he was talking engine capacities. So much to take in, she thought. He continued, 'I think from memory that the blue was a popular colour and they made up maybe 20 per cent of the total so, what's that total end up being, say 1600 blue 186s? But remember that a lot of them haven't survived, so maybe there is less than half that number out there – maybe 800, which seems a lot. *But*, remember again, that is spread right across Australia. Most of them are in the capital cities. Sydney has a lot and Adelaide has a lot because they were made in Adelaide. I reckon in New South Wales there would be, say, 30 per cent of that number and Victoria 25 per cent, and in South Australia say 15 per cent. So, if you wanted to buy one from New South Wales, there would be around 240 cars, outside of Sydney say 60 or 80 cars. But my 327 is much, much rarer than the 186s and the blue is a 'hero colour', which makes mine more expensive again.'

Lucy had her pen and paper out and was writing furiously, trying to keep up with all the information. Her head was spinning but she came back to only 80 cars in New South Wales outside Sydney, and only 200 in Victoria and 120 in South Australia! Whoo hoo! she thought. I am making such good progress. I can't wait to tell Alice.

That evening in bed, she revised the note she had written the previous night, and added, it's a 186s and there are about 60 to 80 in country New South Wales.

On Monday afternoon, she told Alice all about her day at Ber-Beri and what she had found out about Mr White T-Shirt Man. Alice was impressed, but not sure they were any closer to finding him.

'So, we know *all* about his car … But where do we go with this information?' said Alice.

'Well,' said Lucy, 'there aren't that many of those cars in the whole of New South Wales, so it's a start.'

With that, Alice went to her school pencil case and got out a protractor. She then disappeared and returned with a paper map of New South Wales, and laid it out on the table.

'I have a fantastic idea,' she announced. 'How far did grid man say he drove?'

'He didn't say how far, just that he drove most of the night,' replied Lucy.

'Well, if we say that's – I don't know – maybe 10 hours, at an average of say 90 kilometres an hour – because you have to allow for petrol stops and rest breaks – that equals 900 kilometres he could have travelled,' Alice said.

'Good calculations, Mr Pengilly,' replied Lucy, referring to their maths teacher. They both giggled. 'Alice looked at the scale of the map, and set the protractor to 900 kilometres and drew a semi-circle from Little Creek. Lucy was awake to what Alice was doing. 'The semi-circle only needs to be sort of west from Little Creek because that was the way he went,' she guided.

Alice drew the semi-circle. They looked at it silently, then at each other. It was an incredibly large area, dwarfing what they had anticipated.

'But,' Lucy said, interrupting their thoughts, 'the circle represents the way the crow flies, not the actual road distance.' Alice agreed. They discussed how far 900 kilometres would be by road. They calculated some road distances to towns from the map, then measured the distance via the protractor and agreed that maybe the road route would be around 20 per cent more than the straight-line distance. They then re-adjusted the protractor back to 700 kilometres and re-drew the semi-circle.

This was more palatable, they thought. It now didn't reach well into South Australia. It would have been impossible to drive all night from Adelaide and get to Little Creek, thought Lucy. They had now whittled the area down and took note of some of the larger towns within the circle west of Little Creek. The bigger towns were Swan Hill, Robinvale and Mildura, and then the furthest away, Rasp.

Swan Hill, Robinvale and Mildura were all in Victoria, even though they were west of Little Creek. Rasp, meanwhile, was in New South Wales.

'If you could remember the numberplate, we would know if the car came from Victoria or New South Wales, and we could narrow it down. There are also other smaller towns within the circle we need to consider as well,' said Alice.

Lucy had racked her brain for that information. But nothing came to mind. She didn't know his name, where he lived or the numberplate of his car.

'Okay, I'm dumb,' said Lucy. 'What was I supposed to do? There was this guy telling me about my future and I was dumbstruck. I didn't know what to believe – I didn't know if he was cuckoo, and I wanted to listen in case he was right. I got it wrong! I should have taken notes like we are supposed to in school. Go to school and learn, blah, blah, blah. I'm sick of this place!' Lucy then left abruptly without saying goodbye, with tears in her eyes.

'Shit, shit, shit,' Alice murmured to herself. I'll let her cool down and see her at school, she thought. But Lucy didn't go to school the next day. She told Mavis she didn't feel well and wanted to stay home, and Mavis agreed.

It was all getting too much for Lucy. So much to deal with, she thought. Maybe this is just a dream; maybe I should just give up. It's not fair of *him*, she thought again. I just turned 16 and I have all this on my plate. I can't tell Mum – she'll probably put me in a nut house. She cried that night as she thought about her future. I'll probably just marry a farmer and be stuck around here for the next 50 years, she thought, which only made her more upset.

Lucy was still morose the following day but did go to school and did talk with Alice. Alice tried to be upbeat, but Lucy had no spark. Alice was still incredulous about Lucy's story and wanted to help, but was running short of ideas. Lucy had an idea and thought she knew what to do next, but was reluctant to share the idea with Alice. Lucy reckoned that the registration authority in New South Wales, the RTA, would have loads of data about vehicles on the road and where those vehicles were housed, and she knew that Jake Smith worked at the RTA in Barnbale.

She rang Jake later that afternoon. 'Hello,' said Lucy in an authoritative tone, 'am I speaking with Jake Smith?'

'Yes, how can I help you?'

'My name is Lucy Martin from Little Creek and I want some information.'

There was a moment of silence. Lucy knew that Jake Smith was composing himself. She knew he knew her, and that she was very good friends with Alice Blackwell.

'What can I do for you?' he replied coldly.

'I want some information about a car. I would like to know how many of a certain car are registered in certain towns. I am gathering data for a car club,' she ventured.

'I can't really give you that information,' Jake said again coldly. 'Sure you can,' said Lucy. 'We could sort of do an exchange. You give me the information and I don't give anyone in Barnbale *any* information.'

Lucy wanted to say she wouldn't talk to Jake's partner about him getting a 16-year-old girl pregnant, but she preferred to be positive.

'What do you know about my personal life? Any way I've already told her,' he lied, referring, presumably, to his fiancée.

Lucy took a risk. 'You told her that you got a 16-year-old girl pregnant while you were away one Saturday playing football? And you are, what, 30? Not sure who else might like to know as well. I think we should just do each other a small favour, Jake, and I won't have any reason to come to Barnbale.'

Lucy's bad mood allowed her to be feisty and demanding. She was sick of everyone taking advantage of her and telling her what to do, and she didn't even care if the phone call had consequences.

'What do you want to know? This request can be classified as a general search for a car club,' he said, surrendering.

'I also want the name the cars are registered in. I don't need addresses, just the names.' Lucy thought she might be letting him off a little by not demanding any addresses, just the town name. Then again, she wasn't sure of the RTA protocols, and she thought it may be easier for him to achieve this.

Lucy told him all about the car and what she wanted. He promised he would have the information in about three days' time. Lucy told him she would ring him; he was not to ring her.

She rang the following Monday afternoon and he gave her the information – everything she had asked for. 'Now fuck off, you slag,' he said menacingly, and hung up.

Lucy now knew that, in terms of registered HK GTS Monaros with six-cylinder engines in the colour 'Bright Blue', that there were four in Mildura, none in Robinvale, two in Swan Hill and four in Rasp.

Lucy discounted Swan Hill because it was too close to Little Creek. Probably only 400 kilometres away. That left Mildura and Rasp. Mildura was around 500 kilometres away, and Rasp 800 kilometres away. She discounted Mildura, also because of its proximity, and decided they would go to Rasp.

She had been given four names: Peter Browne, Max Bruce, Alan Kerkovich and Maria Sultana. She thought she would not have to talk to the woman unless she found none of the men were Mr White T-Shirt Man. Surely, he wouldn't register his car in his mother's name, she thought.

One evening, Lucy relayed all the information she had gathered over the past few weeks to Alice. She told Alice about the car nut in Ber-Beri who was so knowledgeable she couldn't believe it.

'This guy must have dreamed about cars,' Lucy told Alice, explaining he was a Holden aficionado and owned just such a car. Alice never cared for cars much, but she had brothers and understood that boys keep such knowledge.

'This is getting exciting. I am really impressed with your detective work. But how did you get names and locations of the cars?' Alice asked.

Lucy hesitated. She knew Alice would not be very happy that she had spoken with Jake Smith, but she couldn't think of anything else to tell her. 'Umm, I got it from Jake Smith,' she said meekly, waiting for Alice to explode.

Alice fulminated. She accused Lucy of going behind her back and aligning herself with Jake. She also suggested Lucy was interested in Jake Smith. Lucy could hardly get a word in to defend herself, and scolded herself for not talking to Alice before contacting Jake. Lucy knew she had used Alice to help find Mr White T-Shirt Man, but she believed she was justified because she *had* to find him. She was trying desperately to understand what had happened at the grid, and to put her life in order. She would apologise to Alice when the time was right – but she knew if she had to, she would do it all over again.

Lucy also knew that all the hurt Alice had endured over the past year was unfortunately coming out in her direction. Lucy absorbed all the accusations cast her way because she didn't want to inflame the situation. At the same time, she examined her actions.

The ranting ended in tears from both girls, and it would be two weeks before they spoke again. When they did reconcile, there weren't any 'sorrys' from either. They both understood why the other acted the way they did, and as friends do, they mended their differences without an apology, but with a look that said 'I know' and by simply being friends again, strengthened by another shared experience.

(26)

Rasp road trip

July 1979

Lucy turned 16 in May, and convinced her reluctant mother and father to allow her to go on a road trip with Alice. Alice was only 17, but mature beyond her years following the birth of Jon in January. They planned to travel to Rasp with Jon, to try and find Mr White T-Shirt man.

'Find the car and we find the mysterious man,' was Alice's mantra. She was as intrigued as Lucy was nervous and apprehensive. They were both determined to find out what he knew and why he knew it – and they both wanted to know more.

In some respects, they both had selfish reasons for the trip. Alice wondered if Mr White T-Shirt Man could see her future as well as Lucy's, and Lucy wanted to know where, when and how things would happen.

They borrowed Fred's car for the trip and told their families they were going to visit historic Rasp in the far west of New South Wales, and would be gone for about four days. One day travelling there, one day back and two days in Rasp itself, they figured.

They left early on a Tuesday and planned to be home on Friday evening. During the trip to Rasp, Lucy wondered if she had allowed enough time. She envisaged herself spending time with Mr White T-Shirt Man, getting to know him. Her thoughts were about romance and learning about her future.

It's going to be so great when I find him, she thought. Won't he be surprised! He surprised me and turned my world upside down, and now he'll be the one with his head in a spin. Why do I marry him? I obviously must like and love him some time in the future, and I want to know how it all happens, and what he is like.

Not once did Lucy believe she wouldn't find him. She had looked at the map of Australia a thousand times and Rasp was the only town he could have come from. It was about a night's drive away. There weren't any other towns within 300 kilometres of Rasp, which made them all too close or too far away to undertake a drive from in one night. She was adamant she would find him and look him in the eye again and take him in. Drink in his personality. Learn everything she could about him. Is he smart? What does he do? Is he a nice guy?

Alice wasn't as sure of their success, but kept her doubts to herself. She was, however, secretly hoping to meet the grid guy. Maybe he can tell me about my future. When will I get married? Who will I marry? Is Jon going to grow up and be a nice boy and son? I hope we find him, she thought, but if he didn't tell Lucy his name or where he was from when he met her at the grid, did he want to be found? If he's as smart as Lucy thinks he is and doesn't want to be found, we probably won't find him. Lucy will be devastated and I will be disappointed.

Alice knew nothing about Rasp, but wondered if the grid guy tried to deliberately fool Lucy by driving west. Surely not, because if he had to double back it would be a heck of a long way. This thought kept coming back to her. Australia is a huge place and he could be anywhere, but Lucy had done her homework. Of all people she could have sought help from – fucking Jake Smith, Alice thought. Pretty smart of her to kind of blackmail the bastard though. When she is determined to do something, she can be very stubborn.

Green farming lands gave way to drier country the further west they went. Grazing grasses gave way to blue bushes and spear grass, and rolling hills gave way to plains with fewer trees. Along the dry creek beds were huge redgum trees.

Lucy had studied which was the best route, and the route she thought Mr White T-Shirt Man would take. Alice did all the driving and Lucy gave directions and provided commentary. Lucy still wasn't old enough to hold a driver's licence; 16 years and nine months was the requirement in New South Wales. She had seven months to go before she could apply, but could drive well because of her farm upbringing. She often drove trucks for Mick with hay or grain on the back, and she often rode her motorbike into Little Creek.

Common sense told Lucy that Mr White T-Shirt Man would have gone the most direct route and those were the directions she was giving to Alice. Jon had been sleeping most of the way and had only woken once because he was hungry.

After driving for about three hours they refuelled, changed Jon's nappy and then Alice breast-fed him while they snacked. They had left at about 7 am. Lucy had calculated that with regular stops, it would take them about nine-and-a-half hours to get to Rasp, which would mean they would arrive at 4pm. It was a very long drive with Jon, but when he was unhappy, they were prepared to stop, give him some respite from his car seat, and feed and change him.

Before they left, Lucy had telephoned a small motel in Rasp and booked a room for three nights. Mavis wasn't comfortable that the girls were travelling such a long way, but Mick was more relaxed and, unbeknown to Mavis, had given Lucy enough money to cover fuel and motel costs. They are good girls, thought Mick in a soft moment, they will be careful. The deal was, though, that Lucy had to phone home each night.

They reached Mildura around 1.30pm, a little behind their schedule. They were now about three hours from Rasp. Mick's only instruction to Lucy was 'Don't drive in the dark', because of the risk of colliding with kangaroos. There were no towns between Mildura and Rasp, and Lucy calculated they would get to the motel in Rasp at about 4.30pm, before dark. She had discounted Mildura as the town where Mr White T-Shirt man had come from, because it was a little close. They had taken six-and-a-half hours, with regular stops because of Jon, but he said he had driven all night to get to Little Creek, so it was out.

From her research, she knew that Rasp was a mining town in arid, semi-desert country. It had a population of around 27,000 and most employment centred around the mines and services to rural property. She had wondered if Mr White T-Shirt man was a miner, but for some reason he didn't look like how she envisaged a miner would look.

When they finally reached Rasp, they had been travelling for nearly 10 hours, but neither of them was tired. Lucy could feel that this was where Mr White T-Shirt Man lived, and Alice was also excited. But what a strange town. Many of the houses were built from iron and had small frontages – a legacy of the early mining years when corrugated iron was cheap and easy to transport. There were no lawns in front of most houses, just gravel – a result of the lack of nearby water and very hot summers. It wasn't a pretty town and Lucy, for some reason, was disappointed. She had expected it to be a pretty town. The surrounding landscape was, however, spectacular, with rocky hills that took on an orange hue from the setting sun. The earth was a rich red, with dry creeks that meandered down from the hills. I wonder if Mr White T-Shirt Man has lived here all his life, thought Lucy.

Their motel was at the very western end of the main street and they walked two kilometres right to the other end and back to stretch their legs and give Jon some fresh air. On the way, they stopped at a café and bought grilled fish and a salad to eat back at the motel.

'It really is a holiday,' Lucy said excitedly to Alice, 'and we have no one telling us what to do.' They both laughed.

'Are you keeping an eye out for you know who, because I don't know what he looks like,' asked Alice.

'I told you; he is tall and slim with long blonde hair and some freckles on his face,' Lucy replied.

'That could be a hundred people,' retorted Alice.

'I'm looking,' said Lucy with a huge smile on her face.

Lucy's plan for tomorrow was to go and see Peter Browne, Alan Kerkovich and Max Bruce. They would only visit Maria Sultana if they failed on those three. Lucy had looked up the names in the telephone directory and could only find Peter Browne, Alan Kerkovich and an R & M Sultana. There were a number of Bruces but no Max. Maybe he lived with his parents, she thought, which also made him the most likely. She thought that if she mentioned his name to the others, they might know him and where he lived.

Lucy was well awake when Jon stirred early the next morning. She picked him up and nursed him until Alice woke to feed him. They had brought fruit and cereal with them for breakfast and the motel provided milk and cutlery. Lucy wanted to go early before people would be likely to go to work. She had learned that the mines had three rotating shifts: 7 am to 3 pm, 3 pm to 11 pm, and 11 pm to 7 am. She figured that if they visited a home at around 8 am, if the person was a miner he could have already left for work, or he could just be getting home. They would then do the same around 4 pm to catch someone who had the 7 am shift.

The motel provided a street map and they headed to find Peter Browne. Lucy knocked and an older lady aged around 60 answered the door.

'Hello, my name is Lucy and I'm looking for Peter Browne. I wondered if your son is home?' enquired Lucy.

'Oh dear, Peter is my husband not my son,' replied the lady. 'What did you want to speak with him about, he's just finishing breakfast?' Lucy's heart sank, but she continued. 'I wanted to talk to him about his Monaro. Someone told me he owned a blue Monaro and I was looking to buy one.'

Lucy learned from Peter that he had owned the Monaro since new. It was in the shed down the back if she wanted to look, but it wasn't for sale. 'They aren't making them anymore and I reckon it'll be a collectable car in the future,' advised Peter.

Lucy and Alice went and looked at the car out of courtesy, then had a cup of tea with the Brownes. Lucy probed Peter about other Monaros in town; he said there could be one or two more, but didn't know the owners. Did he know a young man named Max Bruce? Elizabeth, Peter's wife, replied that she knew the Bruces: 'Charlie and June, and they have two sons, Max and David. They live in Tin Street, 145 I think. Both boys work, Max on the mine, but he's not a miner, he works in the office, and David is a mechanic, I think.'

Lucy's heart was now its usual self, but beating faster as she thought about Max. He's a young guy and he's not a miner, she thought. 'So, Max has a Monaro like yours Peter?' Lucy asked.

'No, I don't think so,' said Peter, 'but the young guys change cars like their underpants, so he could have bought one, but I don't really know.'

Lucy clung to the thought that Max could be Mr White T-Shirt Man when they said their goodbyes. He probably bought the car recently, she thought, and Mr Browne doesn't know about it. However, they would not know until after 3 pm when he came home from work. In the interim, they went to find Alan Kerkovich.

When they knocked, a woman in her 30s answered. Alan's wife said that yes, he did own a blue Monaro, but that he was at work at present, and wouldn't be home until later that evening. He worked at a menswear shop in the main street. Mrs Kerkovich thought that Alan could be prepared to sell the car and said they could visit him at the shop if they wanted to talk to him.

The girls then visited Rudy Alagich Menswear and spoke with Alan, just to make sure they eyeballed him, and also to see if he could offer any information on other cars. That he was not Mr White T-Shirt Man was no surprise. He took them down the street not far from his shop and showed them the car. He said he would consider selling, if they made a good enough offer. 'The car is 10 years old now and it's about time I got a new one.'

Lucy told him she had his telephone number and would call him if she was interested. When asked if there were any other blue GTS HK 186s Monaros in town, he said that yes, he had seen Peter Brown's, and there was another one owned by a young bloke, but he didn't know him. He also didn't know a Max Bruce.

Both girls thought that it would be futile to visit Maria Sultana, but they went and found her for the same reasons they had visited

Alan Kerkovich. They wanted to see if she could offer any information on any other Monaros. Besides, they had time to kill before they went to visit Max Bruce sometime after 4pm, when he would be home from the mine.

Maria Sultana's tale was a sad one. Yes, she did own a blue HK GTS Monaro with a 186s motor. She kept the car in a shed at the rear of her property. She kindly showed the girls and they respectfully had a look at the car, even though it was of little help to them. The car was originally owned by Maria's first husband, who had passed away around eight years ago. It was in mint condition. The external paint was perfect, and the interior looked like it was brand-new.

Maria told the girls that her late husband only bought the car about 12 months before he took ill, and it hadn't been used since, but there was no way that she would sell it. She told them she wasn't a car buff, but she had seen a lovely example driving around town on a couple of occasions.

Lucy's hopes now rested with Max Bruce. He was a young man, owned the particular make and model Monaro, and lived in Rasp. This had to be him, she thought. They were both excited about visiting Max, but Alice, ever the sensible one, told Lucy not to get her hopes up.

To ensure they could be at his home promptly at 4pm, they did a reconnaissance. It was a low-set brick home with an iron roof and a low wall at the front with a single driveway and two sheds at the rear. The house looked like there was no one at home when they slowly drove past. Lucy intuitively knew they were close to Mr White T-Shirt Man.

At 4 pm on the dot, they pulled up outside the house behind a pale, early-model, light brown two-door Toyota Corolla. There were no other cars in the driveway. Alice knew that Lucy was expecting to see a blue Monaro parked in the driveway.

They went to the front door, Alice carrying Jon. There was no way in the whole wide world that Alice was going to miss out on meeting the grid man. They knocked and heard footsteps approaching. A young man opened the door and Lucy was taken aback. The guy who opened the door was dressed in a manual labourer's high-visibility shirt and heavy, navy tradesman-like pants. He was about 172 centimetres tall, with longish curly hair that sat like a bowl on top of his head. It wasn't Mr White T-Shirt Man, but Lucy assured herself that this was his brother.

'Hi, is Max Bruce home?'

'Yes, that's me,' replied Max.

Lucy's world started to come apart at the seams. 'You're Max?' queried a disbelieving Lucy.

'Yep,' he replied. 'How can I help you?' Lucy was flabbergasted, and felt sick in the belly.

'Umm my name is Lucy, do you own a blue Monaro?'

It was now Max's turn to feel sick. Harry had told him in January that one day he thought a young woman with long dark hair would come looking for him, which is why Harry had hatched this stupid, stupid plan, recalled Max. Why did I ever agree to this? he thought, as he tried to remember exactly what he and Harry had agreed. At the time, he thought Harry was being paranoid, so he agreed to the plan to calm him down. Those four months after Harry's accident were just plain weird for everyone who knew or was involved with Harry.

Fuck, what do I say? thought Max. During that time of recovery, Harry was right about everything and I didn't believe him – and now he's right about this girl. Fuck, fuck, what do I say?

'Well, I used to own a HK Monaro,' declared Max, 'but I sold it.' Lucy immediately thought that maybe after their grid meeting, Mr White T-Shirt Man had sold the Monaro to Max, or that maybe he had bought it from Max and they hadn't got around to changing the ownership particulars with the road and transport authority.

'When did you sell it?' Lucy asked, without giving Max a reason for them being at his house, or for questioning him. But Max was rattled, and because of that didn't think to ask who they were or why they were there.

'Oh, I only sold it a couple of weeks ago and bought the Corolla,' lied Max. Lucy now reasoned that Max must have bought it from Mr White T-Shirt Man after the grid meeting.

'Oh, you sold it. How long did you have it for?' The information she had from Jake Smith only told her the owner's name at the time she had requested the information, which was June, so that could be right – he could have bought it from Mr White T-Shirt Man after September 1978.

Max thought quickly: to cover Harry he would say a time well before Harry had his accident, because that's when things were normal in Harry's world – and his world, come to think of it.

'I owned it for about 18 months. I bought it from a second-hand car dealer in Adelaide. It was a good car but it cost too much to keep on the road. The insurance was too costly because it was a GTS, so I traded it in in Adelaide,' he lied. 'Anyway, why do you ask?'

'Someone told me you owned the exact car that I wanted to buy, which is why I asked about it,' Lucy said, scrambling for a plausible answer. 'You don't know anyone else who owns a HK Monaro then?'

Max pondered what all this was about. A beautiful young woman with long dark hair was looking for Harry's Monaro, just as Harry had predicted seven months ago. He didn't believe her story about wanting to buy one.

'I think Peter Browne owns a HK, but that's the only one I know of. Do you live in Broken Hill?' Max asked.

'No, we drove up from Adelaide, so maybe we should check out the car dealers down there again. When I last looked, no one had one for sale. Guess I will have to check,' said Lucy trying to elicit a response from Max. She wasn't sure that Max was telling the truth – or maybe she just didn't want to believe what Max had told her. She wanted so much to find Mr White T-Shirt Man, and now she felt defeated.

Max knew Adelaide well, so to authenticate his story, he told the girls the dealer was on a particular road, which just happened to be a well-known car strip.

Lucy had a feeling that Max wasn't being totally honest with her, but she wasn't in a position to challenge him. 'Max, it's really important to me that I find this particular model of car, is there anything else you can tell me about your car?'

Lucy had wounded Max with her apparent mistrust; he felt guilty about deceiving her. He could see that she was upset by what he had told her, and again wondered why she had visited him, what her connection to Harry was, and why she had asked such detailed questions. He felt sorry for her, and at that moment wanted to uncover the mystery now confronting him, and help her by outing Harry, but he remained loyal to what Harry had asked him to do. He had told Harry he would protect him, and he did. 'No, not really, but I hope you find one,' was all Max could offer.

The girls returned to the motel deflated. They had no more leads and Lucy became emotional. Alice consoled her by telling her they must have made a mistake with the town and that later in the year they could do another trip, because it had been so much fun. Lucy was bewildered, but she took some comfort from what Mr White T-Shirt Man had written on his note: 'The next time you see me I'll be in a dark brown 1976 Holden'.

'Alice, he is right again you know,' said Lucy.

'What do you mean Luce?' asked Alice.

Lucy had brought the note with her and showed it to Alice. 'See right here where he says the next time you see me?' ventured Lucy as Alice read the note. 'I don't think we were meant to, or ever will find him,' sighed Lucy. 'He's going to be right again.' Then Lucy smiled mischievously and asked Alice if she could telephone Jake and get details for brown Holdens. They smiled at each other and laughed.

Max on a mission

July 1979

Max reacted as soon as the girls were out of sight. He knew that in some respects talking to Harry would be pointless, because Harry couldn't remember anything between his crash in September 1978 and late January 1979, but Max wanted to complete his assignment and make sure the girl didn't find him.

Max went to the bank, which had closed, and waited on the footpath outside until Harry finished work.

'Heady, what are you doing here?' asked Harry.

'Mate you are never going to believe what just happened,' said Max excitedly. Max knew the explanation would be pointless, but he asked Harry again if he remembered them agreeing to transfer the ownership of his Monaro to him in December, because Harry thought a girl with long dark hair would try to find him?

'I know we did it only because you told me we did it,' said Harry.

'Well Flash, I think we can undo all that because today the girl visited me,' exclaimed Max excitedly.

'Max, I still can't remember why we did that.'

'I know you can't bud, but I remember because you told me she would come looking, and you didn't want her to find you, for whatever reason, and I thought you were crackers, but today she came to my house! So I'm going to protect you from her, because that's what "Vision Harry" would have wanted,' said Max even more excitedly.

Max instructed Harry. 'Don't go cruising, take all the back streets you know on the way home, don't take your car out tonight and make sure you walk to work tomorrow – maybe don't even go to work tomorrow.' He also told Harry to put the Monaro in his dad's shed tonight so no one could see it.

'I wish I could remember what this is all about,' said Harry. 'I can't remember a thing that happened after my crash. Not one thing. It's so frustrating, mate. I can't remember who I spoke to and why. It's just all a blur. I'm bloody happy I met Bridget before the crash or I wouldn't even remember that.'

Harry did what Max told him to that night, but decided he would go to work the next day; Max was being dramatic. He left the car home that night and ran to Bridget's flat in the main street, which was only 400 metres from the motel where Alice and Lucy were staying. He always felt on top of the world when he ran to her flat, chilled with her, made love and ran home again. In the middle of the night when the town was quiet, he stopped on top of the hill on the way home, gazed back at the city and thought he owned the night. He felt bullet-proof; if only he could remember those past few months and what had happened.

Lucy and Alice decided to travel home the next day and take their time. They would stay somewhere around halfway to make the trip easier on Jon. That meant they didn't have to leave so early to beat the dark and kangaroos.

Before they left, Alice needed to go to the bank and withdraw money. They drove to the bank and rather than get Jon out, Lucy stayed with him in the car and Alice went in. She was served by a tall, lean, blonde guy with freckles whose name tag read 'Harry'.

'That teller was so nice,' Alice told Lucy when she got back to the car. 'He even asked where Little Creek was and asked what I was doing in Rasp.' Harry didn't know of Little Creek or where it was, and didn't know Alice. They both had no inkling about each other. Harry wasn't aware that Alice was looking for him, and Alice didn't know Harry was Mr White T-Shirt Man. If Harry had been able to remember September 1978, or if Lucy had come into the bank with Alice, the future may have been very different.

'Maybe we should come back to Rasp,' Alice said to Lucy as she thought of Harry. They giggled as they drove out of town. Lucy was only half-listening to Alice as she talked about boys – a favourite subject of Alice's. Lucy pondered how she might find a brown Holden.

Moving time

August 1979 to June 1981

Mr Hayden was a senior manager with the Australian Rural Bank and the manager of the Rasp branch. His morning routine was to walk through the branch, acknowledging and greeting staff. The women would always offer, 'Good morning Mr Hayden', while the male staff would say 'Morning boss'.

Mr Hayden was in his early 60s with silvery white hair and a deep voice. He would often wear tweed-style jackets with leather elbow patches or dark navy suits with a crisp white shirt and a tie. He was a well-respected boss. On this particular morning, he stopped in front of Harry's desk. Harry was a junior employee and his desk was towards the back of the office close to the ledger machines. It was a treat for Harry to have Mr Hayden's attention.

'Morning Harry. Can you come and see me in my office later?'

'Morning Boss. Yes Boss,' replied Harry.

Harry wondered all morning what Mr Hayden would want to see

him about. He thought he had been a model employee since the incident with Bridget's ex-boyfriend and his bike crash. In fact, he had taken no sick days or days off since then.

Harry knocked softly; Mr Hayden looked up from his desk. 'You wanted to see me boss?'

'Yes, come in Harry,' replied Mr Hayden. 'Well, young Harry, by all reports you have been doing very well, which is appreciated,' he continued. 'I have a letter here from our personnel department … You have been transferred, Harry. However, initially you have to provide relief at our Hollybrook branch for ten weeks, and then you will have a permanent role as a teller in our Ber-Beri branch. You start in Hollybrook in three weeks – I'll give you a letter that outlines your relief role, and your new role and salary in Ber-Beri.'

Wow, thought Harry as he left the boss's office, my first transfer. Harry knew that transfers for single men happened exactly the way his did just then. Single officers, as they were designated by the personnel department, were told about their new role and expected to follow orders. When employees were married, there was often an offer made that could be accepted by the employee or rejected after consideration by the employee and their family. Single employees without ties were just expected to follow directions if they wanted to climb the corporate ladder.

Harry had no qualms about leaving Rasp; he had joined the bank because of the opportunity to go to new places and climb the ladder. But now he thought about Bridget. Her parents lived in Rasp and she had lived there all her life. Is it fair to ask her to come with me? he thought. I don't want to leave her, but I am so excited about moving to another town, into a different role and with a much better salary.

Bridget was surprised that night when Harry told her about his transfer. 'Bridge, I think I can do well in the bank and I am excited about a move, but I don't want us to be apart,' Harry said.

'Well, there's little point in me moving to Hollybrook with you – it's only a temporary position until you go to Ber-Beri. Why don't you go to Hollybrook and we continue to talk about the move to Ber-Beri? I don't want to be without you either, but don't you think that's what we should do?' Bridget asked. 'You can come home some weekends and see me, and we can talk every night,' she added.

It hurt Harry to be thinking about a separation, but she was right. 'So, will you think about moving to Ber-Beri when I go there?' he asked.

'Yes, I think it would be fun to get away from Rasp,' she replied.

'And I thought you were thinking of *me*!' said Harry, teasing her.

Bridget flashed Harry her beautiful smile and Harry thought at that moment that their plan may work.

The next weekend, Harry and Bridget drove to Adelaide and Harry traded in his HK Monaro for a dark brown HJ Holden Kingswood. It was a 1976 sports model with a 4.2-litre V8, four-speed gearbox, bucket seats and GTS instrumentation. It will be much easier for Bridget to drive if we both go to Ber-Beri, Harry thought, but he was heartbroken to part with the HK.

He had had so much fun in that car. She was part of my personality, he thought, and now I feel like I'm just discarding her! He loved the HK and life would never be the same, he thought. Harry consoled himself on the way home by playing Meat Loaf's *Bat Out of Hell* on the new car's cassette player. Eight tracks were out and cassette tapes in!

Harry's time in Hollybrook was not much fun. It was a much smaller branch than Rasp, with five employees: himself, an older male manager, a male manager's assistant and two women. Harry was staying in the local caravan park in a rented caravan. Hollybrook was a small country town with little for Harry to do after work. Both women were married and Harry saw little of them, with the exception of an occasional drink at the local club. The second-in-charge was married and not a very friendly bloke. He is a prick, no wonder they are short-staffed, Harry thought.

Because he was in a rented caravan with little in the way of utensils or cooking equipment, Harry ate out every night. He had bought breakfast cereal and groceries so he could eat in the morning, bought sandwiches for lunch and would go to the café or local club for dinner.

Harry was bored and lonely. He had lived with his mother and father, and had all his mates and Bridget around him in Rasp – then suddenly, no one. He would talk to Bridget every night from a telephone box, staying on the phone with her for about an hour. After two weeks, Harry drove home to Rasp for the weekend. It's a very long 900 kilometres when you can't wait to get home, Harry thought. He left Hollybrook at 5 pm Friday after work and didn't get to Rasp until 2 am on Saturday, then left Rasp around 4 pm on Sunday for the return trip.

'Bridge, why don't you take a couple of weeks' holiday and come and stay with me?' asked Harry after five weeks on his second trip home to Rasp.

'Harry, I miss you so much – why don't I just give notice at work, resign and come to Hollybrook?' Bridget replied. 'If I give two weeks' notice, you'll almost be finished at Hollybrook and then we can go to Ber-Beri. We could even drive to Ber-Beri on the weekends and look for a place to live.'

Harry could not get the smile off his face for the next two weeks as he counted down the days until he would go to Rasp and pick up Bridget. Bridget had agreed to leave Rasp and be with him, and he now felt responsible for her. Their relationship had ratcheted up a notch or two, he thought. She must love me. Harry was being paid very well by the bank now because of his relieving allowance. He got paid extra because he was away from home and not in regular accommodation, which meant his pay would be enough for them both to live off, but Bridget would need to get a job in Ber-Beri.

The final week of work in Hollybrook was a breeze for Harry. He was happy to have Bridge with him and living together was fun. For a 19-year-old guy, that meant sex in the morning and at night. Bridget was happy to oblige, and Harry hoped she enjoyed their time together as much as he did. He didn't feel guilty about his desires, because he was determined to look after Bridget. He wasn't taking advantage of her, he thought, she is an intelligent, mature woman and knows what she wants. Bridget often had strong opinions and would tell Harry what she liked, didn't like or what she wanted to do. Harry liked that. If Bridget has an opinion, she will let me know.

They found a small, two-bedroom unit in Ber-Beri not far from the city centre and Harry's dad made the arduous drive from Rasp in a small enclosed truck with Bridget's furniture. A brown velour lounge, coffee table, her terrarium plants, refrigerator, the usual kitchen oddments and of course, Bridget's stereo. On their first night in the unit, they listened to Boston. Harry loved the song – *More Than a Feeling*, and put it on maximum volume. Once again, thought Harry, life is so good.

Bridget found a job very quickly in a building supply factory on the far side of town and would drive the HJ to and from work. Harry bought a pushbike and rode it to work. It was downhill to work, but a struggle home, particularly in the heat that summer.

Harry enjoyed his work in Ber-Beri. The branch was even larger than Rasp's, and most of the staff were very friendly. Harry was 'Teller D' with other back-office responsibilities, and was made to feel at home because there was a girl from Rasp who worked there. She was older than Harry and had come to Ber-Beri with her husband, who also worked at the branch. She mothered Harry a little and he enjoyed his relationship with her.

Being in a different and larger city also appealed to Harry and Bridget. They both quickly became accustomed to living together. Harry would cook his speciality, sausage casserole, which Bridget would poke fun at. She was a good cook and would do most of the cooking, but didn't really enjoy it unless Harry was involved.

They visited Rasp often. Bridget would go and stay with her parents and Harry would stay with his. It was good for Bridget to visit her mother, Harry thought. He wouldn't bother Bridget while they were in Rasp, apart from the occasional telephone call. Harry kept in touch with Max, Steve and Webby by telephone from Ber-Beri and through his regular visits.

In February 1981, Harry's parents held a 21st birthday party for Harry in Rasp. A few of Harry's new friends drove all the way from Ber-Beri to Rasp for the occasion, and all his Rasp mates were there. It is so great to celebrate like this, thought Harry. He never forgot that night: it was a highlight of his life.

The summer of 1978 was well behind Harry and he was settling into life. He was oblivious to the dreams and visions of that summer and was infatuated with Bridget and life. Harry would play golf on Saturdays, and Bridget would go shopping or lounge at home. It seemed she, too, was comfortable with the life they were making together. Bridget had made good friends at her work, which at times made Harry uncomfortable. Bridget was mature and attractive, and Harry sometimes wondered if she would always be faithful to him. He would think of the Dr Hook song, 'When you're in love with a beautiful woman'. Harry knew it was an issue he manufactured, but at times he underestimated himself, lacked confidence and was insecure. Sometimes, he thought Bridget deserved someone better than him. She made love to him because she loved him, he reconciled. She wouldn't make love to just anyone, he reasoned, but Harry carried that flaw with him.

Harry and Bridget had been living in Ber-Beri for 16 months when he received another transfer, in March 1981. This time, it was to Rosella Bay on the south coast of NSW.

The transfer did not sit well with Bridget. She and Harry had made a home together in Ber-Beri and she had a job that she enjoyed very much. Bridget loved the anonymity of Ber-Beri. She hardly knew anyone, apart from her work friends and Harry's workmates, and she liked it that way. Bridget preferred to stay at home rather than go out to clubs or pubs. She enjoyed going out just with Harry and didn't need a large circle of friends. She was very settled at work and could see there were opportunities to advance within the business – and now Harry wanted to take her away from that.

Harry reasoned that she had also been concerned at first to move away from Rasp, but the move to Ber-Beri had been successful and the same would happen when they moved to Rosella Bay.

'It's okay for you, because you already have a job lined up and it's a promotion, and you will get a pay rise, but I have to start over again,' she lamented. 'Why does your job take precedence over mine?'

'You will get a job Bridge, which could be even better than the one you have now,' consoled Harry.

'You're not listening, Harry, why is your job more important than mine? Why don't *you* work around *me*?'

It was difficult for Harry. He wasn't recognised by the bank as a married employee and he had little choice other than to accept the transfer. He had heard of other young guys refusing transfers and their careers had suffered. They stayed in their existing roles for much longer without promotion and were passed over when there was a really plumb job on offer.

Harry figured the best way out of the situation was a *mea culpa*. 'You are right, Bridge. I shouldn't overlook your career. I should be more aware of your needs and ambitions. I do love you, and I am sorry. I didn't ask for this transfer, but I will make sure the bank is aware of our relationship going forward. Can you please come with me?' pleaded Harry.

Harry was genuine in his pleading; he hadn't thought of Bridget's career and in the future, he would have to balance this against his desire to advance his career with the bank. Harry knew that transfers to different jobs and towns was required for employees to build their knowledge. He was aware of how the transfer system worked and wanted desperately to be more senior, but his desire would have to be tempered against what Bridget wanted. Harry would have to rethink his role as the breadwinner in the family. The future will not be the same as when my parents got married, he thought.

Bridget reluctantly agreed to go with Harry, but only because she loved him. If she didn't care for him as much, she said, she would have stayed in Ber-Beri.

This time, the bank found a townhouse for Harry and Bridget to rent and paid for the cost of moving their furniture. They are listening, thought Harry, but I'll have to take special care of Bridget.

Rosella Bay was a beautiful, relatively small coastal town, but Harry hardly noticed the scenery in the first few months. He was engrossed in his work. He wanted to make his mark with this move – he wanted to do a great job and get noticed. He gave up golf on the weekends to be with Bridget and mollycoddled her as much as he could. But Bridget wasn't happy. She couldn't get a job in her chosen industry of building supplies, and had been applying for just any job without success.

Harry was at work all day and wanted to share his days with her. He knew it hurt her that she didn't have a job. Bridget was alone at home each and every day, and as much as Harry tried, he couldn't please her. But he was forever positive. 'It will happen Bridge,' urged

Harry. 'You are so smart. I'm here for you baby.' Their relationship was still good, but Bridget didn't have the stimulation or sense of self-worth that a job brings, which she needed.

Harry rode his pushbike to work and some days he would even ride home for lunch and take a treat for Bridget. He asked just about every bank customer he met if they needed a great employee, but the economy was poor and businesses weren't hiring in 1981.

Harry and Bridget had been living in Rosella Bay for three months when Harry rode home one June evening. It was a Thursday and he thought that on the weekend they could take a drive to Canberra, about three hours away. Bridget would enjoy that. There weren't any lights on in their unit as he rode into the driveway, and the HJ wasn't in the carport.

Harry guessed that Bridget had gone to the supermarket for groceries to make dinner. I wonder why she left it so late, he thought. He still called out to her as he opened the front door, which was unlocked.

'Bridge?' he called, but there was no reply as he went to the bedroom to get changed. He reasoned she would be home soon, but as he turned the light on, he saw something written on the dresser mirror. He looked and noticed it was written in red lipstick. 'Harry, I love you so much, but I can't do it anymore. I can't be here without a job. I've gone to Ber-Beri. I'll ring you tomorrow, Love Bridget.'

Harry's world collapsed around him. He immediately felt alone and abandoned. It scared him and there was nothing he could do about it. Harry became emotional, not only because of his predicament, but also for Bridget. He wondered how much she must have been hurting to do what she had done – leave him alone. She must have been hurting so much to leave, he thought.

Harry didn't like things left undone or unsaid. He didn't like things he couldn't control, and now his whole life was out of control. He couldn't talk to Bridget and reason with her or plead with her or make it better for either of them. Harry's throat ached as he fought back tears. He didn't know what to do. There was a pay telephone down the street, but where was she? Would she be okay driving all the way back to Ber-Beri? Why Ber-Beri? I can't even drive anywhere to look for her – I don't have a car!

It just happened

June 1981 to September 1981

Harry wandered out of the bedroom to the lounge room, trying to think of who he could contact. His thoughts were scattered. What was the name of her friend at work in Ber-Beri, he tried to remember. I know, in the morning I could ring the business and talk to someone.

Harry then noticed someone outside the sliding glass door at the front of the apartment and went to it.

'Hi,' said Harry.

'Hi,' said the young woman, 'Are you okay?'

Harry recognised her as the girl who lived two doors down in their block of townhouses. He knew her face but didn't know her name. 'It's Becky from number five, you're Harry aren't you?' she asked.

Harry asked her to come in, and she continued, 'I saw her packing the car this morning. She left about lunchtime. I didn't talk to her; I could see that she was in a hurry and obviously leaving. She threw all her clothes in the back seat.'

Becky had her small child with her. He was about two. Harry was not prepared for a visitor. He just wanted to sit and cry then try to figure out what he could do to find Bridget. He didn't want to entertain anyone.

'Umm, thanks Becky. So, you didn't talk to her about anything?' asked Harry.

'No, I was watching out my front window and saw her; Bridget, right? She seemed intent on leaving before you came home, I think. I'm so sorry for you.'

Becky sat on Bridget's velour brown lounge opposite him. Harry was still dressed in his work attire with a tie on. He was mostly looking at the floor, because he knew that if he tried to communicate with anyone, he would probably cry out loud.

He then looked at Becky. He had seen her around. It seemed to him she was a single mother, because he had never seen anyone else living there, only a guy who occasionally visited her on a motorbike. She was dressed in a sleeveless printed summer dress. She wasn't very tall and had short, brown, straight hair. It was clear to Harry that she wasn't wearing any underwear and she was looking at him intently. Her dress had ridden up above her parted knees as she sat on the lounge opposite and he could see her dark pubic hair and make out her nipples. Harry wondered if she was deliberately showing her womanhood, or if she always dressed that way.

'I can make you feel better Harry,' she said as she stood, walked over to where he was sitting and put her hand on his shoulder, then took his hand. Harry stood up and looked down at her as she took him into the bedroom. Without saying a word, Becky let go of his hand, sat on the bed and took her arms out of the dress so it was around her waist exposing her breasts. She then got on all fours on the bed and pulled the remainder of her dress up around her waist so that her backside was exposed. He could see everything she had to offer. Her breasts hung down and her vagina with thick black hair was on show to him.

'Come on,' she urged Harry. Harry undressed and was ready as he got on his knees behind Becky. Harry was confused, hurt, lonely and aroused as he abused Becky's body from behind. She talked to Harry and urged him to fuck her hard; Harry obliged. He didn't care about Becky; he was using her to stop the pain he was feeling. He wasn't in the moment and wasn't interested in making Becky feel good. He was erect and using it on Becky. He folded over her from behind and fondled her breasts then leaned back and thrust his pelvis forward making sure she felt him. He looked out the bedroom window to the vacant lots next door and thought of his messed-up life, all while fucking her furiously. Her vagina provided little sensation around his penis, and Harry thought this may have been because she had had a child. He had never fucked a mother, he thought.

The encounter finished with as little fuss as when it had started. Harry cried out loud as he ejaculated and Becky responded by yelling, 'Fuck yes, yes.' Harry didn't know if he pleased her and didn't care; she had made him feel better, as promised. He now wasn't as emotional and was thinking more clearly. I didn't make love to her, he reasoned, I fucked her to inflict pain on Bridget.

Harry lay on the bed as Becky left. She didn't need to put her dress on. She merely put her arms back through her dress sleeves and got off the bed. She looked at Harry with bedraggled hair, touched him on the shoulder and left. Her son had been walking around the apartment the whole time they had been fucking. Harry didn't care. He was angry with the world. It wasn't his fault Bridget wasn't here anymore, he lied to himself.

It was a long night for Harry. He initially slept because of the sex, which made him tired, but he woke in the middle of the night, hungry and sad. In a weak moment as he lay there, he wondered if he should give up his job for Bridget – would that make things better? He cried. It had hurt so much to come home and find someone you love not there. She said she loved him, but he wondered. I wouldn't have done that to her, he thought.

He had tears in his eyes again as he spoke to his boss the next day.

'Dougie, I have to have next week off,' Harry said with his head bowed. 'What's the matter mate?' asked Doug sympathetically. Harry was choked up and found it difficult to answer, but explained to Doug about Bridget and how he felt.

'Dougie, if you can't help me, I'll have to walk out,' Harry said, with uncharacteristic determination. 'I just can't deal with what's happened to me.'

'Hey Harry, don't be like that. Leave it to me and I'll see what I can do. Where are you going to go – what are you going to do?' asked Doug.

'I don't know. I just need to find her. She said in her note she was going to ring me today, so I just have to wait,' replied Harry.

Harry worked but listened for every phone call to the office. Eventually, Bridget called. Harry took her call in Doug's office so he couldn't be heard. With a broken voice, she told Harry she was in Ber-Beri and wouldn't be coming back to Rosella Bay. Harry was choked up and found it difficult to respond.

'I'm taking next week off. Can you meet me part of the way, in Gidgee?' he managed. 'We can meet at a motel.'

There was a pause, then Bridget replied, 'I still love you Harry, we can do that.' They had both been to Gidgee before when Harry was working at Hollybrook.

Harry suggested a motel that Bridget knew. 'I'll probably get there Sunday, not sure how, but I'll be waiting for you,' he said.

Doug arranged for Harry to have a week off. 'If you want, Harry, you could take two weeks' leave,' Doug offered.

Harry shook Doug's hand: 'That will be great Dougie, thank you,' he replied.

Doug was a family man; he could see that Harry was hurt by what had happened to him and was sympathetic. Harry had taken only a few weeks' leave since he joined the bank in 1977, so he had a lot of leave up his sleeve. Early on in their relationship Bridget had gone to the north coast of New South Wales to stay with her aunt and Harry surprised her by driving all the way from Rasp in one day to spend a few days with her. He remembered how she had recognised the HK and ran down the street towards him with her arms outstretched to hug him. Harry smiled and thought he would never forget that greeting.

It was difficult for Harry to get from Rosella Bay to Gidgee. Eve Smythe, a friend he had met in Rosella Bay, drove Harry to a remote airport, where he boarded a small six-seat plane that took him to Canberra on Saturday morning. He then hopped on a bus to Gidgee and got to the motel he had booked on Saturday evening.

Even though they had agreed to meet on Sunday, Harry was disappointed that Bridget wasn't there yet. Harry was twisting everything in a negative way since he had been abandoned. At the moment, he thought his glass was half empty, not half full. He hadn't spoken to Bridget since the call on Friday and his mind was full of negative thoughts. Would Bridget show up, he wondered. What do I do if she doesn't arrive – I don't have a telephone number, and I don't know where she is staying in Ber-Beri. Who is she staying with?

He felt physically unwell and couldn't eat. His life had been exposed to everyone at work in Rosella Bay and he felt more alone than he had in Hollybrook. He couldn't ring anyone and say, 'Oh by the way, Bridget left me without saying goodbye.' Harry had no one to lean on and confide in and he had no way to get home to Rasp. He grasped on to his favourite saying during those moments, 'Never give up.' He determined he would come out of this mess stronger, but dark thoughts tugged at him incessantly.

Harry had not been sleeping well, and tonight was no exception. He went for a long walk along the Murrumbidgee River after he checked in to the motel to pass time, but bad thoughts continued to plague him. He had fallen in love when he wasn't suspecting it, and wondered if love always acted this way. If it always creeps up on you, makes you feel good – then hurts so much?

The year 1978 was one of the great periods in Harry's life: he did what he wanted, when he wanted and didn't answer to anyone. His confidence was sky-high all through 1978 because everything went right for him, but he now felt the world was against him. He had the respect of his mates and friends in Rasp, he had a great job and then he met Bridget. Bridget was the icing on the cake for Harry. Maybe she was a trophy girlfriend at the outset, but she had captivated and caused him to love her, and now he was broken. When do we go from having no responsibilities or worries to the opposite, he wondered as he drifted from consciousness to fitful sleeping. The walk didn't help him sleep. He watched television and dozed. Anything to pass the time. It was late when he turned the TV off. Harry was thinking of his actions in taking Bridget away from Rasp, her friends and family when there was a soft tap on the door.

Bridget stood still in the doorway looking up at him, neither daring to move, it seemed, for ages. 'Bridge, you hurt me so much,' he said softly, then wondered if that's what he should have said. Maybe he should have asked how she was, but that was the first thing that had come into his head.

'I know Harry and I'm sorry. We are both hurting,' she replied, 'but I couldn't look at you and tell you that I had to leave Rosella Bay. You would have talked me out of it.' They walked to the car, got her bag and she automatically took Harry's hand, which caused some of the wall between them to come down.

Bridget explained to Harry that she had felt insignificant, lonely and worthless in Rosella Bay. 'But you and I are together Bridge,' Harry responded. 'We do everything together – so your loneliness is hard for me to understand.'

'I need stimulation from other people Harry, and I get that from work. I have an urge to build a career and at the moment I don't have that. I want to study and I couldn't do that. It all built up on me Harry, and I need you to understand that I love you, but I want all those other things as well.'

Harry did understand, because his career was also very important to him and he was reluctant to compromise in that regard, but he couldn't tell Bridget that. They had both previously visited Gidgee and liked the city, which was much larger than Rosella Bay, and Harry agreed that if Bridget was able to find a job in Gidgee, he would ask the bank for a transfer there. Bridget asked about a transfer back to Ber-Beri but Harry thought the bank would be reluctant to transfer him back there – and anyway, he wanted a new start.

Over Harry's ensuing two-week holiday, they found a two-bedroom apartment to rent and organised for their furniture to be trucked from Rosella Bay. Harry arranged to move in with Steve, a single guy he worked with in Rosella Bay, and cancelled the lease on their town-house, near Becky.

Bridget got a job in Gidgee within those two weeks and was due to start the same Monday Harry was due back at work. It all happened quickly, but Bridget seemed very happy, which made Harry happy. Bridget was happy with their new apartment and had found work with a building supply company, which made her feel comfortable. The plan was for Harry to go back to Rosella Bay and live with Steve, ask for a transfer and then wait. He would drive the approximately 800-kilometre round trip every weekend to come home to Bridget until his transfer came through.

'Dougie,' started Harry, 'thank you so much for the holiday, I feel much better now, but …'.

Doug knew what was coming in the absence of Bridget living in Rosella Bay.

'I want a transfer to Gidgee,' Harry continued. 'Surely they can get me a job there? It's a big town. I don't want this Doug, but I have to.' The bank wasn't entirely insensitive to personal requests from single guys and Doug agreed to talk to the personnel department and see what could be done. A week later the bank responded to Harry's request. The best they could do was a job in a small country town called Little Creek. Harry had never heard of Little Creek and didn't even know where it was.

'It's about 110 kilometres from Gidgee,' Doug told him. 'Apparently, there weren't any vacancies at short notice in Gidgee and this is the best they can do. It's a very good job, though – you will be second-in-charge.'

Fuck me, thought Harry. I spend all my spare time travelling now and then when I get to Little Creek, I'll be doing more than 1000 kilometres a week. Harry kept his thoughts to himself because he reasoned this was not Doug's fault; he reckoned the bank could have tried harder to fit him in at Gidgee, and the transfer smacked of them using him for their own purpose in an out-of-the-way regional town.

Further back in his mind, he also resented Bridget for forcing this whole saga on him, but would not admit that to himself because he would do anything to ensure her happiness.

'Thank you for going in to bat for me Dougie, you don't know how much I appreciate it, and if that's the best they can do for me, I'll accept the transfer. When will I start there?'

'They are looking to fill your role here, which will hold things up a bit – but hey, who wouldn't want to work on the coast, eh? About two months, early September,' replied Doug.

Who wouldn't want to work at Rosella Bay? echoed Harry in his mind. Well, I know someone.

(30)

Life goes on

September 1979

July morphed into September. Lucy was still annoyed that she and Alice hadn't found Mr White T-Shirt Man. She was so sure of her research, which in the end amounted to bupkis. She racked her brain about how they could continue the search for him, but knew it would be pointless and that she would just have to wait. *No wonder I hate him,* she thought, *all the excitement in my life has now vanished. I just have this guy Arthur Hall bugging me, otherwise I have nothing.*

Lying on her bed one night, Lucy opened her *Thorn Birds* book. There, neatly folded, was the piece of paper Mr White T-Shirt Man had given her. The folds were becoming sharp creases, as Lucy looked at it often and it was now 12 months old. She studied it again, taking careful note of his writing style and trying to remember that morning at the grid as vividly as possible. She remembered the other things he had said to her. He had told her about Alice and Jon, and warned her about a guy she would meet. She re-read the note to herself and looked carefully at the dot point that said, 'The next time you see me I'll be in a dark brown 1976 Holden,' and 'You and I get married.' That will have to sustain me until we meet again, she thought.

Lucy was going through the motions of attending school. She enjoyed athletics and playing netball, but that was about it. She was articulate and smart but didn't enjoy doing stuff she thought would not help her in life. She had made up her mind that she would leave school at the end of the year, even though she didn't have a job in mind. I'll work for Dad, and other farmers in the area, if I have to.

Alice was busy with Jon and they didn't do as much together anymore, and Lucy didn't have anyone else to lean on. She was kind of drifting into a relationship with Arthur, who she didn't really care for. Lucy enjoyed going dancing on Friday nights with her father and Arthur would always be there, watching for her. She was flattered by the attention she caused at dances because she was almost always the most attractive young woman there. Most of the other ladies were older, and young girls generally did not go to old-time dances, but Lucy thought it fun and a good way to spend a weekend, particularly when there was no netball on. This year's competition had just finished and the girls from Little Creek didn't make the final. Alice didn't play the season and without her they were missing something, Lucy thought.

Arthur was teaching Lucy how to dance and working his way into her life. He ingratiated himself with Mick. He got her father's stamp of approval, Lucy thought, in order to pursue her, but she didn't think he was cool, or the type of boyfriend she would like to show off. He wasn't articulate or particularly interesting, and he wasn't mysterious. Mr White T-Shirt Man is mysterious – he would be a trophy boyfriend, Lucy thought. But for now she was stuck with Arthur. Life for Lucy was drifting and everything seemed so ho-hum.

Sometimes, out of the ordinary, things become the norm if they are ignored – and that's what happened with Lucy and Arthur's relationship. He was very possessive and wanted everyone to know that Lucy was 'his'. He would criticise or comment on what Lucy wore, and always wanted to know who she had spoken to and what about. He would become infuriated if Lucy danced with another young guy and would ask her what they had talked about and why she was having so much fun when dancing with him, and he particularly wanted to know where she had been and what she did when she wasn't with him.

Arthur lived about 45 minutes away from Little Creek and usually only saw Lucy on the weekends, which antagonised him because he didn't know what she was up to. What was difficult for Lucy was that her parents and his friends didn't see the dark side of him that she knew; they all encouraged the relationship. But Arthur wasn't liked by Lucy's Little Creek friends. They didn't warm to him and thought him a little strange. Lucy respected her friends' perceptive views and wondered why older people weren't able to see what they could.

Christmas loomed and Lucy perceived that Mr White T-Shirt Man wasn't going to appear like some Santa Claus. She knew he wasn't a figment of her imagination, but she never had the feeling he was just around the corner, so she chose to get on with her life, while often wondering how he would materialise. Would he just knock on the door of Little Creek South homestead one day, or would she see him from a distance in a shop and run to him – or would he see her first and shout, 'Lucy, over here!' She didn't know and that made her glum.

31

Lucy gets a job

May 1980

It was a Saturday and Lucy was leaning on her father's car after playing netball in nearby Rand. She was 17 now and had her licence. She had left school at the end of 1979 and was working part-time while taking a part-time secretarial course at a nearby town one afternoon a week.

She did still think about Mr White T-Shirt Man and their incredible meeting at the grid, but was hurting from not being able to find him last year. The trip to Rasp was nearly 12 months ago, and the grid meeting about two years ago, and she was getting on with life.

I know he'll come to me one day, she thought, I just can't move the dial forward. She used to think, Mr White T-Shirt Man really did a number on me. But now she considered, maybe it was just me who didn't think. I did see him in a blue car, but he did write in his note – 'The next time you see me I'll be in a brown 1976 Holden.'

Since figuring that out, she had been diligently watching for brown 1976 Holdens. She had to get tips from her brother. 'Is that a Holden?'

she would ask him often when she was with him. 'Is it a 1976 model?' Then she would look at car advertisements in magazines and learn about 1976 Holdens. So many cars and so many different models she would think, and he didn't even tell me what model!

Dan asked her one day, 'Why are you so interested in cars these days?' She lied and told him that she was saving for a car and liked the shape of 1976 Holdens. But without a full-time job that was never going to happen. Would I be more motivated if I hadn't met Mr White T-Shirt Man at the grid, she used to often wonder. I seem to have no purpose, and I hate Mr White T-Shirt Man for that.

Her parents were not keen for her to leave school, but she promised that she would find work and if she didn't, she would work for her father on the farm. Mavis tried to talk to Lucy about her future, but Lucy had no firm plans. She was still considering asking her parents if she could go and live in Perth with Janice, where she could easily get a job, but she was hesitant to make such a big leap, and hesitant to leave her mother and father, who she loved very much. On days when she was not very cheerful, she would say to herself, I'm going to join the army and drive a truck – that would be fun – but once again, it was a big commitment and Lucy wasn't good at decisions.

Alice has Jon, and I have a ghost – nothing to hold onto, she thought while watching a netball game, lost in her own world.

'Lucy, just the person I'm looking for!' said a voice which burst her thought bubble.

Lucy was startled. 'Sorry Helen. I was off with the fairies.'

Helen Pratt played netball for Rand: she used to play for Little Creek, including with Lucy, before she got married and moved to a farm near Rand. She still worked in Little Creek but would travel from her farm each day to work in the bank. She was 27 years old and second-in-charge at the Australian Rural Bank branch.

'Hey, I'm giving up netball in a month or so,' she told Lucy. 'I'm getting too old and I'm having a baby.'

'Oh, that's such good news Helen, congratulations,' said Lucy excitedly.

'Matt is so excited,' said Helen. The two went on to talk about what they had both been doing, and of course about netball and keeping fit.

'But Lucy, I want to talk to you about something,' Helen said. 'There are four of us in the branch at the moment and when I go everyone will move up and there will be a vacancy, and I want you to apply. It's not going to be advertised, the boss just said to me, "You know everyone in town – find someone". That someone is you!'

For a moment Lucy was breathless. Mr White T-Shirt Man said that she would get a job in the bank, and now she was being asked to go and work there.

'I don't know anything about banks Helen, and I have been taking lessons, but my typing sucks.'

'The reason I picked you is because of your personality and attitude – we'll teach you everything you need to know on the job. I'm not going to take no for an answer. I know you are only working part-time at the moment so it's perfect for you. I'll tell Mr Small that you'll come in and talk to him on Monday – at, say, 9.30 before we open, okay?'

Lucy was flabbergasted and excited. Everything Mr White T-Shirt Man had said was coming true. He had said, 'You will get a job in the local bank!' Lucy couldn't wait to get home and tell her parents.

'Okay Lucy?' repeated Helen.

'Yes, thank you Helen. Thank you for thinking of me. See you on Monday.'

Alice couldn't believe the coincidence – or as Lucy would have it, 'the prediction' by the grid man. Alice wanted to believe after the birth of Jon, and did collude with Lucy when they searched for him, but she still had her reservations. There was a good chance that Lucy would get a job either at the council or in the bank, or at the post office – what other jobs are there in Little Creek for a young woman, apart from working on a farm? She shared Lucy's excitement when Lucy told her, but wondered if Lucy was excited about getting a good full-time job or about the fact that her Mr White T-Shirt Man had predicted it.

Lucy had run up to Alice at the netball and told her excitedly that Mr White T-Shirt Man 'was right again' – she was going for a job in the bank. Big deal, thought Alice, what about the past two years? Where is he and when will he meet Lucy again?

Mick and Mavis were very pleased for Lucy, and relieved. Mick didn't want her to drift through life and just get married – and he didn't want her leaving home while she was so young, like Janice had done. She should have a job, and experience responsibility and life, he thought. Mick was also harbouring hopes for Lucy's relationship with Arthur Hall. Mick loved his youngest daughter and wanted her to stay close. The job in the bank would mean that she would stay in Little Creek for the foreseeable future, and maybe further her relationship with Arthur, who worked on a farm not far away. Mick thought of Arthur as a responsible, respectful young man who shared his interest in farming. Maybe he and Lucy would take over the farm one day, he wondered, as Dan wasn't interested in farming.

Lucy wasn't as enamoured with Arthur as her father was. She told Alice, 'Dad thinks the sun shines out of his bum, but he doesn't excite me.' She had been on a few dates with him, and saw him at old-time dances when she accompanied her father, but was going through the motions of a relationship, she thought. He always presented himself differently to her parents than he did to her. Lucy saw him as controlling; he probably wouldn't want me to take a job in the bank, she thought. I would be interacting with lots of people and it may open opportunities for me that he wouldn't like. After she failed to find Mr White T-Shirt Man last year, Lucy decided that she had little alternative other than to allow life to happen. Mr White T-Shirt Man had said they would get married and that was good enough for her, if not frustrating. She was, at least, reinvigorated by his prediction about her job in the bank.

Lucy dutifully presented herself at the bank on Monday morning at exactly 9.30. Lucy was never punctual in her life, but on this day she was ready. Ready to get the job and fulfil Mr White T-Shirt Man's prediction – and build her independence, she thought. Mr Small was an old-school banker and liked Lucy's respectfulness and attention. She was also a well-dressed, attractive young woman, which went in her favour, and was halfway through a secretarial course.

Mr Small decided she had been brought up by a good, honest local family, and was exactly the type of young woman he wanted working in the bank. Lucy was hired on the spot and would start in a week's time. That would give Helen time to ensure everyone was trained in their new jobs before she left. Lucy would start as the junior in the branch – the ledger keeper. Marion would move up to general hand and James Bond would take over Helen's job as second officer. James had been at the branch for over a year now and the promotion would mean his tenure would be extended by another 12 months.

Lucy was right about Arthur's reaction to her job. Indifferent at best, she thought. I will be interacting with lots of people, including young men, and he won't like that. His jealous streak will surface at some point.

Mick and Mavis were very happy for her. A job in the bank was a respected role in the community and they were proud of her.

Alice was happy that Lucy's demeanour changed with the new job, but again wondered if that was because she was hoping for the grid man to show up soon. Alice didn't like Arthur much. She sensed he was not a nice person and she had good instincts for people, except when her thoughts were clouded by lust or love – hence the Jake Smith error. Arthur was a little strange, and had a condescending attitude; maybe he is a gold digger – after Mick's farm, thought Alice.

Lucy enjoyed the interaction at her new job. She was working in a team environment and quickly learned her role. Lucy's attitude did change with the job, not only because she thought she was a step closer to Mr White T-Shirt Man, but also because she enjoyed the challenge of something new, which boosted her confidence, and it was entirely different to farming life. People talked about interest rates and budgets and balancing the books, things she had never heard of before. It was exciting, and then on Fridays after work the staff would usually go to the local bowling club to socialise and have a few drinks.

Arthur didn't like that he couldn't manipulate her time and would become angry when she said that she had been to the club with her workmates, or that she couldn't visit him during the week because of work. Lucy wondered if she should try to end her relationship with him, but he always seemed to visit the farm on the weekends and her parents would ask him to stay for dinner. They liked him, but Lucy again wondered about Mr White T-Shirt Man's comment – 'Be careful of someone you meet at a dance.'

The job at the bank made life generally agreeable for Lucy, but her weekends became more difficult. She was torn between what she wanted to do and what everyone else wanted her to do. Working in the bank made her realise there was a whole other world out there. James Bond had worked in many towns over his eight years in the bank, and said that each time he was transferred to a new branch in a new town, it was like a new job. Different people, different experiences and he had learned so much.

Lucy didn't think that James was that professional at his job, but his stories about working in different branches piqued her interest. Lucy would try to go for the usual drinks on Friday night, then rush home to see her mother and father, or go to a dance with her father, then she would be berated by Arthur if she told him she couldn't visit or go out. She played netball during winter and tried to mix with the girls after netball, but even this was difficult, because after netball she would often travel to see Arthur and his family. Then her parents would ask after Arthur and suggest they invite him to the farm for lunch or dinner. It was all getting too hard, but the bright spot was her work. It was nearing Christmas time, Mick was harvesting and Lucy was intent on helping him, which distracted her from her problems.

After the 1978 harvest, Mick would ask around harvest time, 'Well Lucy, when should we harvest?' smiling in her direction.

'I'll have to rub some wheat in my hand and check,' Lucy would reply. Her relationship with her father was close, but Lucy was increasingly concerned that he was pushing another relationship on her that she didn't want and she resented that. For some reason, Mick wanted the relationship with Arthur to work. Mick enjoyed the company of Arthur's parents at the old-time dances and he enjoyed that he could talk with him about farming. Lucy thought that Mick would be very pleased if she married Arthur and they took over the farm – but he's not thinking of me. I don't want to marry a farmer and I'm not fond of Arthur.

Lucy worked over the Christmas and New Year period that first year in the bank, which she understood and didn't mind, but that only gave her the few public holidays off. This enraged Arthur, and on the Saturday before Christmas he exploded, 'You don't really want to spend time with me do you?' Lucy said nothing. 'You just want to be with your bank mates, don't you? You should think yourself lucky you have me – not try to avoid me.'

Arthur was arguing with himself. Lucy was becoming used to him berating her and found that the best course of action was to not say anything, but this would make him try harder to elicit a response from her. Arthur grabbed her by the shoulders and shook her violently. Lucy remained stony-faced. She wasn't about to let him see that he had upset her. She left, drove home and sobbed on her own. She was sobbing not because of the fight, but because of her predicament. She had fallen into an abusive relationship, she thought, and she didn't know how to get out of it. She couldn't tell her mother and father because they would ask if she had been fair to Arthur, she thought – and who else could she talk to? Alice would say, 'If a bloke ever did that to me, I'd tell him to fuck off and never talk to him again.' Advice is easy to prescribe, she thought, but a difficult medicine to swallow.

The next day Arthur visited the farm and was warmly greeted by Mick and Mavis. In private, he was apologetic to Lucy, but she knew the apology carried little weight. She knew he would do it again and maybe become more violent towards her. She was beginning to be scared of Arthur and wished she had taken Mr White T-Shirt Man's advice and kept away from him. Lucy was now wishing that Mr White T-Shirt Man would come into her world soon, because it was deteriorating rapidly.

32

Cracks

August 1981

Living with Steve was a hoot for both guys. They usually ate and drank at the Rosella Bay Returned and Services League Club. Steve loved a beer and playing darts, and Harry drank because it allowed him to forget about his predicament and feel better.

He was going to work in a backwater; he would have to drive 1000 kilometres a week and would be time-poor, he thought. He also thought about his reputation at the bank. Had he burned any bridges? Harry's performance reviews were always very good. He was consistently ranked in the top five per cent of performers within the bank in like-for-like positions and even though he had doubts about working in Little Creek, he would do his very best.

But right now, it was a Wednesday night and he was inebriated and forgetting life with an equally inebriated Steve. 'You are fucking hopeless at darts Dirty,' quipped Steve, using a new nickname he had invented for Harry over the past month. 'Fuck off Phantom,' replied

Harry, using Steve's nickname. Everyone called Steve 'Phantom' because of his surname, Walker.

'I am very good at women though,' retorted Harry. 'Not from what I see,' ridiculed Phantom.

'Well mate, I can tell you, I fucked the girl next door the day Bridget left, so there,' boasted Harry.

The next day, Harry regretted saying this. Over the past month, he had often thought about his encounter with Becky and could now see that she was as lonely as he had been that night. He often thought of visiting her to see how she was, but he didn't trust himself enough not to be intimate with her again. Harry was lonely. He had been living with Bridget for two years and he missed their daily contact and the feeling of them both being aligned and unafraid of the world. But Harry never went to Becky's door. He wasn't clear about why in his mind. Was it that he would be cheating on Bridget? Or was he concerned about Becky? He really wasn't sure, but scolded himself for not admitting he didn't want to have sex with anyone else and hurt Bridget.

Harry dutifully left work every Friday night and drove to Gidgee to be with Bridget. Harry would arrive around 9pm; they would have a late dinner, usually a takeaway, then spend the weekend wasting time together, shopping and talking or cooking a Saturday night dinner. Harry wanted to spend as much time as he could with Bridget and would leave late on Sunday night after making love to her. As the weeks went on, the journey became tiresome for Harry, even though he loved to see Bridget, who would excitedly tell Harry about her week at work. Bridget missed Harry's constant companionship, but was happy to be working at a job she excelled at. Harry always gave his best at work, but wasn't excited about his job now, and was killing time, he thought, before moving to Little Creek.

Eve Smythe and Harry became friends not long after he moved to Rosella Bay. She and her husband owned the newsagency next door to the bank, and Harry would call in every day on his way to work and buy the paper. The newsagency also conducted its business with Harry's bank, and Eve would come in each day to do their banking. Harry was usually on the front counter. Eve was a year older than Harry, had lived all her life in 'the Bay' and had married her childhood sweetheart, Peter, two years ago. She was short with wavy, blonde shoulder-length hair, a soft brown tan, as most coastal girls have, and a small, upturned nose.

She had a shapely body with small breasts and more than once Harry drank in her beauty. She was gregarious and enjoyed banter with Harry. She liked Harry's work ethic and intelligence and enjoyed his after-work laissez-faire attitude. Eve was building a home with her husband and didn't go out often, but was full of giggles when she was out and chanced upon Harry.

'Dirty Harry!' said Eve to Harry one Friday morning as he bought his newspaper. 'You and I are going out to lunch today, because you have been in a shitty mood all week.'

'Yes boss,' replied Harry. 'But I haven't been shitty this week, just not feeling the greatest.'

'Well, you and Steve party too much and that's your problem,' Eve said. 'My friends have seen you two at the club playing up.'

'Guilty mum!' Harry shot back. Harry had often talked to Eve about personal things and she was a good listener. He had confided in Eve about how Bridget had left him, and how that made him feel. It made Harry feel better to express his feelings to someone, and he was grateful for her understanding. Harry looked forward to again chatting with Eve over lunch before he left that afternoon for the trip to Gidgee.

Eve didn't disclose too much about her personal life, but Harry had seen her with her husband and they appeared to have a close relationship. They would often lean on the newsagency counter together as they chatted to Harry.

'Pete will look after the shop, won't you hon?' directed Eve. It seemed to Harry that because they were both born and raised in Rosella Bay and had their family in town, life must be simple for them. He envied them this.

'Harry,' Eve leaned forward and whispered when they had nearly finished lunch. 'I had a dream about you.'

'What about?' Harry answered naively. They were sitting across from each other at a small wooden table in a busy café. Eve was at pains to ensure that her lunch was seen as a casual luncheon with a friend as she was well-known in town, but she was now looking intently into Harry's eyes without smiling. Eve didn't say anything.

'Who else was in the dream?' asked Harry.

'Just you and me,' she whispered again while still watching Harry. Harry suddenly caught up with the conversation. 'You and I,' he said, seeking clarification, 'sort of …'.

'Yes,' said Eve.

'Was it good?'

'It was wonderful, and I can't get it out of my mind.'

Harry couldn't believe the conversation he was having. Eve was attractive, and he had sometimes looked at her in a sexual way because of her shapely body, but the thought of being with her never entered his mind. She was always glued to her husband, and they seemed so happy.

'Wow,' said Harry now, also whispering.

'You are so attractive Evie … Do you want to?'

'Yes.' Harry didn't ask about her reasons or about her relationship and didn't even consider his relationship.

'Steve is going to the club straight after work. I don't have to leave right after work to go to Gidgee. You could come around to our flat after work if you like?'

'I will,' Eve replied.

The afternoon was a blur for Harry. He couldn't believe that Eve made an advance to him. They were friends but nothing more. He had seen her breasts at the beach once when she was sunning with a friend. She had small breasts with thick brown pouty nipples. At the time, Harry tried to look everywhere but at her breasts, and was bashful about the experience, but now she was offering herself to him. She came in to do the afternoon banking and carried on as if nothing had passed between them, which he guessed was what she wanted. She was married, older than Harry and didn't want anyone to know.

Harry's brown Holden was packed ready to leave from work, but instead he went back to the flat he shared with Steve. Steve had already left work for the club so Harry knew that if Eve visited as she said she wanted to, they wouldn't be interrupted. When he returned home, he went and had a shower so he would smell nice if Eve showed – and if she didn't, he would be fresh for the trip home. Harry did wonder if Eve would be as brave as she seemed at lunch, but as he got out of the shower, he heard a soft knock on the door, wrapped a towel around his waist and opened the door just a little so he could see who it was.

When he saw Eve, he opened the door quickly so she could get inside. 'I didn't hear your car,' said Harry. 'I parked around the block a bit so no one would know I'm here,' she replied. She came close and Harry dropped the towel from his waist, exposing his penis, which was already erect. They kissed passionately as they shuffled towards Harry's bedroom. Eve was so enthusiastic about making love, thought Harry, it's like she's been starved of sex.

Harry recounted the experience as he drove to Gidgee. It was probably the best sex he had ever had, he thought. She was so responsive and alive to his touches and made sounds the whole time they were making love. She had taken her clothes off and he admired her beautiful body with wispy blonde pubic hair, before they kissed standing and then lay down on the bed. Harry touched her vagina and found it soaking wet. Never had he felt such lubrication before. She grasped his head in both hands and moaned as she lay beneath him when he suckled her breasts, and opened her legs when he stroked her. She had said to him 'please', and he had tried to enter her, but her vagina was so tight he had to try gently a number of times. After he was able to enter her, she cried with pleasure as he carefully but rhythmically made love to her, slowly at first then faster and faster until they climaxed together. It was such a memorable experience – he couldn't get it out of his head. She seemed so desperate and willing that it was difficult to comprehend.

Afterwards, she held Harry closely without saying much. Harry had to remind her he had a long way to go that night, as he unwound himself from her. She was reluctant to leave and asked him if they could meet again when he got back. He had enjoyed the sex so much he readily agreed – after all, he had only three weeks left in Rosella Bay and some part of him still wanted to punish Bridget for what she had done to him.

He did fuck her the following week, more than once, and each time the sex was crazy and unforgettable. Eve was absorbed with making love to Harry. She couldn't get enough of it. Harry wondered if her husband had ever made love to her. Her pussy was so tight it felt new. Did her husband ever have sex with her? Did he have a small cock that didn't spoil her vagina? Why was she so keen to have sex with him?

She seemed obsessed, and Harry didn't care. He didn't care about Bridget; she was in another town hundreds of kilometres away. He still loved Bridget but he loved fucking Eve. She seemingly only wanted to use Harry for sex and that suited him. Harry fucked her in her car, and at the flat every time she asked, and was able to meet with him without arousing the suspicion of her husband, friends or workmates. Harry couldn't talk to anyone about it. He couldn't talk to Phantom about it for obvious reasons. His mates were all back in Rasp – and in any case, what would they say? Harry wondered. Stevie would probably say 'You lucky dog, Flash.' He had no one that could help with the conflict going on inside his head.

Harry was leading a very busy life. Going to work, travelling to Gidgee on the weekend, fucking Eve every time they had an opportunity, making love to Bridget and driving back to Rosella Bay. Harry thought he had fucked Eve for the last time the Friday night he finished up at Rosella Bay. He told her how beautiful she was and how much he had enjoyed their tryst. In another time, in another place, Harry had said to her, maybe we could have worked out.

Eve cried when Harry left. Harry could see tears welling in her eyes as she said goodbye. 'I'll come and visit you Dirty Harry,' she shouted as he got in his car packed full of possessions.

(33)

Harry and the brown car

September 1981

Lucy's favourite task at work was sorting cheques and deposits, collected the previous day. In the morning prior to the branch opening, she would sort the cheques into alphabetical order before posting them to their relevant accounts later that day. She would get the pile of cheques and deposits, spread them on the front counter, go and make a cup of tea for herself and the boss, then lose herself in the sorting and her thoughts while having a nice warm drink to wake herself up. She had been working at the bank for 16 months and had a work routine that she enjoyed.

It was a Monday. Kev gave Lucy some money and asked her to go to the grocery store and buy a cake. He thought it would be a good way of introducing Harry Barnes to everyone. A slice of cake and a cup of tea. Kev reminded everyone that Harry Barnes would start around 9.30 that morning. James Bond had left last week bound for Shepparton. Shepparton was a much larger town and James was keen to meet new people; he would use his tired introduction of 'Bond, James Bond', which all the staff in Little Creek had grown used to. Lucy figured that at school, James would have been a nerd, but decided during the time they worked together that he was an okay guy.

Six months ago, Marion had left work because she was pregnant, replaced as general hand by Brandon Wheeler, from Canberra. Brandon lived in a two-bedroom flat arranged and leased by the bank. Lucy had built a friendship with Brandon, who was only two years older than her. They would often go to the club together, which gave her an excuse to not see Arthur – but this gave Arthur an excuse to get angry. Mr Small was also transferred around the same time that Marion had left. He had been the manager for four years and was due to be replaced. Lucy didn't warm to Kev McKay, his replacement. Kev, as he liked to be called, was more familiar and that didn't sit well with Lucy. He liked to know about the personal lives of his employees and didn't distance himself from the staff as a bank manager should, thought Lucy.

When James's transfer was announced, Kev informed everyone that the new guy would be starting the following Monday. He was coming from the coast, so Little Creek would be a surprise for him, laughed Kev. 'Apparently, he has a girlfriend in Gidgee, so will commute each day. She must be a keeper if he's going to do that,' quipped Kev.

Lucy liked the changes they were going through at the bank. She had only been there for 16 months, but was already the longest-serving staff member. She also thought it was great working with guys rather than all girls in the office. Kev and Brandon both had stories about the bank and where they had been. It's fun to hear about it, she thought as she sorted her cheques that morning. I wonder what the new guy is like: he must be older because he is living with a girl.

Harry arrived in Gidgee late on Friday with all his possessions packed around him in the HJ. Bridget was outside to greet him when he pulled up. 'Hi you,' she said warmly. 'Home at last. You must have left late.'

'Yeah, everyone wanted to say goodbye and shake my hand,' Harry lied. Harry wondered if Bridget could smell Eve on him; if so, he would blame hugs from the girls. Harry felt sheepish about his encounter with Eve just hours ago. He didn't feel guilty, just contrite, but he appeased himself by reconciling that the Rosella Bay part of his life was now over, and this was like a fresh start. He also believed that Bridget deserved his unfaithfulness by abandoning him. He did still love Bridget very much and told her so as he made love to her that night, but his head told him he would need to sort out their future to ensure an ongoing commitment from both of them.

Harry was pleased to be home with Bridget and felt relaxed all weekend. He would wait a few months before they had a serious conversation about his career versus her career. He just wanted to get back in a routine with Bridget.

Harry contacted Kev McKay on Friday from Rosella Bay and assured him he would be there on Monday. Kev told him not to come in early, as he knew Harry was travelling from Rosella Bay to Gidgee in his own time over the weekend, which he appreciated. Harry thanked him and told Kev that in that case, he would be there around 9.30. But as ever, Harry wanted to be prepared, and on Sunday he and Bridget took a drive to Little Creek. Harry wanted to know how long the trip would take from Gidgee, and where the branch was. He also wanted Bridget to experience the trip so she could understand Harry's daily grind.

They approached Little Creek and turned right at the 'T' junction, then drove over the railway tracks and past the silos. Harry had never been to Little Creek, but knew it was a very small town with only four staff at the branch. He knew the bank would be in the main street, as they always are in country towns.

'Gee, it's only small Harry,' said Bridget.

'Yeah, but I'll be the second officer, so it's a good step up – then who knows where,' he said, without thinking that Bridget would argue against any move that didn't suit her in the future. The branch was a small brick-and-tile fronted building with a glass entrance door and a large window onto the street. Harry cupped his hand against the glass and looked inside.

'It's got a lovely old wooden counter and tellers' box Bridge,' said Harry. The trip had taken them a little over an hour because Harry was hesitant with the route, but he knew that if he drove like Flash, and knew the way, it would probably only take 45 minutes. On the first day, however, he would allow an hour.

They drove around the streets of Little Creek and looked at the homes and businesses. There was a small hospital, two pubs, a grocery store, café, a stone post office building and a police station. Harry also noticed a service station that displayed prices not too dissimilar to Gidgee, which he thought he could use to fill his car.

Harry was confident that given the size of the town, he would be able to competently handle his new role. 'It's not very big is it?' Bridget remarked again as they turned to leave. 'Now at least I'll be able to picture where you are working. You will kill it, Harry.'

Harry left Gidgee at 8.25 on Monday morning. Bridget's work was only a kilometre away and she was used to the walk, but Harry dropped her off on the way. Once he turned off the highway about 20 kilometres out of town, he was able to drive at over the speed limit without much risk of getting caught for speeding, and he was in Little Creek at 9.20.

Harry turned down the main street and angle-parked across the road from the bank. There were no other cars on the street, but Harry didn't want to take customer car parks.

Lucy looked up as she saw a car out of the corner of her eye while sorting cheques. The car slowed and turned to park opposite the bank. It was a brown car. Lucy stopped sorting and stared intently at the car. She had been looking at pictures of 1976 Holdens for over 18 months now and it looked like a Holden Kingswood. She knew the difference between a 1976 Holden Kingswood and the later model was a crease on the boot lid. The HJ model, which was made from 1974 up until mid-1976, had no crease, but thereafter there was a crease. It was around 50 metres from where she was standing in the bank to the car, and Lucy could see there was no crease. It was a metalflake brown with aftermarket chrome wheels and wide tyres with chrome exhaust tips. Lucy knew that Holden made the Kingswood in a number of brown shades, but the colour of the car across the street was the darkest shade of brown they had made – Sierra Tan.

Lucy continued to stare, taking in the type and colour of the car and referencing that against what she had learned. She held her breath and clutched the bundle of cheques with both hands as she waited for someone to get out of the car. The driver's door opened and a tall young man stepped out with a brief case in one hand. He was dressed in beige pants and a light-green body shirt. He leaned forward with his back to Lucy and locked the car. He hadn't yet looked towards the bank, but Lucy could see he had long, blonde surfer-style hair. Lucy didn't yet dare think it was the Mr White T-Shirt Man she had talked to three years ago, until he turned and started walking towards the bank.

It was him! She recognised him as he reached the middle of the street. She had waited three years for this moment and suddenly the person she had been dreaming of had arrived. Lucy was overwhelmed with emotion and everything went black; she fainted. Brandon saw her fall slowly as she tried to grasp the counter and concertinaed onto her bottom with her legs under her as she fell.

'Boss!' Brandon shouted loudly as Harry reached the door, 'Come quick!' Kev rushed out of his office to see Brandon talking to Lucy, who was in a pile on the floor, just as Harry knocked on the door. Kev waved to Harry as if to say 'I won't be a moment' as he made sure Lucy was okay. She was conscious and Brandon was helping her to a chair as Kev went to the door.

'Harry is it?' Kev asked. 'Come in mate, our ledger girl Lucy has just fainted, but come in.' Harry came in past the counter and waited and watched while Kev and Brandon talked to Lucy. 'Are you okay Lucy?' asked a concerned Kev. Some colour was coming back into Lucy's face.

'I'm ok,' she replied. Harry took Lucy in. She was tall and slim, with beautiful long dark hair and long shapely legs. She had on a blue one-piece tunic with a zip that ran down the front and low, comfortable shoes.

'Did you have breakfast this morning?' asked Kev. 'Breakfast is really important. I think I'll ring your mum and she can come and get you.'

'No, no, please don't. I'll be okay – I just felt a little faint and my legs went to jelly,' she replied.

'I'll get you a glass of water then, just sit there,' instructed Kev. 'Make sure she doesn't fall off the chair Brandon.'

Once Lucy seemed to have recovered, Kev introduced Harry. 'Everyone, this is Harry Barnes. Harry, this is our fainting ledger girl, Lucy Martin; Brandon Wheeler, and obviously I am Kev McKay.'

Harry leaned forward and took Lucy's hand while she was seated, and said 'Hi', then talked to Brandon and Kev. Lucy was drinking in the sight of Harry and wondering when he would talk to her about all those things he told her three years ago. Why doesn't he pick me up and sweep me off my feet – why doesn't he hug me or even look at me in a longing way? Maybe he doesn't want everyone to know what happened between us, surmised Lucy. But it was him. There was no mistaking him for anybody else. He was the Mr White T-Shirt Man she had met years ago – and now here he was in Little Creek in his dark brown Holden.

She was embarrassed that she had fainted, but she was so startled by Harry's sudden appearance after three long years that she was over-whelmed. All her thoughts, wants, desires and fears came before her in a matter of seconds and she wasn't able to process it all.

Lucy couldn't wait to be alone with Harry and ask him all the questions she had stored in her mind over the three years since she had seen him. She wanted his love and support and assurances about their future. It was strange, but she felt she already loved him, even though he had only spoken one word to her, because her feelings had grown for him over the past three years in his absence. She knew Harry was what she wanted; she wanted Harry to be her rock, to take her away from her parents, her boyfriend and make her excited about life.

34

Why doesn't he remember?

September 1981

Harry spoke frequently to Lucy that day, but seemed cautious and professional. He carefully told her what he was looking for and worked with her to find the problem, but he seemed a little defensive. She thought he would be warmer towards her, even though others were present. He was congenial to everyone and knew his job well, which is all he wanted to talk about. It infuriated her.

Harry had been through other transfers and was accustomed to feeling his way in the first couple of days, evaluating people and looking at how they were doing things, and considering how he might change things when he was properly settled. Kev was likeable enough, he thought, but seemed to be a bit of a ditherer and too involved in back-office matters. His job was customers, thought Harry, he should leave the office to me. Brandon seemed to be competent, but a relatively new recruit who lacked some banking experience. Prior to this job he had only worked at one other branch and although he seemed smart, he wasn't bank-wise mused Harry.

Harry chided himself for thinking that Lucy was an attractive young woman. He should have thought more about her abilities and strengths, but her beauty was the first thing he had noticed about her. He sensed she was also a warm and considerate person who would help anyone who asked. She was the longest-serving person in the branch and knew all the customers, so Harry could rely on her for feedback or a 'read' on someone. Her banking skills were adequate for the job she was doing, but he thought he would upskill her into Brandon's job when he understood the branch more.

Neither Harry nor Lucy had any idea of the other's thoughts. Harry was in a new job, trying to understand the branch and thinking about his future with Bridget, while Lucy was obsessed by Harry and wanted him to hold her and make her feel safe. Lucy wasn't aware that in January 1979, around four months after they had met at the grid, Harry lost his intuitive ability to see his future – and more than that, the period between September 1978 and January 1979 was lost to him as well.

It frustrated Steve and Max constantly; they had been living with it for nearly three years. As Stevie put it, 'Harry can't remember if he tied his shoelaces in those four months.' Harry reckoned he could remember it, because he didn't lose any of his knowledge over that period.

'I still know my job, you bullet heads,' he had said to them 'and I still love Bridge, and I don't know what I don't know, so as far as I'm concerned, I haven't lost anything.'

Max had replied, 'But Harry, you don't know who you talked to or what you said, and we don't know everything you did during those four months because you wouldn't tell us – and that's what worries us. Why did we have to hide the Monaro? Explain that to me.'

'Shit – I don't know Heady, I bumped my head, what can I say?' replied Harry.

'But the other thing you did Flash, was you predicted the future, which is how we won on the Cup and why we bought those shares,' ventured Steve.

'Yeah but I only shared the future with you two, no one else. Not a soul.'

'Yeah right,' replied Steve sarcastically. Steve continued to worry about what Harry had 'fucked up', as he put it, during those four months, but was ready to defend him. 'If someone turns up and says he robbed a bank in December 1978, I won't be surprised,' Steve had told Max.

'Yeah, remember I told you about that girl who turned up at my place in July 1979?' said Max. 'I had to lie to her. I just can't figure out what he had to do with her. I don't know if he knew she was coming, or if he guessed she might come looking for him, and now we'll never know.'

'Yeah, fuck mate, I wouldn't have transferred the registration. What if he shagged her and she was pregnant, and he doesn't remember any of it?!' exclaimed Steve.

'He told me he hadn't done anything wrong or illegal and he hadn't rooted anyone, so I just did it,' replied Max.

'You know what they call you when you do something like that?' Steve said, laughing. 'An accomplice,' to which they both laughed.

Lucy stayed late on Harry's first day, hoping to get him alone and talk to him, and talk about their meeting in 1978. Kev left work early, which was his usual routine, and Brandon shortly after.

'You've got a bit of a drive Harry; how long will it take you?' Brandon asked.

'It's only about an hour,' Harry replied. 'I'm just going to finish the general ledger then go, and get an early start tomorrow. I'm fine mate, you go.'

'Luce, want to grab a drink?' asked Brandon.

'No, I better not after my blackout this morning. I'll show Harry how to lock up and leave with him,' she replied carefully.

'Okay, I'm out,' Brandon said.

Harry started packing up his desk as Lucy watched and pretended to be busy, but she couldn't endure her feelings any longer. She stood up and walked towards Harry.

'Harry, I think I have met you somewhere before,' she started. Harry stopped what he was doing and eyed Lucy.

'Really?' He searched his memory.

'You don't remember?'

Harry was thinking about his stint at Ber-Beri, which wasn't far from Little Creek, but couldn't place Lucy. Surely he would remember such an attractive girl, he thought.

'Did you relieve in Ber-Beri or come to Ber-Beri Branch for a function?' he asked.

I cannot believe this, thought Lucy, whose world was starting to crumble.

'No, I was on a motorbike and you were at my grid and I stopped and we talked,' Lucy said.

Harry put the book down and studied Lucy's forlorn face. She truly believes we have met, he thought and tried to put some meat on the bone.

'I can't remember that, remind me where was this, Lucy?'

Lucy paused, all the while studying Harry. 'It was here in Little Creek.'

This time it was Harry who paused, wondering if Lucy was well. She had fainted this morning and he could tell she wasn't really concentrating on her work today, but what should he say in reply?

'Umm, are you sure it was me; I haven't been to Little Creek before,' he eventually said.

They both now stared at each other for some time as tears welled in Lucy's eyes and silently began streaming down her cheeks onto the front of her blue tunic. Harry wasn't sure what he had said that had upset her and wasn't sure what he should do as Lucy started sobbing quietly, her chest heaving.

He moved forward, gently put his arms around her and pulled her towards him to comfort her. 'Hey Lucy, please don't cry – tell me what's the matter,' said Harry softly. Lucy continued to cry more loudly as she stood leaning against Harry.

'My life is a mess,' she said between sobs. 'I hate the world and I hate everyone in it. I just wanted to end the dream I've been having and I thought you could help.'

'I will help if you tell me what this is all about,' said Harry encouragingly. With that, Lucy pulled away from Harry, grabbed her bag angrily and ran towards the front door.

'Lucy, please don't go!' shouted Harry as she went outside, jumped in her car and sped away.

'Fuckin' hell,' Harry whispered to no one. Harry was distressed by what had just happened. He didn't understand how any of their conversation should have caused Lucy to become upset, and he wondered if she was well. He wondered if he should talk to Kev about what had happened, but dismissed it to protect Lucy.

She's obviously had a stressful day and I shouldn't exacerbate that, he thought. Fuck my life is complicated, he thought, as he drove home to Bridget. Should I even tell Bridget about what happened, he wondered, then dismissed that idea as well. I will try to talk to Lucy about it tomorrow, if she shows up. If she doesn't show, I'll have to tell Kev.

Lucy went straight home, charged past Mavis to her room and flung herself on her bed, continuing to cry.

'Are you alright darling?' asked Mavis, as she poked her head into Lucy's room. 'Yes mum, I'm just not feeling well, maybe I'm getting my period,' she lied. In one day, Lucy had gone from such a high to feeling depressed, all because of Mr White T-Shirt Man, who she now knew as Harry Barnes. It wasn't how she envisaged their meeting would be after three years. She pictured them running towards each other with open arms, and hugging and kissing.

Instead she got, 'Who are you?' What am I missing, she wondered in a moment of emotional clarity. She grabbed her *Thorn Birds* book and re-read his note. She had looked at Harry's handwriting very closely today and she could see that it was exactly the same as that on the note. It is him, and if it is him, why doesn't he acknowledge it? Is it because he has found someone else and now doesn't want to acknowledge me? What if he has changed his mind about me? He should at least have the courage to say 'Look, I stuffed up all those years ago and just want to say I am so sorry.' Instead, he just flatly denies meeting me, which is so unfair – I hate him.

Lucy went to talk to Alice that night and told her what had happened. Alice was incredulous.

'WHAT? HE IS *HERE*?!' she yelled.

'Shush,' cautioned Lucy.

'He's here and he denies meeting you, despite the note and the fact that everything he predicted that came true?' Alice asked.

'Yep,' replied Lucy, who was feeling a little better sharing her story with Alice.

'I don't get it Lucy, let's think about this. Let's think about all the reasons he could be acting like this. Number one – it might not be him,' reasoned Alice.

'IT IS HIM!' Now Lucy was the one to shout.

'Don't interrupt – let's think about this. Let's just think of everything that could be causing him to deny he knows you. One, it may not be him; two, what you said, he may not want to damage his existing relationship; and three, he may not remember the meeting because … '

'Alice, he found me at the grid; I didn't go looking for him. It was his choice to meet me three years ago,' interrupted Lucy.

'But Luce, you said he could see the future and he proved that. What if he is a little loopy and genuinely doesn't remember the grid meeting?' This was a palatable solution for Lucy. That would mean he just doesn't remember what happened, and in the future we will be together. She could live with that scenario, and gently encourage Harry to like, trust and maybe love her in the future.

Lucy smiled at Alice. 'Do you think that could be the reason?'

'It stands a chance,' Alice replied. 'Tell you what, I'll come into the branch tomorrow and eyeball him.' Alice's smile was returned by Lucy.

It seemed to take Harry no time at all to drive home, probably because he was thinking so much on the way. Now he had three women on his mind, he thought. Bridget, Eve and Lucy. I have some time to come to some arrangement with Bridget, he thought. He could get another job in Gidgee that he would be able to stay with for many years and not move, which he discounted immediately, or he could talk to Bridget about accommodating his career, because it seemed to Harry that at the moment, I am the one who is bending, not Bridge.

This prompted him to think about why he had been with Eve. Eve was like a 'take that' message to Bridget, even though Bridget didn't know about it, he reasoned. When he arrived home, Bridget was her usual happy self, but because he was a little late, Harry had to find himself something to eat, prompting Harry to think, 'Am I getting the wrong end of the stick at the moment?'

Harry was worried about going to work the following day, but his fear lessened when Lucy walked in as he was counting cash in his teller's box.

'Hi Lucy,' he said cheerfully.

'Hi Harry, hi Brandon, hi Kev,' she called out. Lucy was determined not to get upset. She had been thinking; Alice's assessment of Harry could be correct. All savants are a little left-field aren't they? she thought.

'Would anyone like a tea or coffee?' asked Lucy as she set up to sort her cheques and deposits on the counter near Harry.

'That would be nice,' replied Harry, hopeful all the tears from yesterday had been erased. Harry wanted to get to the bottom of the tears – but he also didn't want any more tears. Maybe she just had a bad day, or maybe she's a psycho, thought Harry, but he wanted to like her. He got the impression she was a very down-to-earth person with values he admired.

Then again, Harry didn't like leaving matters unresolved – it was a bugbear of his. When we are alone again, I'll ask her about it, he thought, as he finished the cash count and readied for opening.

Alice was the very first customer after the doors were opened. Alice flashed a smile and nod to Lucy, who was still sorting near Harry's teller's box, as she went to be served by Harry and introduce herself. Harry opened her passbook and looked at some of the entries in her book as Alice filled out a withdrawal form.

'You know what Alice; we have met before!' exclaimed Harry. Lucy, startled, stopped sorting and quickly looked at Harry, then Alice.

'What do you mean?' asked Alice. Yes, what *do* you mean? Lucy thought to herself, suddenly intrigued by what Harry was going to say. The whole branch seemed to go quiet at that moment as both girls waited to hear what Harry would say.

'Well, see right here in your book?' replied Harry, 'You took out $100 in Rasp some time ago, and that's my stamp and initial where I served you.'

'You know what, I think I remember you,' replied Alice. 'I was visiting Rasp with a friend and did go to the bank there. I'm Alice, by the way – a friend of Lucy's.'

'I'm sorry, but I don't actually remember you coming in – my memory from Rasp around that time has holes in it like Swiss cheese. Let me see, the date says July '79. I had a bad crash on my motor bike around that time and my mates from Rasp always chide me about my memory since then; you know what mates are like,' said Harry.

'So, you come from Rasp?' asked Alice while looking devilishly at Lucy. 'Lucy didn't tell me that. Rasp is a great place to visit.'

'Yep, I went to school there and joined the bank there, and have been travelling around the state since,' replied Harry. 'Oh, I was told you came from Rosella Bay,' said Alice, again giving Lucy a quick look.

'No, I just worked there for a bit,' Harry replied. 'You know what, why don't you get Lucy to bring you around to my place for dinner one night? I'm a good cook, aren't I Lucy?' Alice said.

'She makes very nice cakes,' chimed in a chastened Lucy.

'That would be great,' agreed Harry. Alice smiled, said her goodbye to Harry and Lucy and went to go out the door, but turned back again. 'Is that your car Harry?' asked Alice motioning towards Harry's car. 'It looks great – I bet it's a 1976 HJ.'

This time, it was Lucy glaring at Alice. Lucy had been bombarding Alice with details of cars for two years – notably HK Monaros and 1976 Holdens, and Alice fed off this knowledge.

'Yes, it's mine and you are correct, it's a HJ,' Harry informed her.

'My brother used to have a HK Monaro, and it was a great-looking car,' Alice lied.

'Really?' said Harry. 'I used to have one of those. I sold it to buy the HJ.'

Lucy could not believe what was happening between Harry and Alice. Her mouth was agape as she learned as much in five minutes standing there as she had tried to learn over the past three years. 'See you Alice,' encouraged Lucy, '*bye.*'

Alice smiled all the way home, knowing that in a few hours Lucy would rush to her place for lunch to unpack everything that had just been said. *Now* I believe, thought Alice as she walked home.

* * *

'WHAT THE HAY ALICE!' Lucy yelled as she arrived at Alice's for lunch. 'No Luce, I'm on your side,' replied Alice. 'You know, I do now believe everything you have told me about the grid man and his predictions. You were even right about where he lived, but why didn't we find him when we went to Rasp? I'll suss that out when he comes for dinner.'

'You will not! I need to take in everything that he just told you then do some planning,' instructed Lucy. 'He is cute though, right?'

'Yes, I remember saying that to you when we left Rasp,' Alice replied. 'I am sure now that I remember him serving me. I wonder if he has such a poor memory, does he still see the future?'

'Please don't ask him that Alice. Just give it a rest until we figure this out a bit more,' pleaded Lucy.

Harry was adjusting to work in Little Creek well. He often stayed for a couple of drinks on a Friday night, but only drank soft drink because he had to drive home. Lucy enjoyed his company very much. He was different to guys from Little Creek, she thought. He has drive, ambition and is smart, and it seems he is not afraid to move from town to town to further his career.

'I really like him,' Lucy told Alice.

'Just as well, because you are going to marry him,' Alice replied.

Lucy had wondered about that. Perhaps she was too late, she thought. No one in the branch had met Bridget yet, so Lucy wasn't able to make a judgement, but thought that it wouldn't be about the competition, it would be whether or not Harry loved her, which meant that Lucy did give Harry some attention without being obvious. She didn't want to change her personality or life to suit Harry, she just wanted to make sure he understood her.

In the interim, life went on as usual for Lucy. She had only become involved with Arthur because she met him at an old-time dance. She acknowledged to herself that Arthur was a good dancer and she enjoyed dancing with him, but couldn't find a spark that told her she cared for him. They would dance together and other couples at the dances would watch them and comment on their prowess, which drew Lucy towards him, but as she grew to know him, she liked him less. She felt he preyed on her via her parents. He was a different person when in the presence of Lucy's parents than when he was alone with her.

Arthur was often angry with Lucy because she had said or done something he didn't like. If she talked to his male friends she would be in trouble; if she was late, he would want to know where she had been. He was extremely possessive and Lucy would usually be upset when they were together. He didn't hit her, but would grab her roughly and shout at her and degrade her. Lucy's parents and Arthur's parents could not see that she was unhappy in the relationship and actively encouraged them to be together. After a while, being with him was the norm.

Lonely and the blonde

35

September 1981 to March 1982

Harry was tiring of driving between Little Creek and Gidgee. He reckoned he wasted 10 hours a week in the car, and hardly had a life outside work. He didn't have any time to build relationships in Gidgee, because he wasn't involved in sport there and had no work ties that would lead to friendships. He hadn't played golf since he left Ber-Beri and that irked him. He would generally get home around 8 pm on Friday, be with Bridget over the weekend and then it was time to go back to work again.

At least in 'the Creek' he was friendly with Brandon and Lucy, and had met a fellow motorbike rider who he would sometimes mix with. Harry hadn't been home to Rasp since his 21st birthday in February, and missed the contact with his mates and his parents. He felt alone and isolated.

In October, he and Bridget had 'that' conversation. But Harry didn't think that they had resolved anything, other than make Bridget feel better. Harry wanted Bridget to give some commitment that she would support him in his job if he was transferred again. Bridget refused. She wanted Harry to consider other jobs where he didn't have to move every few years, but he could see there would be no significant opportunities for him if he did that. Harry pleaded that the bank was a national company and even had international branches that would be of interest to him. It wasn't an angry argument, there was just friction between Bridget building a career versus Harry's existing career.

Harry had told Bridget before how much she had hurt him when she left the way she did at Rosella Bay, and he told her that he doubted she loved him as much as he loved her.

'Harry, I left my job in Rasp to be with you, I left my job in Ber-Beri to be with you, I agreed to live in Gidgee to be with you, and what commitment have you shown me?' asked Bridget.

'I love you Bridget,' was all Harry could say.

'Well, when you commit to me, I'll think about following you,' she said.

Love isn't simple, thought Harry. I just wanted to be with her and build something with her, and now I'm unhappy and stressed.

'Bridge, will you marry me then?' asked Harry as they sat together on the lounge one Friday night. 'If I have to get engaged to you to prove my love and commitment to you I will.'

It wasn't the most special of proposals, but Harry had nailed his colours to the mast. Bridget accepted. But still, Harry wasn't happy. He remembered coming home to an empty house in Rosella Bay, and how he had a lump in his throat that night and couldn't eat, and how he was so worried about where Bridget had gone, and if she would contact him. It scarred Harry, and he knew he would carry that feeling with him forever.

Even after he proposed and she accepted, Harry didn't regret fucking Becky, and he didn't regret fucking Eve. I didn't love them, I just wanted to use them, he thought, use them to hurt Bridget the way she had hurt me. Once again, stewed Harry, Bridget now feels better and I haven't advanced at all. My career is very important to me and Bridget won't acknowledge that.

Harry stayed in contact with Eve. She had called him at work in Little Creek, the week after he arrived there. The way she talked to him felt like phone sex to Harry and she cajoled him into meeting her at a town about halfway between Gidgee and Rosella Bay a few weeks later.

Harry told Bridget he was staying in Little Creek on Friday and Saturday night, but would be home on Sunday sometime. He was going out with the guys from the bank on Friday night, then helping a friend with his bike at a race on Saturday, he said.

Instead, Harry drove from Little Creek through Gidgee and on to Elong, where he fucked Eve many times over the 36 hours or so that he was there. Eve was already at the motel when he arrived and dressed to kill, thought Harry, in a very small white silk nightdress. It was the first night they had ever slept the night together and Harry knew that she had orgasmed over and over again as she cried while he thrusted into her tight vagina.

Harry wasn't sure why he had agreed to see her again; she was married and he was trying to repair his relationship with Bridget. Harry was losing perspective and trying to hurt everybody, including himself. Shouldn't he be chaste, and spurn advances by other women, and not be attracted to other women? Harry was disappointed with his choices, but didn't care. Eve's marriage would probably break down – and what would happen to his relationship? Deep down he was miserable, he thought – at least Eve cheered him up. She loved sex with Harry, and that made him feel special.

It was nearing November when Eve came and stayed for five days in Little Creek. Harry told Bridget that work was really busy and he wanted to spend the week at Little Creek – which he did, but in the company of Eve. He rented a room at the pub for a week and he and Eve slept together, enjoying sex every morning and sometimes more than once a night.

The first night she arrived, Harry took Eve in the shower up against the tiled wall. She was little in stature and Harry picked her up under her buttocks as she wrapped her legs around him and he roughly fucked her. Her vagina was as he remembered months ago, very wet and so tight it clenched around his cock. She still had a beautiful light brown tan with no suntan strap marks across her back or chest. Her breasts were brown and her nipples an even darker shade of brown, which stood out when she wore a T-shirt or tight-fitting blouse.

The sex was great, but the liaison only made Harry feel worse. He was confused and didn't have anyone to talk to. He didn't have anyone he could cry to or express his feelings to. He was lonely and lost. During Eve's time with him, they went to Ber-Beri so Harry could look at a motorbike. He had decided he needed something outside work and bought a new Yamaha IT 465 enduro bike. Harry was $600 short of the purchase price, but Eve said she would lend it to him, so he went back to the Creek with a new bike, which would help him forget about his deception and philandering ways. He would leave his bike at Lucy's farm and drive out there after work to ride it. It wasn't registered, but Harry didn't care. He would ride through all the sandhills in the common areas around Little Creek for hours by himself. To ride really fast and dangerously was an outlet for him.

'Harry, I want to come and live with you,' Eve declared before she went home.

Fuck no, thought Harry, I can hardly live with myself now let alone Eve – and what about Bridget.

'I'm engaged to Bridget now Evie, I can't do that,' replied Harry matter-of-factly.

'But we are so good together Harry, and I told my husband I'm not coming back.'

Maybe it could work, thought Harry. Maybe he didn't need or want Bridget anymore. That would hurt her.

'Go home Eve and think about it, you don't just want to do it because of the sex,' instructed Harry.

'But I love you, Dirty,' she said, and suddenly Harry's world was darker than it had been before. Harry told Eve he did care for her and would think about their relationship, but she had to go home. Eve cried and Harry cried later. He didn't cry for Eve, he didn't cry for Bridget, he cried for himself. He didn't know what he was doing to himself and couldn't see where he was going with his life. He was hurting people he cared for but had no one to confide in or to help him.

On the way back to Gidgee after Eve had left, he played Jon and Vangelis' *I'll Find My Way Home* at full volume. 'Well I'm near the end and I just ain't got the time/And I'm wasted and can't find my way home.' That was how Harry felt. Where was his home; did he have a home to go to? He didn't have any time, he was just wrecking everyone's life, including his own.

He sobbed to Bridget that night and told her how hard he felt his life was. Bridget was always soft with Harry and that's what he loved about her – and that night was no different.

'You'll find yourself Harry. I'll always love you,' said Bridget softly, but it was that night that Harry knew he couldn't trust his heart to her anymore. He loved her, but their relationship had been irreparably damaged and was tearing him apart. He wanted to blame Bridget, but he knew he couldn't – it wouldn't be fair. It's all my fault, he reasoned – I'm a cunt.

Harry didn't travel home every night anymore. He started staying with Brandon at his flat a few nights a week. He stopped at a phone booth one night on his way back to Gidgee and rang Eve, so he could talk to her without fear of being heard. He told her she could come to Little Creek and live there if that's what she wanted.

He didn't want to hurt Eve any more than he already had. He wanted to repair his life, but wasn't sure if this was the right move. Was he going to tell Bridget he was moving out and that their relationship was over, or was he going to hide from her and continue with his lies? Eve was excited and told Harry she would be there in early December. She hoped that would give him time to end his relationship with Bridget.

Harry was still making love to Bridget and enjoying her company but something was missing: Harry's total commitment to her. He still loved her but wasn't sure that they would be together forever and that hurt. She was so trusting and loving towards him, and that's what hurt him the most. I am a cunt and she doesn't know it, and I can't talk to her about it.

Harry didn't know what to do as December arrived. I am a gutless coward, he thought. He wanted the security of Bridget but wanted to continue to fuck Eve. Harry felt he had nowhere to turn. I wish my best mate Ben was here right now. He would straighten me out and tell me what a fool I have been. Harry would occasionally ring his mother from work to say hello, and Ben would ring occasionally, but he couldn't bring himself to confide in either of them over the telephone from work.

If Ben were here, we would get drunk and open our hearts to each other, thought Harry, and Ben would say, 'You stupid prick, what you need to do is … ,' but he didn't have that luxury.

Harry was agitated about Eve's arrival in a week's time. He hadn't talked to Bridget, as he had agreed with Eve. He couldn't do it. He reasoned he still loved Bridget, and wanted to hang onto that forever, but knew the relationship wouldn't work for the next 40 or 50 years as he had planned. She had opened a small wound and he couldn't stop it festering.

'Are you okay Harry?' asked Lucy one evening as they were working late. She had walked over to Harry's desk and put her hand on Harry's shoulder as he sat working. It was the end of November; at the end of each month they would both work late. Harry would balance the branch books as Lucy posted all the entries. Harry looked up at Lucy, who had been so kind to him since he had arrived in Little Creek. She drank with him and helped him home when he was drunk, and would help him clean the flat on weekends. She was quiet and unassuming but very beautiful and her personality so warm.

Lucy had asked nothing of Harry in return for her friendship and he felt like blurting out all his feelings to her right there and then. Lucy had been watching what Harry was doing and knew he had problems. He had a girlfriend he was engaged to and then a relationship with a surfie chick called Eve. He had no money because he was travelling all the time, and few friendships for the same reason.

Harry put his hand on hers but remained looking at his ledger lest he start thinking about what he had been doing and what was waiting for him and become emotional. Lucy brought her other hand on top of his as they both remained silent. Harry turned and looked at Lucy and saw care in her eyes. Her eyes were an oasis for Harry. No one really cares about me, but Lucy seems to, he thought. Harry turned in his chair and put his head on her belly as she stroked his head, gently caressing him. Harry didn't move for minutes, enjoying the care being bestowed on him and getting his feelings under control.

Harry stood up, put his arms around Lucy and kissed her passionately. Lucy responded. They continued to kiss and explore each other before realising it was dark outside and the lights were on inside, and anyone passing would be able to see them. Once again, Harry wasn't thinking about his life and relationships, he was just doing what he wanted to do. Worse still, he wasn't thinking about Lucy's feelings. They were both focusing just on each other. Lucy had been thinking about this moment for years and just wanted to be close to Harry and hold him.

If this is as good as it gets then I'm happy, thought Lucy. I don't care if I don't have him forever, I've just never felt this way about anybody before and I'll take what I can get. They made love later that night in Harry's car. Lucy was reluctant, but after three years just wanted to taste Harry, hold him and feel him, and she allowed him. Harry wanted to be kind and gentle. He wondered, had Lucy made love to anyone before, and asked if she was okay. Lucy nodded and Harry hoped she felt as good as he did.

Harry was chastened by the experience with Lucy. She had been so loving towards him and so giving that he felt guilty about making love to her, but she had already had an effect on him. Harry rang Eve two days later and asked her not to come to Little Creek. 'Evie, this is not easy for me to talk about and I know it will be harder for you, but I don't want you to come to be with me. I don't think it's going to work and I'm all messed up,' confessed Harry.

He didn't tell Eve about Lucy, but she had seen them look at each other and guessed. 'I bet you're fucking Lucy, aren't you Harry?' she replied. 'You are, aren't you? You're a prick Harry. Not two girls, but three. Really. You are fucked up.'

That was the last time Harry ever heard from Eve, apart from a letter from a solicitor threatening legal action unless her loan of $600 was repaid immediately. Harry didn't have the money, but Lucy kindly gave it to Harry and the debt was paid. Harry didn't want the Boss or Brandon to know that Lucy had gifted him some money, so he took from the day's deposits and withdrawals the two matching entries: a debit to Lucy's account and a credit to his from the day's vouchers. The entries did go through as normal; they were just taken out after the work was posted then put back in after the boss and Brandon had reviewed the vouchers for the day.

Harry was truly sorry he had broken Eve's marriage, but figured for her to be with him in the first place that the marriage must have already been severely damaged and in trouble. But then, who was Harry to cast stones or apportion blame?

Harry and Lucy's relationship did not move quickly after their initial encounter. Lucy was still kind and caring towards Harry, and it seemed to Harry she was allowing him time and space to make up his mind and consider his future. Maybe she's more mature than I am, Harry wondered, or maybe she cares more for me than I care for myself?

Lucy wanted to find a way out of her existing relationship but didn't want to confront Arthur, or her parents – and she didn't want Arthur's parents to be disappointed in her. Until Harry knows what he wants and how he is going to achieve it, I'm not putting myself through any more pain. I should have listened to Mr White T-Shirt Man's warning years ago about Arthur, she thought.

One weekend before Easter, Harry went and bought Bridget a kitten. Bridget loved 'moggies', as she called them, and immediately fell in love with 'Frecks'.

They sat on the lounge as Bridget cooed at Frecks. 'Are you giving me something to love when you aren't here anymore Harry?' she asked, looking closely at Harry.

Bridget's comment stung and hurt Harry because they were partly true. Harry felt responsible for Bridget because he had taken her away from Rasp, her family and friends.

36

The protection racket exposed

April 1982

'Why don't we go to Rasp for Easter?' Harry asked Brandon and Lucy. 'You can meet my friends – we'll go and stay at a property north of Rasp that I know, and spend the weekend riding bikes and exploring. You'll love it.'

Harry was still seeing Bridget and staying with her some week-nights and weekends, and in his confused mind still had a relationship and was engaged, but the relationship was gradually breaking down as Easter approached. Harry wasn't sure that Bridget loved him as much as she used to, and he couldn't blame her. He was heartbroken, but couldn't bring himself to repair the rift, because he knew it would never work for him in the future. He would have to leave the bank and a career he loved, get an ordinary job and be an ordinary person.

Harry had made love to Lucy a number of times following their first encounter and the more he got to know her the more he liked her and wanted to be with her. He was still travelling back and forth to Gidgee to see Bridget and to maintain their relationship, but more often he was staying in Little Creek and having fun with Lucy. Lucy would come to his flat and they would make love after work, and Harry knew that if he let go of Bridget, he would allow himself to admit that he loved Lucy.

Harry knew that Bridget would want to go to Rasp for Easter as well. Bridget would want to stay with her mother while they all 'went bush'. She was just happy to spend time with her mother and no doubt talk about Harry. Harry would drop her off when they arrived in Rasp and pick her up on the way out of Rasp on Monday afternoon. It would be difficult with two women he cared for in the car together, but everyone was keen to go.

It was Thursday afternoon when they all met up in Little Creek. Bridget had driven over in her car. Harry had arranged a loan for Bridget and found a car for her to buy. Bridget had also started night school and needed to get around Gidgee when he wasn't there. Harry knew that Bridget would think of the car as something to give her greater independence, making her less reliant on him – and making his exit easier.

Lucy would often drive Harry's HJ while he stayed in Little Creek, and the week before they left for Rasp, she gave it a good clean while Harry tinkered with his bike nearby. 'Harry, why have you got my dad's name on your key ring?' asked Lucy.

'What do you mean Luce?'

'I was just wiping the dash and I looked at your keys and it says "Mick" on the leather key tag,' she replied.

'I don't think it refers to your father – it's been there for as long as I can remember. I think I carved it there one night when I was drunk, because I can't remember doing it or why.'

'Oh, just thought I would ask,' said Lucy. Both were oblivious to Harry's intention when he carved Mick's name on the tag two years earlier: to save Lucy grief, and Mick his arm.

Lucy had already been to Rasp, knew that it was a very long trip, and was worried about being couped up with Bridget and Harry together for so long. Brandon was taking his girlfriend Beth Ridge; they would be in the rear seat with Lucy while Harry drove and Bridget sat in the front passenger seat.

They were also towing a trailer with Harry and Brandon's bike strapped in. It was the first time Lucy and Brandon had met Bridget. Brandon suspected that Harry and Lucy were an item, even though they were both careful about when Lucy would visit and how much time they spent together, but he said nothing to Lucy or Harry about it. Harry guessed Brandon knew they enjoyed a relationship, but took it for granted that he wouldn't talk about it to anyone.

Bridget was a mature, beautiful woman and Lucy could see why Harry was attracted to her. They had little in common, and there was limited conversation between them on the journey, but Lucy treated Bridget as she would any friend of Harry's, with courtesy and friendliness. Lucy underestimated Bridget's beauty and wit and wondered why Harry was interested in her. It scared Lucy somewhat. What if he chooses to stay with Bridget, she thought – but she remembered how unhappy Harry had been, and this placated her.

Harry had told Steve and Max that he was bringing some friends with him, along with two bikes, and that he would arrive very late on Thursday night. They were to meet at Harry's parents' house early Friday to go to Windy Creek station.

Harry was so excited to be going home and said that even if he got in late on Thursday, he would be ready early Friday. 'So be ready to go then,' he told the boys. The plan was to meet Harry's brother Ryan at the station.

Max and Steve arrived early on Good Friday to Harry's parents' home, with their car loaded with supplies and a trailer with their bikes and riding gear packed ready to go. Max sauntered in and greeted Harry's mum: 'Hello Mrs B, long time no see,' and embraced Harry as he appeared from his old bedroom. Lucy and Beth had stayed in the guest room together, Harry in his old room and Brandon in Ryan's old room. 'Bloody Hell mate, good to see you,' Max said to Harry and Steve chimed in shaking Harry's hand, as Harry introduced Brandon to the boys.

'Where are your other friends?' asked Max.

'In the shower mate, they'll be out soon. Come on Stevie, let's look at the trailers,' he said as they went out the door with Brandon to make sure everything on their trailer was secure after a long trip the previous night.

Max stayed talking with Harry's mum as two young women emerged. Max was initially surprised to see the two young women. When Harry had said 'friends', Max assumed they were guys, but he had been talking to Mrs Barnes and hadn't really taken any notice, until she introduced him to Lucy and Beth.

Max was lost for words as Mrs Barnes told Max, 'This is Lucy.' There was an instant icy stare from Lucy towards Max. Lucy remembered Max from three years ago in an instant – and Max recalled the tall girl with long dark hair who had visited and asked him about the Monaro.

Max stumbled, 'Hi Lucy, nice to meet you,' hoping she wouldn't recall their meeting in 1979. But Lucy did remember Max and quickly started to put two and two together. Bloody hell, thought Lucy, when I found Max, I did find Harry's Monaro – it was just in Max's name! I waited three years for Harry to turn up at Little Creek, and if Max had been honest with me in 1979, I would have found him then.

'Hi,' frowned Lucy. Max had so many thoughts running through his head and was trying to comprehend how this girl was standing in front of him. He wanted to run out and grab Harry, but knew it would be pointless. Harry couldn't even remember asking him to transfer the car into his name, let alone why. Fuck, he thought, I've been caught red-handed. Max couldn't wait to get out of the house to the safety of Steve and let him know what had just happened. She hasn't said anything yet – maybe she has forgotten about it, he thought.

'Hi Beth, nice to meet you too,' continued a still-stumbling Max. 'Do you work with Harry?'

'Hi. No, I'm Brandon's girlfriend – Brandon and Lucy work with Harry.'

'Oh, I see, Harry just told me some of his friends from work were coming with him. You'll have a great time out bush; I better go and talk to the boys and get ready,' said Max as he escaped to the safety of the backyard with the other boys.

'Fuck Steve, we've got to get out of here,' said Max quietly so Harry couldn't hear. 'Harry, we'll go and fuel up. Meet you on the edge of town in, say, 15 minutes, okay?'

As they got in the car, Steve questioned Max. 'Heady, what's going on? I hardly had time to talk with Flash. Are you alright?'

'Harry's brought Brandon and two girls with him and one of the girls, Lucy, is the one who came and saw me about Harry's car back in July '79,' explained Max.

'Are you sure?' asked Steve.

'Mate it's her alright. I clearly remember that day because it put the wind up me when she turned up at my place – and now she's here! What do we do?' said Max excitedly.

'Fuck, did she say anything?' asked Steve.

'No, but I could see from her look that she recognised me. I could say "I'm crook and you could go by yourself", and that way I can avoid her and she doesn't know that you know anything, so you would be safe from questioning,' reasoned Max.

'You're not thinking straight, Heady. We could just be honest with her and then we can find out why Harry was agitated about her finding him. We'll know more than Harry because he's clueless about all this; he can't remember if he was Arthur or Martha during that time. He won't even know that you and Lucy have met before if neither we, nor Lucy, tell him.'

'Good point. I was just doing what Harry asked; I didn't set out to deceive her,' Max said with conviction.

Windy Gap was around 240 kilometres north of Rasp. It was a large sheep station owned by friends of Harry's father. The country was dry and stoney, thought Lucy as they travelled north. It was nothing like her father's farm at Little Creek. The country didn't support cropping, only sheep – and in the better seasons, cattle. The bush track from the main road into the homestead was around 20 kilometres in itself and Lucy was awed by the distances and sheer size of the property.

They were all to stay in the shearer's quarters, used at shearing and crutching time each year and then left unoccupied. There was no hot running water and limited electricity. There were eight rooms in a rectangular iron-clad building, four rooms back-to-back, a kitchen and separate shower block. The shower block was fed by water from a nearby earthen dam and was not filtered in any way. To get hot water, a fire was lit under a large drum laid on its side on a stand. Water would pass through the drum and become warm to shower in.

The water made Beth and Lucy's hair frizzy, which the boys laughed about. It was all very basic, but so quiet, the sky festooned with stars as far as you could see. Harry took Lucy up to the top of a nearby hill and they sat and watched a full moon rise. It was spectacular and Lucy loved the whole experience, especially being alone with Harry. Lucy thought it was the biggest and brightest moon she had ever seen and felt she could reach out and touch it if she wanted.

Max was careful to avoid being alone with Lucy when they arrived at Windy Gap. But later, as they sat around the campfire, Max found himself alone with her when Harry and Steve went to tinker with Harry's new bike.

'So Max, do you run a protection racket for Harry all the time – or only when women come looking for him?' asked Lucy pointedly. 'You told me that the Monaro I was looking for was yours when I asked you about it; do you want to come clean?'

Max had readied himself for such an inquisition and agreed with Steve: the best form of defence would be the truth. 'Harry asked me to do what I did,' responded Max.

'What, lie to me and cause me to waste two years of my life? You don't understand how what you did affected me; I desperately wanted to find him when I came to your place,' pleaded Lucy.

'I didn't set out to deceive you; Harry wasn't Harry at the time and Stevie and I just wanted to protect him. We thought he was going cuckoo from about September 1978 until January 1979. He was telling us about the future, and we didn't know if he was well or not. Then he came around to my place one day in December 1978 and asked me to transfer the Monaro into his name because he thought a girl would come looking for him and he didn't want her to find him.

'That's all Steve and I know, apart from the fact that after January 1979, he was totally clueless about everything that had happened and everything he did from September 1978 until the end of January 1979.'

Lucy calmed down as she took in what Max had just said. That explains so much, she thought. It explains why he didn't recognise me when he came to Little Creek. As Alice had said, 'Maybe he doesn't remember the grid meeting; maybe he doesn't remember what he said to you.' It explains everything about his behaviour. Shit, I can't wait to talk to Alice about this, she thought.

Max went on to tell Lucy all about Harry's motorbike crash in early September 1978 and what happened when he recovered. 'We don't know everything he did when he could see the future, because he wouldn't tell me and Steve about it all, and now even he doesn't know what he did. But you know, Lucy, everything he did tell us has come true. He even told Stevie that he would marry a girl called Sandra, when Stevie was already going out with a girl called Debbie. Stevie said at the time he was talking shit. Well, guess what? Two years later, about three months ago, Stevie started going out with a girl called Sandra.'

Lucy could hardly believe what she was hearing because her experience with Harry was similar. Everything he had said so far had come true, yet he didn't seem to know anything about that period in his life – including the grid meeting, which she went on to tell Max about.

'Fuck, so he drove all the way to your home town, told you that he was going to marry you, then three years later he turns up and doesn't remember you?' repeated Max. 'That must have been tough on you.'

Lucy nodded. 'But Max, why do you think he didn't want me to find him?' asked Lucy.

'I'm not sure, he didn't tell me why, he just didn't want you to find him, is what he said.'

'But Max,' Lucy persisted, 'now that you know the full story, why do *you* think he didn't want to be found?'

'I got the impression he didn't want to tell us everything he saw in his visions – that he wanted to protect us in some way and maybe that's what he was doing with you. He did only just start going out with

Bridget around that time and maybe he wanted to protect her. I'm not sure about his motives … But what about you and Harry and Bridget now – what's the go?' questioned Max, somewhat insensitively.

'He doesn't tell me everything, but we are kind of having a relationship. He's been down on himself ever since he left Rosella Bay to come to Little Creek and I just want to be there for him. He's told me he's been lonely and he's been emotional. It would be good if you and Steve could cheer him up, but until he decides about Bridget, I think he'll be down in the dumps,' explained Lucy.

'Harry down in the dumps?' Max asked. 'Really?'

'Bridget walked out on him in Rosella Bay and I don't think he's been the same Harry since,' advised Lucy.

'Shit, he didn't tell Stevie or me about that. So all this time he's been keeping that to himself?' Harry hadn't told anyone about Bridget leaving him in Rosella Bay. He had been embarrassed and hurt and couldn't bring himself to share the incident with anyone.

That night, Harry went to Lucy's room and made love to her as she held him closer than she ever had before. She wondered what Harry had been going through since September 1978 and wanted to sympathise with him – not with words, but with love. Lucy reasoned that Max may be right. Maybe Harry wanted to confirm his future but didn't want others to know much about their future, which could cause them angst. Pity he told *me* so much, thought Lucy, but I think he sought me out to find out if he was right about his dreams.

They rode bikes all day and drank too much at night around the campfire, and Lucy elicited everything she could from Max and Stevie about Harry. The three of them laughed out loud when Stevie told the story of how Harry had predicted the winner of the Melbourne Cup, then laughed again when Stevie said Harry then convinced them to buy Berkshire Hathaway shares, which were still at about the same price as when they bought them.

At Lucy's expense, Max animatedly recounted how this long-legged, dark-haired girl walked up his drive and asked him bluntly, 'Do you own a HK Monaro?' Brandon and Beth weren't privy to the conversations, as they only knew Harry as just plain Harry, and weren't aware of the extraordinary happenings that had engulfed Harry and Lucy over the past few years.

Lucy was so pleased to have found Max and Steve and have these conversations, which set her mind at ease. She couldn't wait to get home and tell Alice. She was determined that when she got home, she would break her relationship with Arthur and devote herself to Harry – after all, he was going to marry her. But when would he make up his mind about Bridget, she wondered.

It was a long trip home via Rasp to Little Creek. Three hours' drive to Rasp then a further eight hours to Little Creek, punctuated by a short stop at Harry's parents' home and to pick up Bridget.

Yet Lucy was energised by the weekend. It had been hot and dusty, but the scenery was spectacular and she had seen Harry in his element. He was a different person in the bush, she thought – or was that the old Harry re-emerging? They had ridden hundreds of kilometres together in a group and Harry was the ring-leader, riding way too fast, thought Lucy as she clutched Harry around the waist, watching Ryan and Max up on one wheel skylarking.

Lucy and Harry, it seemed, had forgotten about all their problems and were having fun. Lucy knew that Max and Steve wondered about their relationship, but she didn't care. The three of them were privy to a much larger secret about Harry, and she knew that they were aligned with her in that respect. They all wanted Harry to get well and remember what he had done and said when he had been able to see the future.

37

Broken

April 1982

The week following the trip to Rasp was eventful for Harry and Lucy.

Lucy received a cold response when she got home. Her parents hadn't been keen for her to go away with Harry, but she had insisted. Lucy was 18 and thought she had the right to make up her own mind, but that didn't deter Mick and Mavis from expressing their feelings. Mick had dance plans for that Easter, and Lucy being away took some pleasure away from him. Mick was also disappointed Lucy didn't see Arthur, and knew that Arthur was very concerned that Lucy was away.

Lucy was uncomfortable at dinner on Tuesday night after arriving home late the previous night. 'Arthur asked after you at the dance,' remarked Mick knowingly. 'Did you tell him you were going away?'

'Yes,' replied Lucy. In fact, she hadn't told Arthur the full story – about who was going and where they would be staying. 'He said that you told him you were going away with Beth,' questioned Mick.

'Yes, I did Dad,' replied Lucy.

'Did you tell him about the boys going as well?'

'No, I didn't Dad, because I didn't want him to be querying what I am doing. I don't need him second-guessing what I am doing. It's none of his business.'

'I thought you were keen on Arthur – we like him,' said Mavis. Lucy was always respectful and loving towards her parents but was seething that they were questioning her choices that didn't favour Arthur. Mick and Mavis weren't aware that when Arthur was last at the farm, he had slapped her across the face when they were down near the creek, out of sight of everyone.

Arthur was conscious that he was losing Lucy and losing control of her. A one-sided argument had started about why they were seeing each other less and Lucy wasn't keen to provide him with answers or argue back, and he had become angry that she wouldn't respond or concede. Afterwards, Lucy went to her room in the homestead and he didn't follow her. She wanted to be honest with her parents and ask for their help, but it seemed to her they were simply pushing in the direction they favoured.

Lucy had been on top of the world when she arrived home from Rasp; she felt she knew where her life was heading. But in an instant, her feelings were crushed. At that moment she wanted her parents to love her and trust her unconditionally, but she felt abandoned by the two people she loved very much.

She retreated. 'I might go to bed Mum, I'm really tired,' said Lucy, and left the table as she became emotional.

Lucy wasn't at home when Harry drove to her farm the next day. She was keen to tell Alice all she had learned when she met Harry's mates, and told Harry she was going to visit Alice after work, but he said he would go to the farm anyway because he wanted to clean his bike and then give it a 'run'. There was no one to be seen when he arrived at Little Creek South; he figured Mick and Mavis were in the paddocks working. He cleaned the IT then started it as Mick and Mavis arrived back at the homestead.

He waved to them both as a courtesy. He sat on the bike while it was idling and was starting to put his helmet on as Mick approached.

'G'day Mick,' ventured Harry as he got close, but Harry was taken aback as Mick spoke to him.

'I don't think you should leave your bike out here anymore, and I don't want you on my property,' Mick declared.

Harry didn't know how to respond. He was trying to rationalise his feelings and understand why Mick was being so cruel to him – but he soon had the answers. 'You've been rooting every girl you can find; everyone in town is talking about you and I don't want you here,' said Mick, as Harry considered what he should say to defend himself.

But he couldn't defend himself. He wasn't about to argue with Mick about his life. He didn't have to tell Mick he was a young guy who had made mistakes and was lonely and searching for a way forward. He didn't want to tell Mick he loved his daughter and would be a better person in the future.

'Mick, you can kick me off your property, but you can't stop me seeing your daughter,' replied Harry with sincerity.

Harry rode away without looking back. He was astounded that Mick would talk to him like that. Mick considered himself a Christian man, but in the eyes of Harry, not on this day. Harry knew that he was a threat to what Mick and Mavis wanted for their daughter, but he wasn't going to concede unless Lucy told him she didn't want to see him again. He decided that Lucy would not want to see or know about that side of her father and kept the conversation with Mick to himself.

Conversation at work on Friday was muted. Lucy was still upset with her parents; Harry was chastened by Mick's nasty approach to him and Brandon was still recovering from lack of sleep and all the alcohol he consumed at Windy Gap the previous weekend. There was no visit to the club or drinks on this Friday night.

Harry was going to Gidgee to visit Bridget, and Lucy decided she would stay home and mend bridges with her parents – maybe she would tell them what she wanted in life, she thought.

When Lucy arrived home from work, Arthur was waiting for her, sitting in the kitchen having a drink with Mick and Mavis. Lucy had recognised his car as she came down the drive and wanted to turn around and go to the safety of Harry, but she couldn't, because he was already on his way to Gidgee and wouldn't be back until Sunday.

Lucy was patient with Harry and understood his reasons for continuing to visit Bridget. She understood that Harry felt responsible for Bridget and didn't want to abandon her. Even though his behaviour had been unpredictable and complicated, Lucy knew he was a good man who had made mistakes. In the near future he would put his life in order – and she hoped to be a part of that.

'Hi Lucy,' said Arthur cheerfully. 'I hope you had a good weekend. We missed you at the dance, didn't we Mick?' Mick nodded as he sipped his glass of brown muscat, something he enjoyed once a week, usually on Friday. Mavis hardly touched alcohol but had a glass of muscat in front of her as well.

Here we go, thought Lucy sarcastically, a nice Friday night together with loved ones. But something was amiss – she sensed a formality in the air. She was annoyed that she had been short with her mother and father on Tuesday and wanted to make amends, but here she was again in a situation where it was her alone against the will of her parents and Arthur.

Yet before Lucy had a chance to compose herself, Arthur spoke. 'Your father and I had a chat tonight, Lucy, and he gave his consent to us being married, and I would like you to say yes.'

Lucy was all at once pressured to do something she didn't want to do. She felt betrayed by her parents and coerced by Arthur. She had been so happy last weekend, and thought she had her life mapped out. Harry had not yet committed to her, but she believed he would, and that would make her so happy. She had made love to Harry because she loved him and she believed that what he said would come true.

She didn't care about her relationship with Arthur, which made her decision to be with Harry a simple one. If Harry didn't commit to her, she had emboldened herself and taken what part of Harry she could get. Surely this is not how couples commit to each other, she thought, as she took in the kitchen. Surely there is an understanding between couples about such a commitment. Lucy had never told Arthur she loved him, and because he had abused her, she never would, she had decided.

Lucy was speechless as her father went to her and offered his congratulations. Mavis took a bottle of pre-organised chilled champagne from the refrigerator as Arthur took her hand and offered a ring. Lucy cried again for the second time this week. Her tears were mistaken by all in the room. Only Lucy knew why she was crying.

The remainder of the weekend was a blur for Lucy. On Saturday morning, the couple visited Arthur's parents and family to give them the good news and Lucy was captured. She couldn't escape and yell to anyone, 'This is not what I want!' Everyone was happy, apart from her. It was a charade she couldn't control. This wasn't what Mr White T-Shirt Man had predicted. I am supposed to be happy, thought Lucy. I should have stayed away from Arthur as Harry had warned.

38

Just because you can't be with someone doesn't mean you don't love them

April 1982

Bridget was in the shower when Harry arrived on Friday night following their trip to Rasp. His visits to Gidgee were less frequent now, but he couldn't bring himself to hurt Bridget and end the relationship. He still cared for her very much and loved her – but wasn't *in love* with her, he thought.

He knocked at the bathroom door and she said, 'I hope that's you Harry, come in.' Harry went in and watched and talked as she showered. She is beautiful thought Harry, and she knows how I think, and we get on so well – how did we get to where we are?

Harry knew how they got there, but in his mind, he refused to apportion any blame to Bridget. The trip to Rasp had helped Harry come to terms with himself. He was contrite about his relationships with Becky and Eve and ashamed of his conduct and the way he had treated Bridget. Harry had allowed their relationship to collapse and disintegrate because he had been hurt. But more than that, he was thinking of his future, not their future. His banking career would be in tatters if he didn't agree to transfers, which trigger promotions, and he was falling in love with Lucy.

Bridget talked about her work and the university course she was doing. Harry continued to watch her as she washed her hair and soap suds slid down her back and over her body. He didn't have sexual thoughts; he was just reminding himself of how pretty she was to him and how kind she had been to him.

He had made love to Bridget last week when he visited and stayed the night. She had given herself to him and he enjoyed their time together, but he felt guilty about it. He felt he was stealing from her, and he felt that he was betraying Lucy, who he was in love with. Tonight, though, he felt like he was doing a welfare check on Bridget – and reprimanded himself for thinking that way. He knew Bridget was a capable woman and didn't need him as a monitor.

Harry followed Bridget into the bedroom. She sat on the bed leaning forward, her hair cascading in front of her while she massaged it with a towel. She still had no clothes on; Harry had seen her naked thousands of times and she wasn't shy in front of him. Bridget stopped what she was doing, put the towel on her lap and looked up at Harry, holding his gaze with a sad face. Bridget always had a cheerful disposition unless something was wrong. She recognised they were growing apart, but still welcomed Harry into her heart.

She has been so strong, thought Harry. 'Harry … I made love to someone else,' said Bridget, without removing her gaze from him. A lump formed in Harry's throat as he felt tears streaming down his face. Bridget continued, 'You haven't been here and I want company, and I need to get on with my life.'

Harry continued to stand in front of Bridget, but now looked at the floor as his tears dripped down onto the carpet. 'I'm so sorry Harry.' Harry understood her reasons and didn't say a word as he turned to leave the room. 'I do love you Harry, please don't leave like this,' were the last words he heard as he went down the stairs and outside towards the HJ.

Bridget had done what Harry didn't have the courage to do. With those few words, she had ended their four-year relationship.

Harry was truly heartbroken, but didn't say, 'I understand why Bridge, but we can get over that.' He knew that Bridget was doing what she had always done for him. She was being honest, kind and caring, and helping him get on with his life.

That night was difficult for Harry. He didn't sleep and was in a dark place and wondered if he was depressed. He incoherently blamed his parents and friends for not being there to help him, and wondered if anybody cared for him. Sometimes nights are very dark and you don't know if the morning will come, thought Harry. You hope for the light and a new day, but wonder if it will bring better things.

Harry stopped on the way home to Little Creek and cried loudly in the dark on the side of the road where no one could hear or see him. Bridget was right again, he thought, in a moment of clarity. This will be good for both of us.

Harry never went back to Gidgee. He left his home and all his possessions with Bridget – a way of saying sorry, he thought. He hoped she would keep their engagement ring and remember him, but he never found out if that happened.

39

It's a charade

April 1982

Mavis and Mick were keen to let their friends know the good news. Kev McKay learned the news before Monday and was ready to act. Harry was usually the first to work each day and was well into his routine when the others started arriving. He couldn't wait to see Lucy and feel loved. She is so kind and will understand what I am going through, he thought. He had come back to Little Creek late on Friday after his gut-wrenching night with Bridget. He was thankful that Brandon was staying with Beth, leaving him alone in the flat with his feelings all weekend.

His bike was now at the flat and he had taken a long ride all day Saturday. He stopped in the sandhills and again cried about Bridget, but knew she was doing the right thing for himself and for her, and he admired her courage in being honest with him. He wasn't angry, he was sad and dismayed. He had been the contributing factor and hoped that Bridget would now be happy and able to move on with her life.

Harry didn't want to see Lucy at that moment, but was hoping that when he saw her on Monday, she would fuss over him as she usually did and help him piece his life back together. He decided that now he wasn't with Bridget, he could be fair with her and build their relationship properly and tell her he loved her.

Brandon arrived, then Lucy and Kev came in together and went into Kev's office. I just want to talk to her, thought Harry as she emerged from Kev's office. Lucy looked at the floor while Harry tried to catch her eye. He wondered what was going on.

'Harry, Brandon. I want to make an announcement,' said Kev theatrically. 'I am happy to announce that Lucy is engaged to be married! She got engaged on Friday and I think we should celebrate with a cake and a cup of tea. Show them your ring Lucy,' encouraged Kev.

Harry remained seated as a myriad of thoughts flashed through his head. Lucy walked towards him with her hand outstretched. Harry searched for eye contact but it seemed Lucy was avoiding him; she didn't seem at all happy. It seemed to Harry that she wasn't ecstatic or proud of her engagement as a bride-to-be should. Was there something Lucy was hiding, he thought, as he maintained some sensibility and offered his congratulations, all while hiding his confusion and unwillingness to accept what he had just been told.

Harry tried to talk to Lucy during the day, but she remained aloof. 'Luce, can we talk so I know what's going on?' asked Harry when Brandon and Kev were at lunch.

'I can't Harry, or I'll cry. It seems you have your life and now I have mine,' replied Lucy as she turned away. Harry was shocked by what Lucy had said and worried that Lucy had decided she didn't want to be with him.

Lucy went home early after speaking with Kev. After work, Harry decided he couldn't go to her farm because of his altercation with Mick, but desperately wanted to see her. At his wits end, he went to see Alice.

'Alice, what the fuck is going on?' asked Harry. Alice knew what Harry was talking about.

'You understand it as much as I do Harry,' replied Alice. 'She came here crying but couldn't get any words out. She's a wreck. She just sobbed and sobbed without saying anything, so I took her to the doctors. She wouldn't stop crying.'

'You know she got engaged to Arthur, don't you?' asked Harry. 'Yeah, she got engaged to the prick who abused her. He hit her Harry, and demeans her. She told me. But please don't go looking for her. Leave her at the doctor's office.'

40

Lucy lost

April 1982

Dr Greene recognised that Lucy was suffering from anxiety. He was a small-town regional doctor who knew all the families in the district, and thought his wife may be able to help. He figured that she would be able to unlock Lucy's concerns and worries without him sedating her, which is what he told Mavis when he rang her.

'Mavis, I just want you to know that Lucy is resting at my home with Cheryl. She left work at lunch time and Alice brought her here because she was very emotional and wouldn't stop crying. At the moment she is very fragile, but we will look after her and I think she will be fine. I'll talk to you before Cheryl and I bring her home.'

Cheryl was a mature, worldly woman, raised on a farm near Little Creek. Her marriage to Dr Greene was her second. Her previous marriage was to a local farmer and she understood the pressures that young women in the country face.

Cheryl sat with Lucy and held her hand. She had known Lucy for years but had never seen her in such a state and was worried. Lucy had stopped crying and was drinking tea with her. 'Would you like to talk to me Lucy? Whatever we say to each other will go no further than these walls. I am not going to judge you; I just want to help.'

To start the conversation, Cheryl talked about Lucy's engagement. Little Creek was a small town and Cheryl had heard about Lucy's dalliance with young Harry and also about Lucy's engagement to someone else. 'I understand you got engaged a few days ago. How do you feel about that?'

Lucy erupted, talking and crying all at once. 'I didn't want that to happen. I'm just stupid, I couldn't say no!'

Cheryl hugged Lucy. 'No one can make you do anything you don't want to Lucy. I know it may feel like people can make you do things you don't want to and sometimes it's easier to travel the path of least resistance, but sometimes the hardest walk is the walk that will make you feel stronger and better. Do you want to be engaged?' asked Cheryl.

'No!' bawled Lucy. 'I just want Harry, and now he'll think I'm stupid, and will never love me.'

Dr Greene and Cheryl took Lucy home later that evening and chatted to Mick and Mavis about Lucy and how emotional she had been, but Cheryl didn't divulge her discussion with Lucy as promised. She simply encouraged them to talk to Lucy about what she wanted in life and to trust and support her.

'I gave her a light sedative. Perhaps she shouldn't go to work tomorrow – I'll call Kev and explain, and maybe you three could take the time to have a chat together tomorrow,' advised Dr Greene.

Lucy didn't go to work on Tuesday and the branch wasn't the same. Kev had a conversation with Mavis and told her that Lucy could take as much time off as she needed. Brandon was aware of a simmering relationship between Harry and Lucy and thought the whole engagement thing had brought things to a head. Little Creek was a small town and nothing went unnoticed. Harry was quiet and only spoke when he needed to, but wondered about Lucy all day. I've been an idiot, thought Harry. Right in front of me is the person I've really needed and now I might have lost her.

There was a quiet knock on the door of the flat just after Harry got home from work on Tuesday evening. Harry looked out the window, saw Lucy and rushed to the door.

'Hi Luce!' said Harry. 'Are you okay?'

'I didn't know if you would be here, but I saw your car and wanted to talk.'

Harry thought this was a bold statement coming from a usually reserved Lucy.

'Yeah, I'm here and will always be here from now on,' replied Harry. He would tell Lucy about his estrangement from Bridget when he thought the time was right, but at the moment he was focused on Lucy. 'Why, Lucy?' asked Harry as he hugged her to his chest, 'I thought we were going good together.'

'We are going great, I just stuffed up,' Lucy replied. 'I didn't tell my parents about my feelings and I didn't stick up for myself, but I'll fix it, starting tonight.' Harry didn't tell Lucy about Bridget but he did give her a very important message.

'I love you Luce.' Lucy cried again, but told Harry she loved him too.

41

Lucy takes control

April 1982

'Mum, I'm not ready to get engaged,' said Lucy as they were washing up together that evening.

'What do you mean dearie?' asked Mavis.

'I mean exactly what I said, Mum – or maybe not exactly that. I should have said I don't want to be engaged to Arthur. There is so much I could tell you Mum, but I'm trying to protect you.'

Mavis stopped washing and looked at her youngest daughter. 'We only want what's best for you Lucy.'

'I know you do Mum, but you need to let me make my own decisions, and then if I make a mistake, you can help me. You should let me try to walk by myself and be there to catch me when I fall, just like when I was a baby. I'm not a baby anymore Mum, and yesterday showed me I shouldn't be pushed into anything I don't want to do.'

'Well, I don't understand Lucy,' replied Mavis, shaking her head.

Arthur arrived the next evening when Lucy and her parents were feeding the pigs. He had phoned the house the previous night, because he hadn't heard from Lucy for a few days. Mavis told him she was unwell and couldn't come to the phone.

Arthur walked into the shed as the family were finishing feeding the pigs and immediately went to Lucy as she poured her last bucket of grain into a trough. She kept her head down as he tried to kiss her on the side of her forehead.

'Are you okay Lucy?' he asked.

'Yep, I'm fine,' she replied curtly.

'Let's go up to the house and have a cuppa,' urged Mick.

'What was the problem then Lucy?' queried Arthur as the four of them walked. Lucy felt as if she was being interrogated, but quietly said, 'I'm not ready to be engaged Arthur.'

'I don't understand what she wants,' chimed in Mavis.

Lucy turned and walked quickly backwards so she was in front of and facing all three of them. She thought she could have been nasty, but reverted to type. 'I'm sorry Arthur, I don't want to be engaged to you,' she said loudly as she fished in her jeans pocket, reached out and handed the engagement ring back to him, then turned and started running towards the house.

Arthur lengthened his stride and started to follow her until Mick spoke. Mick was a man of few words and a deep thinker. When Janice had left home, he blamed himself for not being a better parent, and being closer to his eldest daughter. Now he was being tested again, and this time he would not fail his youngest daughter. The girl that had provided much pleasure to him throughout her life by being there for him, and by being a friend as well as a daughter. He had seen how distraught Lucy was a few nights ago and he didn't want to see her like that again.

'I think you better leave Arthur,' he said sternly.

42

Is it love?

May 1982

Harry introduced Lucy to his extended family in May 1982 at a reunion, and they officially became a couple. Late in 1982, they went to Steve and Sandra's wedding. Max was there with Emma Forrest, who later became his wife.

It was great fun for Steve, Max and Lucy to again talk about that special summer of 1978. Everything Harry said during that time came true, but Stevie rued lost chances. He would offer 'what ifs' all the time because he could hardly believe what had happened.

'We could have made a lot of money,' he would say. 'Imagine if his visions lasted longer and he told us more.'

'Don't wish that on me,' would be Lucy's typical response. 'I wouldn't have been able to handle it.'

The legacy from that time were the Berkshire Hathaway shares. Steve and Harry had bought 12 shares each for $2200, and Max six shares for $1100. Four years later, the shares were worth around $6000 and $3000 respectively, but Steve was adamant that there was no way he was going to sell until at least 2015 when 'Vision Harry' had said they could be worth around $3,000,000.

Lucy laughed at Steve. 'That's 33 years away Stevie, do you trust vision Harry that much?'

Harry was laconic about the discussions between Lucy and his mates. He wasn't able to recall that time when he had been extraordinary, and more importantly what he had done over that summer, but Lucy told him he had 'done good' and played it right, as far as she understood his actions and what he had done. The only loser, she thought, was probably Harry. If he just lost his ability to see the future, but kept his memory of that time, he wouldn't have hurt himself, and some others that mattered to him. She was sad for Harry that he couldn't remember and often coaxed him to try to recall what had happened.

'Well Luce, I was in about fourth gear and I had it "pinned"; I was really motoring,' cajoled Harry. 'I remember it promised to be a great weekend and I was feeling good. I had a Monaro, a fast bike, a cool chick, and I didn't have a worry in the world. I reckon if I faced that bend and gutter again, I could take them.' He was taking the mickey out of Lucy and she knew it. 'But that's all I remember,' he smiled at Lucy.

'Sometimes I hate you, Harry Barnes. You know all that stuff you went through; I think that if you remembered what you had seen, you may have been able to avoid a lot of your problems and life would have been simpler for you,' advised Lucy.

'Alternatively, at least I can remember the past four years, imagine if I get another bump on the head and forget all that ... forget those beautiful girls,' continued Harry, smiling.

'I do hate you, you know that, Harry? That's one of the things I said to you as you drove away from the grid that day, and I was right!'

Harry built a life in Little Creek and fitted into Lucy's lifestyle well. He would travel with her to her netball games and cheer her on from the sideline. She would cook for him after work and make sure he had neatly pressed clothes. He would take her away for weekends in the HJ and she would drive it far too fast and they would make love every chance they got. Lucy was beautiful and Harry treated her like a princess and in 1983 they were married. Harry was due for a transfer and Lucy told him she would go anywhere with him, but he had learned his lesson. 'I don't want to live with you. I want you to marry me because I want to commit to our relationship.'

(43)

Bill, much later

March 1998

Bill did meet Harry again, in 1998 at the Rasp Golf Club. Harry and his family had come to Rasp for a holiday to visit his parents and Harry and Max played golf on a Saturday. Even though Harry was 20 years older, Bill recognised him and rushed over to greet him.

'Harry, I've been waiting years to see you again!' he announced in front of Max. Harry didn't recognise Bill and tried to hide the fact he couldn't remember him. Harry dealt with a lot of people; often he would have people recognise him and he couldn't remember their names. Lucy loved watching him dig a hole for himself, and would later laugh and say to Harry, 'You didn't have a clue who that was, did you?'

Harry would chide Lucy for not helping him out and for laughing at his predicament. Max stepped in and said, 'Harry, you remember Bill don't you? I'm sure you two played a round sometime when you lived here?' Harry lied and said, 'Of course Bill, how are you?' Max and Harry didn't have anywhere to be and stayed drinking at the club until closing.

Harry confided in Max, 'Mate, I don't know Bill.' Max garnered Bill's attention from across the table, 'When did you last see Harry, Bill?' Without hesitation Bill replied, 'December 1978. We played golf and went to lunch.'

Max took Harry aside and told him, 'I know why you don't remember Bill, it was the summer of 1978.' Max, Steve and Lucy had told Harry about those hot summer months, which were still a mystery to him. Who he had spoken to and what he had said remained a riddle to Harry, apart from what those three had told him.

More than anything, Bill was happy to be reunited with Harry. Bill had played golf often with Max, but the thought that they had a common acquaintance never crossed their mind. Bill had conceded to himself years earlier that Harry was telling the truth, and it forever haunted him that he hadn't taken more interest in Harry's plight. Arwon had won, the share market had behaved the way Harry had forecast, Berkshire shares had gone through the roof, and Bill's family would be financially comfortable for the rest of their lives. But Bill was a man of few words, and that night when they were talking all he said to Harry about the past was, 'Buddy, you know how many holes in one I have had don't you? I've had five. You told me 20 years ago that the next time you see me I would forever nag you about my five holes in one and I will,' said Bill.

Bill didn't tell Harry about how he'd followed the market for years after their initial meeting or that he had invested in Berkshire shares. He just wanted to be mates with Harry, which he hoped would make up for the lack of help he offered Harry when he was young and alone.

Harry visited Bill often, but he never told Bill that he couldn't recall their original meeting. He didn't know how he had helped Bill, or if Bill had helped him, but they spoke regularly and enjoyed a very close friendship, which lasted until Bill passed away in 2016. Harry and Lucy flew to Adelaide where Bill was in hospital. Bill told Harry that the doctors advised they couldn't do any more for him.

Harry spoke at Bill's funeral and although everyone knew, he told them once again that Bill had five holes in one – four more than he had.

44

Sunlight is wonderful

26 January 2024

Lucy was dozing, holding Harry's hand as he lay still, breathing rhythmically, in his hospital bed. Her mind was drifting, as if she were lying on a beach in the warm morning sun.

Lucy and Harry weren't raised near the ocean, but they both loved to visit beaches. Their favourite was Mission Beach in far north Queensland. They had often visited and wasted time there, walking along the beach, eating fish and chips and lolling in the sun. She remembered the first time they visited Mission. They were towing a camper trailer and had travelled through the outback of Queensland and the Northern Territory. They both loved the isolation of the outback. They weren't partial to caravan parks and would look for isolated camping spots instead where they could have a campfire at night and watch it flicker while they talked about their family and everyday things, undisturbed by crowds and noise.

They were the best times, thought Lucy, even though she occasionally went crook at Harry for getting them bogged or lost – or both. Harry's friends were very aware that when Harry said he knew a short cut, be careful. Most of his short cuts were shorter in distance, but took much longer, which is why no one else used his 'special short cut'.

Lucy didn't admit it to Harry, but those times when she was frustrated with him were usually the best of memories: years later Harry would say something like, 'Remember when we got bogged out near Thargomindah and you cried because you thought we were going to be stuck there until we died of dehydration?' Maybe Harry won't be able to relive memories like that anymore, she thought. Maybe Harry won't be Harry. She knew Harry wouldn't like being a shell of his former self.

If Harry was well, my life would be wonderful, she thought. The kids are doing great and managing their lives. Harry would say, 'You know I used to tell them how to do things and now they tell me, "Not that way Dad, if you do it this way it's easier." '

He reckoned he still had them on toast on financial issues though. They all sought his opinion on where to invest or how to structure their businesses or other financial matters, and he would still beat the boys at golf.

It was 26 January – Australia Day 2024. Harry had been in a coma since Saturday 9 September 2023, and the doctors could only tell Lucy that it was a waiting game for her and Harry. She was dozing and lazily thinking about the implications of what they had said.

It was cold in Harry's room when she arrived that morning, even though it was midsummer, and she had opened the curtains to get some sunlight and warmth into his room. She had rubbed his arms and legs and talked to him as she always did, and tried to roll him over a little so she could rub and inspect his back. This was difficult, because even though he had lost significant weight, he was still heavy to move. He had a feeding tube inserted into his stomach via his nose, and a catheter, but he was able to breathe without assistance. The doctors always noted that Harry had a good capacity to maintain his own breathing, but he had wires attached to his chest and fingers that provided feedback to a monitor beside his bed.

Lucy had her eyes closed and the morning sun made her sleepy. She thought she heard the sound of someone entering the room and opened her eyes to look towards the door, but there was no one. She looked at Harry and jerked her head forward to look more closely.

Harry's eyes were open and he had moved them slightly towards her. She moved her hand slowly in front of his eyes and they lazily followed its movement. Tears were welling in Lucy's eyes when she asked, 'Harry are you awake?'

It seemed to take Harry forever to respond but he moved his eyes again and with a coarse voice that could barely be heard slurred, 'The sun woke me.'

Harry was trying to say something else. Lucy held her hair back with one hand and moved her ear to right near his mouth. She thought she heard, 'You were so beautiful at the grid.'

Lucy sobbed silently with tears running down her face onto Harry's gown. She had her head on his chest with her arms wrapped over him and she didn't want to move, she wanted to hold him close forever. Her chest was heaving uncontrollably as she now sobbed freely. Lucy hadn't fully comprehended what Harry had said – she was overcome with emotion and stayed glued to Harry. She didn't register that perhaps she should sound the alert buzzer to rouse hospital staff. Harry still lay quietly as she pulled away to look at him to make sure he was still conscious. He gazed back at her, seemingly with confused concern etched on his face. He didn't appear to be agitated in any way, but seemed to be trying to understand why Lucy was crying.

Lucy knew she couldn't keep this time to herself any longer. She pressed the alert button at the end of a cord hanging on the side of his bed. The duty nurse appeared, then a second nurse. Lucy continued to clutch Harry's hand as they began examining him. He flinched, screwed up his face when they lightly pinched his thigh, and shut his eyes when they shone the ophthalmoscope into his eyes and refused to open them until the torch was turned off. He was yet to move his arms or legs, but Lucy knew it was very positive that he was having reactions to their touches and to the pupil examination.

The nurse told Lucy that Dr Lynch had been notified and was on his way to the hospital to examine Harry. Soon, there were four nurses in Harry's room, all chattering about his observations. Lucy knew two of

Harry's regular nurses and each of them came and hugged Lucy and shared in her emotions. Both of them had huge grins and shed tears with her as they went about their duties.

Harry seemed to be awake and cognisant for about 15 minutes, until he closed his eyes again. Lucy was worried that he may have relapsed, but a nurse told her that she shouldn't be worried about that. 'I think he's sleeping. That last 15 minutes would have put a strain on his resources,' she said. 'I think he'll wake again.'

Around 40 minutes later, Dr Peter Lynch arrived, said a quick 'Hi' to Lucy and started looking at Harry's clinical notes and discussing the nurses' observations. 'Lucy, I think what has just happened is wonderful news for us,' he said. 'I am not concerned that he is sleeping again now. I'm hopeful that we may get some intermittent waking before he is fully back with us, but for now I am excited with this development and I think you should allow yourself to be excited as well. I expect he was exhausted by his waking, which is why he is now sleeping, and I am loathe to try to wake him. Did he say or do anything that you saw?' asked the doctor.

Lucy told Dr Lynch what had happened with his eye movement and that he had tried to talk, and he affirmed that that was very good news.

Over the following few days, Harry did wake again and each time he seemed stronger and stayed awake for longer. Ben, Susie and Albert all visited in the days after he first woke. Lucy could not get the smile off her face. Harry said very little, but seemed to be assessing where he was. He certainly knew Lucy, however. When he was awake and she was there, she would reach for his hand and he would grasp it and look at her.

During the second week, he started talking a little. What he was saying was eclectic and haphazard, but it was very clear he was trying to communicate, and Lucy would talk endlessly to him until he fell asleep. The hospital physiotherapist unit was now involved and had been doing vigorous limb exercises on Harry. He was responding and they could feel his movements.

Three weeks after he initially woke, Harry was communicating with Lucy by answering her questions. He hadn't yet questioned her, but was capable of responding to her queries. Harry had a number of CT scans and Dr Lynch was very optimistic about Harry's prognosis. Harry started to recognise people; he knew the role of the nurses and smiled when his children visited. Dr Lynch directed that the feed tube be removed and they started with soup meals via a straw, which he managed propped up in bed.

Lucy was keen to discuss what Harry had said to her when he first woke. She thought she heard him say, 'You were so beautiful at the grid.' She had been mulling those words over ever since. For 42 years, Harry had told Lucy he didn't remember meeting her in 1978 at the grid. It was initially a point of friction between them. She clung to the grid meeting from September 1978 until she saw Harry three years later. Her whole life centred around that meeting.

Harry had told her about their future together and to prove he could see the future, he told her of the impending big rains, Alice being pregnant, Jon's name, that she took a job with the local bank, and that when she saw him next, he would be in a dark brown Holden. All those things mattered to Lucy and were crucial events in her life. Each prediction had come true.

Lucy still had that note folded carefully in her book, *The Thorn Birds*, and read it from time to time. Only one other person in the world was privy to what Lucy had gone though and that was Alice. Lucy still remembers driving to Rasp and searching for Harry, to no avail. After that event, she looked at the note and read what Harry had said in it: 'The next time you see me I'll be in a dark brown Holden.' He was right again – she never located the blue HK GTS Monaro.

During their friendship, she had often spoken with Max and Steve about Harry and what happened in 1978. All they could tell her was that Harry crashed his motorbike and for a period of about four months after the crash was different. He was able to tell them about their futures, but post-January 1979, he couldn't recall a thing about the previous four months. He remembered going camping, but that was it. He didn't remember their big win on the 1978 Melbourne Cup; he didn't remember their investment in shares. There was nothing, they said.

And now *after 42 years* Harry mentions the grid meeting! What the hay, thought Lucy. Lucy mentioned what Harry had said to her to Max and Stevie, with whom she had a special relationship because of their shared experience with Harry. They were astounded that he had remembered something from 1978. Lucy was keen to talk to Harry and try to find out if he did really remember, but she was afraid she would interfere with his recovery.

She decided she would wait until he was out of hospital, but Harry had other ideas. In the fourth week of his recovery, Harry said to Lucy, 'That day at the grid, I only had a T-shirt on, you know. I didn't have a windcheater with me and I nearly froze, and you turned up with a big jacket on. I should have asked you for it,' he smiled.

'I remember the white T-shirt Harry, but after all these years do you still remember that?' questioned Lucy carefully.

'Yeah, I do. I can't remember what I had for breakfast today, but I remember that, because it was the first time we met, and I remember you thought I was a looney because I was telling you about your future,' replied Harry.

Lucy couldn't understand what was happening inside Harry's head – or more correctly, his brain. First, he crashed and could see the future, then he did nothing and lost that ability. Then, he could no longer remember that he had had that ability – or remember what he did while he had that ability. Now, he crashes again and the ability to see the future isn't back, but the memory of being able to see that future and what he did when he had that ability is back!

What Lucy understood now was that both changes to Harry's cognitive abilities occurred when he suffered head injuries after crashes, with the exception of when he lost the ability to see the future, which strangely disappeared around the end of January 1979. Lucy wondered how that could happen.

Lucy contacted Max. 'Max when did Harry have the crash on his bike in 1978?' she asked. 'Oh, let me think for a bit – yeah, I got it. It was the Saturday before the big hail storm that year in Rasp, which was on 14 September, so it was 9 September – yeah that's right,' replied Max.

'Can you be more specific Max?' asked Lucy.

'What, that's the date,' stated Max.

'No, was it in the morning of that day?'

'Yeah it was at about 11.45. I looked at my watch when we found him and saw he was unconscious, because I thought that if we got him to hospital the doctors would ask how long has he been like this,' said the anal Max.

'Good thinking,' said Lucy, happy that Max had taken note of this.

'Why are you asking me all this Lucy?' questioned Max.

'I don't really know, I'm just trying to solve this bloody riddle of Harry's, and I think there is some link between what happened in '78 and what we are going through now. Did you know Max that Harry's crash last year also happened on 9 September at 11.30 and it was also a Saturday!' exclaimed Lucy.

'Really?' responded Max. 'Well, of course I looked at my watch at 11.45, but he could have been there for 15 minutes because we got tired of waiting for him to return. He went looking for the right track to an old homestead.'

'So, this is probably tough for you to answer,' Lucy continued, 'But two questions: how far into the future could he see; and secondly, exactly when did his visions stop?'

'The second question is easy, because I remember it was on the long weekend in January, the day after Australia day, the 27th it would have been. He came over to my place I think, and Stevie asked him a question about Sandra or Debbie, as Stevie always did, and Harry said something to the effect of "What are you talking about Stevie?" And I thought Stevie was going to bash him. It was so funny.'

'Max, do you know what day Harry woke in January this year?! It was the 26th.'

There was a period of silence over the phone between the two sleuths. 'Shit Lucy, I can't believe that!' said Max excitedly. 'I'm not sure how far into the future he could see though – I think he kept that to himself, but why are you asking that?'

'Well, what I am thinking is, and I know this sounds crazy, but what if when Harry crashed in 1978, and in 2023 at the same time, what if old Harry's memories somehow went back to young Harry? I mean they crashed at the exact same time and day, 45 years apart, and it seems that old Harry was unconscious for the exact same period that young Harry was able to see the future.

'Old Harry wakes and suddenly young Harry, 45 years earlier, loses the ability to see the future. So, if we can determine what period young Harry could see forward to, it might tie it together. If, for example, young Harry could see forward up until 2023 when old Harry had his crash, we have a theory. Then the other bit we haven't talked about is that when old Harry just woke, suddenly he got his memory back for that period from September 1978 to January 1979!'

What Harry doesn't know now, mused Lucy, was that for 45 years he hasn't been able to remember the stuff he's been talking to me about, such as the grid meeting. He doesn't know he didn't know! It's a mess, she thought.

Max felt bludgeoned by all the information Lucy had just provided, but said he would try to think about all the visions Harry had had to see if he could recall what future time period Harry had spoken about.

45

Harry comes home

March 2024

Lucy took it slowly with Harry when he came home, but it was soon evident to her that Harry was the old Harry she knew and loved. To celebrate, she bought him a gift. 'Go look in the shed,' she told Harry one Saturday morning. Harry opened the garage and there, gleaming under the lights, was a 1968 GTS HK Monaro with a 186s engine.

'I love you Lucy! It's just fantastic, it's in such great condition.' Harry looked at the odometer, which read only 5300 kilometres. 'How did you find one with such low kilometres – they are like hens' teeth?'

'Remember I told you I came looking for you in Rasp and visited four people who had HKs?'

'And I had hid mine by transferring the registration to Max?' interrupted Harry.

'Yes, I am glad you remember that because that really pissed me off,' Lucy continued. 'Well this is Maria Sultana's car. Her husband only drove it for about a year after he bought it, and then passed away, and she kept it for 55 years. I spoke to her in 1978 when she was about 40 years old, and she is now 85. I rang her and she agreed to sell the car to me because she knows we will cherish it. I even found your old leather key ring; let's take it for a drive?' said a proud Lucy as she handed the keys to Harry.

'My old key tag, with your Dad's name on it! Wow, where did you find it?' asked Harry. Lucy was staggered by what Harry had just said.

'My Dad's name?' Lucy asked. 'What do you mean?'

'Remember I said that I carved your father's name on my key tag so I could remember to warn you and him about his accident so he wouldn't have his arm amputated?' said Harry.

'Harry, Dad lost his arm in 1987,' Lucy told him regretfully.

'No Luce, I warned you about it … Didn't I?' Harry asked, unconvinced.

'No, you didn't Harry.' Harry could now remember what he had done in the summer of '78 and '79 but was yet to reconcile in his mind that in the intervening 45 years, he hadn't remembered the summer, and Lucy would need to tell him that.

'Ahh shit Luce, I am so terribly sorry … I didn't warn you about that accident? I fucked up. Please tell me what is happening: what do I know and what don't I know, and what should I tell you? Please Luce, I didn't mean to hurt you,' said Harry.

'I know you didn't, we just need to sit for a while, and you can tell me all about that summer and what you did and who you spoke to, and then I'll tell you how that might have affected us. Deal?' asked Lucy.

Harry told Lucy as much as he could remember from that summer, including his visions from that summer. He told her about his visit with Bill and what they had talked about, and his interaction with Max and Steve at that time and their investment in Berkshire Hathaway.

'I guess now you and I know how I made such a good investment,' he smiled to Lucy, 'and you just thought I was smart! You know how Bill left me so much money; I reckon it was because we talked about Berkshire shares as well.'

Steve rang Lucy from Rasp to check on Harry and during the call told Lucy that Max had asked him if he knew how far into the future Harry's visions went. 'I know that he saw up until 2023,' Steve informed her.

'How do you know that, Steve; Max said he didn't know or couldn't remember?' queried Lucy.

'Well, I remember because it was important to me. Max wasn't really listening, but when we bought the shares, I distinctly remember Harry saying that in 2023 each share could be worth about $500,000, which is why in June 2023 I suggested to Harry that we sell our shares. I remember in 1978, he actually said he saw himself trading in 2023 and each Berkshire Hathaway share was worth over $500,000.'

Lucy wasn't sure how such things happen, but she was sure that when old and young Harry crashed something very strange happened. Old Harry stayed in a coma for four months and during that time young Harry, who wasn't in a coma, had old Harry's memories. Then when old Harry recovered from his coma, young Harry's insight into the future was lost. But then when old Harry recovered, what young Harry did in the summer of '78 and '79 entered old Harry's memories.

'Luce, I forgot to tell you about my dad,' said Harry, interrupting Lucy's thought bubble. 'I think I saved him from death, or at least a debilitating head injury. At the time, I couldn't tell Mum about my dreams, but I did see Dad dying in hospital in my visions because of a blow to his head. He was working under a tripod hoist when the pulley broke and struck him on the head. I told Mum that he should always wear a hard hat – and you know what, he always did after Mum and I talked, even though I didn't tell her I saw an accident. I think maybe I did do something good in 1978!'

Lucy thought that at least she now had an explanation for the tortured time she shared with Harry in 1978, and for the following 40-odd years when he couldn't remember what he had done or what had happened to him between September 1978 and January 1979. Most people wouldn't believe the story about what had happened to her and Harry, let alone her explanation, but those who shared that time with them would agree with her explanation, she thought.

46

Hope

June 2024

Alice married a farmer in 1985 and settled not far from Ber-Beri. She had two more children and is now a grandmother. Jon works as a builder and lives not far from Alice in a small country town. Alice is busy with visits from her grandchildren but come regional show time, she offers herself as a tarot card reader – looking at the past and future for people. Without providing names, she regales her customers with her true-life story about when she didn't believe – but then came to believe in the ability to see the future.

'Life works in mysterious ways,' she tells people. 'And, I believe that it can happen to anyone.'

Max married Emma Forrest in late 1982 and is still happily married. They had two sons, just as Harry had seen. Harry reckoned at the time that even though he had visions of their marriage, that he didn't need his special powers to see that they would marry. Max was smitten right from the start and everyone could see it. Max sold his Berkshire

Hathaway shares in 1997 and received around $300,000, which he told everyone was approximately a 43,000 per cent return! Max did well in life, as Harry predicted.

Steve and Sandra had a daughter and a son. Despite Stevie's best efforts for 45-odd years, he never again won money on the Melbourne Cup – nor the AFL premiership for that matter. He occasionally sees Debbie in Rasp, prompting him to think about that weird summer and their time together. It seems he is the only one of the select group who would have liked Harry's visions to continue.

Steve and Harry each sold their shares in 2023 for around $6,500,000. Together they bought a pastoral property called 'Hope', near Darling, where they meet with all their friends to ride motorbikes and kick back.

'You know Harry,' grinned Steve one night as they enjoyed a drink beside the open fire at their property. 'The only thing this place doesn't have is a large round concrete tank we can swim in.'

'Listen mate, with the money you have, I am sure you can have a tank built just like the one we swam in in 1978,' quipped Harry laconically. 'And then I'll tell you who is going to win this year's Melbourne Cup.'

www.ingramcontent.com/pod-product-compliance
Lightning Source LLC
Chambersburg PA
CBHW030019200726
48283CB00012B/692